Lock, Stock and Harold

Ebberley Finch

ISBN: 978-1-0685454-0-5
First edition 2024

To Ellie, Freddy and Ivan – follow your dreams!

Table of Contents

Chapter 1

Noah peered up and down the street searching for a landmark he recognised. The rest of the world were striding confidently towards their destinations. If they could do this, why couldn't he? He reached for his phone and the security of Google maps, a tight band squeezing his chest. Perhaps everything would become clear at the corner? He slipped the phone back into his pocket and continued walking, but without conviction.

A small well-worn backpack contained the reason he had come to this part of town. Fresh lemongrass and curry leaves, galangal and rice paper wraps. When Daisy found out he was cooking spring rolls and kari ayam curry on Saturday, her face was sure to light up. Something he didn't see very often these days.

He had been to this part of Slough a couple of times before and on reaching the corner, he scanned all directions for something to spark a memory. A rush hour street full of ethnic supermarkets, tattoo parlours and barber shops met his searching gaze. Buses and vans squeezed past cars parked on either side of the road, adding to the chaos of the scene. He had no idea which direction to take. Defeated, he pulled out his phone, keyed in the address of his flat and sloped back down the street he had just walked up. A cloud of inadequacy tailing him all the way home.

He climbed the stairwell of his apartment block, all towering magnolia and musty odour. Reaching the fourth floor, he glanced out over Slough's urban sprawl, where heaving traffic emitted a steady rumble. How different would life feel if he lived somewhere with open space and the sound of the sea? Surely he wasn't the only person unhappy to be sitting like a battery hen at his computer, laying golden eggs with the press of an 'enter' key and receiving crumbs of salary in return?

Giving himself a shake, Noah unlocked the door to his flat, pausing on the threshold. Thursday was Daisy's tennis club evening and he didn't expect her to be at home, but the place felt so bleak and hollow he couldn't help calling out.

'Hello, are you there?' His words echoed into an empty space.

The living room could have been photographed for a magazine. This was Daisy's preferred look, even though it was his flat. Swinging the backpack off his shoulder, he poked his head into the kitchen. Every surface gleamed. Not so much as a crumb on the toaster. It hadn't been like this when he left for work in the morning.

Had his girlfriend been in one of her *'I'm spring cleaning because you've done something wrong'* moods? A chill ran down his spine and he slowed his steps. A piece of lined paper torn roughly out of a pad lay next to the kettle. It was out of keeping in the pristine kitchen. Daisy's looping script filled the page. He prodded it with a finger. As it moved the words swam and circled. He made a half-hearted attempt to focus on what she had written, but it wasn't going to happen. The note would have to wait.

One step into the bedroom confirmed she was gone. Had he sensed it the moment he opened the front door? He checked the wardrobe anyway. No dresses, no jackets, no shoes. Nothing that belonged to Daisy. The room felt bigger without any of her in there. Bigger and uncomfortably bare.

To stamp out the last vestiges of hope, he checked the bathroom. A Sargasso Sea of plastic had vanished. Plastic was the only issue where he had held the moral high ground in their debates. No one person needed that many polymer-clad beauty products, least of all Daisy. His palm-oil free soap, shampoo and shaving bars were all that remained on the side of the bath.

Perched on the bed chewing his nails he mulled over her complaints. In the first year there hadn't been too many, but three years on they were legion. And (so she told him) justified. Putting his head in his hands he sat until the pain in his stomach drove him to move. Was it hunger or loss? Either way, making supper would help. He imagined the comforting heft of a chef's knife against his palm and the rhythm of chopping.

Back in the kitchen, the note's critical eye followed him. Snatching it up, he put it face down on the coffee table in the lounge. He would de-stress before deciphering. Cooking was Noah's go to for relaxation, second only to volunteering at the animal sanctuary where he worked every Sunday.

The heavy oak chopping board was comfortingly solid under his fingers. The chop, chop, chop dulled thoughts of the missive waiting in the other room. Soon the aroma of frying garlic and onion filled the kitchen. After adding tomato purée, fresh cherry tomatoes, the remainder of a pot of mascarpone and some black pepper, he stirred the colourful sauce and watched his pasta boil. He ate standing up in the kitchen, not wanting to be in the same room as the note. Scraping his empty bowl, he knew the knot in his stomach had not been hunger. The time for prevarication was over.

He had finally mastered reading in secondary school, scarred by years of not understanding why others could do it and he could not. Derision and mockery had been mostly veiled, but occasionally overt. Both hurt. Today, anxiety and Daisy's cursive script stripped him of his hard-won ability. He held the note in trembling hands for several moments before starting to read. Putting the note flat on the table and tracing each word with a finger, he spoke them out loud.

3

Dear Noah,

I guess you were expecting this. I've finally left for good. Our relationship was never going to last, we're just too incompatible. It's best if we split now and get on with our lives.

I hope you find someone new and have a happy life, but to do that you need to focus and get your act together. You constantly forget things you've promised to do and things I've told you. You're too laid back and you don't care. I need someone who does care. There's only so many times you can apologise, after that the 'sorrys' become meaningless. Being nice isn't enough. Not having me around to organise you will make you responsible for organising yourself. It's a good thing.

I've threatened to leave before, but this time I really mean it. I can't deal with you calling and telling me things will be different, then coming back and finding they are not. I need a clean break.

Don't try to contact me. It's over and I'm moving on. Good luck.
Daisy x

He ploughed through the note again, looking for and failing to find a crumb of hope. Had he been expecting it? He didn't know. It wasn't the first time she had left, but it was the first time she had taken everything. He phoned. The call went to voicemail after one ring. She had never blocked him before.

Wandering aimlessly round the space they used to share, he searched for something he could return. There was nothing. Every shred of her had vanished. Eventually, he went to bed and stared at the ceiling, the orange glow of the streetlights creating strange shadows, the sound of sirens blaring in the distance.

Despite her request, Noah tried in vain to contact her. He called her work and most of the friends he had a number for. They had all been briefed. Daisy was nothing if not thorough. He wondered if she'd sent a copy of the letter to everyone, so they were clear on his shortcomings. Or had she detailed them in person?

It took him a week to accept he was not going to be able to speak to her until she was ready. Her terms, as always. Making himself a cup of tea, Noah took it up to the roof terrace. Out of curiosity, rather than with intent, he peered over the railings and pondered the potential extent of damage if he were to step over and hurl himself to the ground. Four floors up looked a long way, but would it be enough? He could end up in a wheelchair for the rest of his life. The thought of his mother's expression on being presented with a son who required her to give up her life and provide twenty-four/seven care was wretched. The thought of actually relying on her care, alarming.

He stepped back. Life wasn't that bad. His burden was disappointment not devastation. Not so much disappointment that Daisy had left, but with himself because he couldn't do the things normal people seemed to find easy. Reading and writing were fine except when he was stressed and he was good at his analyst job. Words might swim on the page, but numbers remained still and had patterns. He could manipulate them into recommendations and conclusions that made sense. It was basic day-to-day challenges that troubled him.

He thought back to his last argument with Daisy. It had happened exactly a week before she left. Had it been the final straw? Daisy's Thursday night tennis was something he looked forward to. It meant he had a whole evening on his own relaxed schedule, rather than on her more frenetic one.

Last week, on getting home from work, he had thrown the post and his shopping on the side in the kitchen and put on his pyjamas, looking forward to culinary creativity and relaxation. Before long, he was on the sofa, a plate of fried sea bream and new potatoes together with a fennel and orange salad in front of him. Daisy wouldn't be back until after ten o'clock so there was plenty of time to clear up and remove all evidence of fish; her most hated food. His feet were resting on the coffee table next to his empty plate when the front door burst open and Daisy marched in.

'What are you doing?'

Something was wrong. Noah searched his brain, dread pooling in his stomach. He didn't think it was just the fish. 'I thought you had tennis tonight.'

'Do you ever listen to a word I say? I've told you a hundred times it's Jenny's birthday tonight and we're out for dinner.' Wrinkling her nose, she glared at his plate. 'It stinks of fish in here. Don't tell me you've eaten already.' She turned her back and marched off to the kitchen.

Noah scoured his memory. Daisy had said something about Jenny's birthday, but that was ages ago. A shrill voice came from the next room.

'What's all this shit? The kitchen was immaculate when I left this morning.'

He went to inspect the offending mess. Pans littered the hob. Chopping boards, vegetable shavings and a sticky residue of orange juice covered the limited workspace. He couldn't very well deny having eaten. Before he had worked out whether to answer the eating or the mess question first, she had changed tack and pounced on the post.

'There's orange juice all over these bloody letters. Look at them. They're sticky and disgusting. Don't you ever think?' She started to paw at the damp post with a tea towel, ripping the soggy envelopes and contents rather than waiting for them to dry, she then threw up her hands in an overly dramatic gesture. 'I despair.'

'I would have cleared it up.' Why was he always on the back foot? If she had arrived home at the proper time, all would have been in order – mostly anyway.

'That's not the point.'

What was the point? He hesitated wondering how not to make things worse.

Daisy huffed and slammed a hand on the worksurface. 'We're leaving in five minutes. Get changed. You'll have to eat two dinners and clear up this crap later.' She swept into the bedroom. Her voice echoed down the corridor. 'Your clothes are all over my side of the bed, including your dirty pants. For God's sake. Don't you ever put anything away?'

He heard the door to the bathroom slam and leapt off the sofa. It would be best to change while Daisy was not in the bedroom.

Why hadn't she reminded him about Jenny's birthday this afternoon? Was this some sort of test to make him 'more responsible'? He pulled on clean trousers and the shirt she had bought him last Christmas. It was her favourite.

Returning to the kitchen, he started clearing up.

'I said leave that until later.' Her strident tone cut through his thoughts and he jumped. Somehow the spatula in the pan he was holding flipped up, depositing a hand-sized greasy stain and slivers of fish scales onto the front of his shirt. Daisy put her hands over her face.

'For fuck's sake.' She never swore.

How had everything degenerated so quickly? One minute he was enjoying a tasty meal and a peaceful evening. Now he had upset Daisy to the point of tears and landed himself with a tsunami of guilt, which would swamp him for the whole evening. Looking Daisy in the eye or joining in with banter over dinner would be almost impossible.

She waited in the hall, coat on and handbag over her shoulder while he put on a clean shirt.

'I'll drive, then you can have a drink,' he offered, taking her nod as one small step back up the ladder into her good books. They walked to the car in silence and were almost at the restaurant when Daisy suddenly yelled, 'Where the fuck are you going? I said turn left.'

Hadn't he gone left? He glanced at his hands doing a quick

7

right-left check. He had turned right.

'Are you trying to make us even later?' Daisy's voice broke; she was close to tears, if not actually crying. He couldn't tell which.

'I'm sorry. I didn't mean to. Sometimes I mix up right and left, you know that.'

Now he was languishing well below the bottom rung of Daisy's 'good books' ladder again. It was pretty commonplace lately.

'You're not in kindergarten. Get a grip. Carry on down here then turn right at the lights – that's the road on your side of the car.' Daisy addressed her remarks to the windscreen rather than to him. Whenever something went wrong it was always his fault.

He brought his thoughts back to the present. Not having Daisy around had its plus points.

The rooftop terrace was Noah's place to contemplate life. It was late and the orange streetlights gave the scene about him an eerie glow. Staring out across the busy suburban street he longed for answers and inspiration. How could he get his life back on track? What was 'on track'?

A plastic bag blew down the street, drifting and shapeless like his thoughts, until a police car raced past sending the bag up in the air. Blue lights flashed and the siren wailed. A couple of drunks shouted obscenities after the car for no apparent reason. Noah felt as though he were being dragged down into quicksand. This wasn't how he wanted to live his life.

A lone bright thought swirled through the grey in his brain. He could leave Slough. Without Daisy he was a free agent and could start anew. The 'where' and 'how' were too big for him to cope with, but the thought was clear and enticing.

Sunday morning had been Noah's favourite time of the week for a couple of years. It was the time he looked forward to as he trawled through spreadsheets on his computer or sat in meetings where the same things were discussed month after month. It was the space he had longed for when Daisy was berating him for some unwitting crime. His solace from a world that moved too fast.

He had started volunteering at Feathered Friends two years ago, after taking in an injured magpie he found struggling in the grounds of his flat. Handing the bird over, he spotted a notice asking for volunteers. Without even checking with Daisy, he had signed up.

Just thirty minutes' drive from his flat, the sanctuary was the passion of pensioner Javier Garcia and his wife Elena. In the ten years since their retirement, they had devoted all their spare time to tending mainly birds, but any and every creature that was brought in.

Situated in a couple of acres behind Javier and Elena's house, the small sanctuary was surrounded by mature trees and the sound of birdsong. Bark paths led between the cages and a large natural pond provided a peaceful place to reflect.

Cleaning up animal poop wasn't everyone's cup of tea, but there was a satisfaction in sprinkling fresh sawdust for the ferrets, inhaling chopped straw as he packed it into the duck house and admiring freshly hosed concrete in the aviaries, while the birds flapped their wings and dipped feathers in newly filled baths. His favourite task was feeding the new chicks, proffering tasty morsels at the end of tweezers and seeing their beaks open wide to take the food. With the right care they would get stronger every day and soon be transferred to one of the aviaries in preparation for release back into the wild.

It was late October, so the sanctuary was relatively empty, but come spring they would have up to two hundred birds at a time, together with hedgehogs and even the occasional fox or badger.

Noah had finished for the day and was about to head home when Javier called him over.

'How about a cuppa before you go?'

'Sound's good.' He followed Javier into the multi-purpose garage. It served as tea-room, storage, incubator room, bird feeding station and when necessary, reptile house.

Short and stocky with dark features and weathered olive skin, Javier was originally from Colombia where he had worked for an organisation trying to reduce the trafficking of endangered species. An avid parrot enthusiast, he owned a couple of African greys and a cockatoo. They had been acquired when their owners died or a bird had become too destructive to live in its previous home.

Apart from his brother James, who lived in Australia, Javier was the one of the few people with whom Noah felt completely relaxed. Most of his friends had been acquired through Daisy's social circle and were into sharing achievements and ambitions. He did not anticipate keeping in touch with them.

'How are things?' Javier handed over a steaming mug. His hands were rough, with dirt under the fingernails, but the tea was strong and hot. His tanned face and dark eyes had a warm empathy about them.

Noah sighed. 'They've been better, I suppose.'

'What's happened, amigo? You've not been yourself these past couple of weeks.' Despite living in England for over twenty years, Javier had a thick Spanish accent and a habit of calling his volunteers 'amigo'.

Noah paused, then the words came tumbling out. 'Daisy and I have broken up. I can't message or phone because she's blocked me. I've called her work, but she won't speak to me and I've phoned her friends, but they won't tell me where she is. I'm at a loss. I know it's over, but I'm struggling to work out what's next.'

'It's hard when someone leaves, amigo,' sighed Javier sitting quietly, waiting to hear the rest of what Noah had to say.

'I'd at least like to speak to her face to face. It feels so weird that she's just gone.'

'Is that what they call ghosting?'

Noah shrugged. 'She left a note telling me she'd gone and how useless I am. So technically it's not ghosting.'

Javier jabbed a finger towards Noah's chest. 'If there's one thing you're not, it's useless. You're by far my best volunteer. You're fantastic with the animals and equally great with the people who bring them in. They go away confident that you care and the animals are in good hands.'

'Animals and animal people are easy. It's the rest of the world I struggle with.'

'That's the reason I do what I do,' said Javier. They sat in comfortable silence for a while.

'I'm not sure where to go from here.' Noah put down his mug next to a bag of birdseed.

'Could you use Daisy leaving as an opportunity to rethink your life?' asked Javier. 'You've often said you'd like to live by the sea and that job of yours doesn't seem to inspire you.'

'I don't know. The job pays the bills and I'm good at it, but you're right, it's not how I want to spend my life.'

He had to face it, the job didn't inspire him and Slough didn't either.

Chapter 2

Climbing out of his car (currently doubling as a removal van), Noah shivered in the chilly December afternoon. Hitching his rucksack onto his shoulder, he looked up at his mother's house. Situated on the outskirts of Dorchester, it was a three-storey townhouse, fronted by a herringbone pathway and a small, square patch of grass. The everyday exterior masked the alternative reality inside. The only give-away was a multi-coloured VW camper van parked on the drive, 'Love and Peace' emblazoned on its side.

Taking Javier's advice to heart, he was starting afresh with his life. Perhaps he would get it right this time. In a flurry of activity, totally alien to his normal style, he had resigned from work and put his flat on the market. The sale of his former home had proceeded smoothly and the proceeds were now in his account. The time he had allowed himself to decide on his next steps was ticking down.

Still reeling from the speed at which his relationship had transformed from all consuming to non-existent, he was spending Christmas with his mother. Squaring his shoulders, he braced himself for a few days of well-meaning but unhelpful advice and rang the doorbell.

Since meeting her new boyfriend, Radagast, at a 'Finding Your True Self' retreat, his mother's behaviour had progressed from an obsession with crystals, alternative therapies and tree-hugging to devoting herself full-time to embracing the spirit within. As far as Noah could see, this consisted mainly of pandering to her boyfriend's next brainchild.

In keeping with her new persona, she had changed her name from Julie Wood to Shayleigh Woodrose. Radagast, self-professed innovator and guru (former names unknown), had chosen the name himself. Shayleigh, meaning fairy princess in Celtic and Woodrose, a hallucinogenic plant. Fortunately, she still answered to 'Mum'.

Always one step away from changing the world, Radagast's enthusiasm was boundless. Tigger would have been a more apt 'nom de plume'. Privately, Noah questioned the income potential of his many ventures, especially as he suspected his mother funded them, although he had no proof of this.

The door opened revealing a bare, dark-skinned torso oozing muscle definition and a handsome smiling face offset by beaded dreadlocks. Orange harem pants hung low on the man's hips, blinding charisma oozed from every pore.

'Welcome to the land of the free.' Radagast gave Noah a high-five followed by a peace sign.

Land of the free lunch, thought Noah, stepping into the hall. 'Hi Radagast.'

'Congratulations, dude. You're single, homeless and jobless. Now adventure and self-discovery can begin. The planets are aligned in your favour.' His grin broadened. 'Shayleigh and I are running a self-discovery workshop in January. You could join us and help prepare your spirit for the way forward.'

Noah sighed. He hadn't even got his coat off yet. Should he turn around and leave now? How long could he 'go with the flow' before an outburst of unwelcome and unheeded reality sprang from his lips? Any reality would probably result in him being requested to take his negative energy elsewhere.

He loved his mother and apart from his brother James, she was the only close family he had. Recently, he preferred her in small doses and without her new sidekick. Sighing again, he followed Radagast up the stairs, as only the garage, utility room and a dingy spare room were located on the ground floor of the townhouse. The first floor living room had been transformed since his last visit and was now dark purple. A large 'Om' sign dominated the ceiling and the aroma of incense lingered in the air. The sofas had vanished having been replaced by bean bags. Bean bags! His mother was fifty-five for God's sake.

She wafted towards him. Her hair was red and green today, possibly to celebrate the festive season. A flowing robe brushed the leather thongs on her feet. Putting her hands together in prayer she gave a yogic bow before hugging him as normal.

'It's wonderful to see you. And without that dominating girlfriend. Your soul is free now. The universe can lift you to greater and better things.'

'Hi Mum,' said Noah. His mother had never liked Daisy, but since their break-up, she had become markedly more outspoken in her antipathy.

'I never understood her obsession with "proper jobs",' she continued. 'And all that harping on about "reality". Reality is in the mind of the beholder you know. She had too many sharp edges for you that girl.'

The last bit might have been right, but Noah didn't want to get into a debate, so he kept quiet. He wondered if his mum was still working as a freelance editor, or if she had discarded the job (and its income) in favour of having a free soul.

'You can't move forward in life unless you have spirituality,' Radagast made a weird gesture with his arms, presumably indicating spirituality.

Noah changed the subject. 'Any chance of a cup of tea?'

'Of course!' His mum beamed. 'We've got ginger, hibiscus, echinacea or sage. I'll make it while you put your things in your room.'

Noah had been hoping for builder's, but opted for ginger and headed for the staircase to the second floor and his old room.

'Not that way, darling.' A raft of bangles jingled as his mum flapped her hands. 'Did I not tell you? We're letting a lovely couple who've been attending our mindfulness sessions stay in your old room. There didn't seem any point in keeping it empty and we weren't expecting you home.'

She didn't need to rub it in. 'You're renting it out then?' he asked.

'Of course not.' She looked shocked. 'They're friends of Radagast's. You'll be off again soon though, won't you, so you'll be okay in the spare room? No young man wants to live with his mum at thirty.'

He *didn't* want to live with his mum and he certainly didn't want to live with Radagast. He was supposed to have made something of his life by now, but here he was moving back into his childhood home.

Relegated to the dark and uninspiring spare room on the ground floor, he inhaled the faint scent of diesel wafting from under the garage door. He had anticipated having the bright and spacious haven of his old bedroom for when the alternative reality of his mother's home got too much. This new accommodation had him wondering how soon he could move on. The tired grey walls had not been redecorated to match his mother's wacky lifestyle and the space felt more storeroom than bedroom. Under the window was a small desk and next to this a couple of filing cabinets. A futon garnished with a lurid mandala coverlet took up most of the floor space; the remainder being storage for yoga mats and large gongs. The shelves had long been purged of trite novels and reference books and now contained an untidy mix of singing bowls, small drums, wands and blindfolds, together with a few self-help books. He was not going to ask what the blindfolds were for.

Christmas came and went. Despite Noah's fears it had been less trying than expected, mainly because of Yusuf and Ayla the houseguests staying in his old room. They were pleasant, articulate and good fun, although the frequency with which they apologised for taking his room became embarrassing.

Despite Radagast's insistence that they should really be

15

exchanging gifts at the Pagan ceremony of New Year, presents were opened on Christmas day, although only after he'd offered protracted and earnest thanks to a plethora of spirits and obscure gods. The interminable process strengthened Noah's urge to move on sooner rather than later.

He had bought a book on the Shamanic kitchen for Radagast, who professed to enjoy cooking more than he actually cooked, but, as expected, he enthused wildly over the book anyway. For his mother he had chosen a monogrammed yoga tote bag (SW for Shayleigh Woodrose, rather than JW for Julie Wood). She was delighted. Summoning every shred of his limited dramatic prowess, he feigned delight at his own gifts. These included an alpaca wool poncho, similar to the one Clint Eastwood wore in *The Good, the Bad and the Ugly* and a weighty self-help book filled with dense, uninviting text. These were from his mother. He was as unlikely to read the book as he was to wear the poncho.

Yusuf and Ayla, having not known he would be there, opted for sending him positive vibes. In the absence of a ready gift, Noah returned the favour. The final push to move on was a card presented to him, with great fanfare, by Radagast. It proffered free entry to the self-discovery workshop in January. In order not to put a damper on celebrations, Noah agreed it was the perfect present.

The best part of the day had been a long call with his brother James in Brisbane. Older than Noah, he had gone to join his father there three years after their parents' divorce and had now been living on the other side of the world for almost fifteen years. A light had gone out in Noah's life the day James left. His brief visits and calls were too few to compensate for the loss. A loss compounded by the fact that his father had died from a heart attack within a year of James's arrival in Australia.

James managed to put a positive spin on almost everything. He entertained with tales of his whirlwind social life, latest surfing success and anecdotes from his surf shop. Noah was grateful his brother hogged the conversation that day. There wasn't much he wanted to talk about.

After a week of enforced health-kick and biting his tongue, Noah woke up longing for a shot of caffeine and an artery-clogging breakfast. It was early and the house was silent, so he tugged on well-worn trainers and his favourite puffer jacket and walked to the high street. His preferred café had changed hands a few times, but still retained the same welcoming ambiance and large, south-facing windows. Settled in a corner, he relished his double shot cappuccino, big breakfast and normality.

January was his allocated breathing space to explore options and decide where he wanted the future to take him. Ideas were already beginning to form. On the way to the café, the sight of a child's plastic bucket peeping out of the top of a recycling bin reminded him of building elaborate sandcastles on the beach with James, calling on their father's muscle and superior engineering skills to perfect the structures. Buckets of water would be poured into the moat in a vain attempt to fill it up and they would cheer when the sea finally came in to do the job properly and claim its prize. Fish and chips on the promenade was their tea-time treat. Even the memory of disasters, like a seagull stealing his chips and knocking his supper to the ground, brought a smile to Noah's face. The holidays he remembered most fondly were those when they stayed with his uncle in Appledore in North Devon.

Uncle John was a larger-than-life character who had the knack of making everyday activities fun. The day would start with pancakes. Even James and Noah were allowed to have a go at tossing them, with no comebacks if one (or more) landed on the floor. Long days on the beach would end with a barbecue in the sand dunes or a family meal around John's sturdy kitchen table. Helping his uncle with meal preparation had sparked

Noah's love of cooking. A love that still took him to his happy place today.

Sitting in the café and longing to recreate the sense of peace and belonging those holidays had given him, Noah took out his phone and Googled short-term rentals near Appledore. Bookmarking the ones with a good price and a sea view, he pictured crashing waves and wide-open spaces. Could he make his childhood dream of living by the sea into reality, even if it were only for a few weeks? Walking the long way back to his mother's house, his thoughts flitted between sandy shores, salty spray and windswept clifftops.

Arriving back, he did not get to relax for very long. The double-pronged ambush that was waiting for him made him thankful he was fortified with coffee and a hearty breakfast.

His mother delivered the first salvo.

'Noah, New Year is the time to find direction and make positive change. You need to work with the universe and align your life's path. Drifting damages spirituality.'

Drifting? The injustice! Should he even bother defending himself? If anything, he had spent too little rather than too much of his life drifting. An inner voice driving him to 'do the right thing' had always overridden more frivolous ideas.

'What do you even mean? Which bit of a maths degree, a Masters, a gap year working in Australia, building a career, buying a flat and having a social life is drifting? That's normal. It's what people do.'

'You're missing the point.' His mother sighed and looked helplessly at Radagast who picked up the baton.

'Dude, it's your soul that's been marking time. All that kow-towing to corporate norms and social conventions. It kills self-expression and personal growth.'

'I was completely happy with my life before the break-up with Daisy.' Noah's voice lost some of its conviction here and he hoped Radagast and his mother would not pounce on this.

He *had* been fairly happy, he told himself.

'I've got savings to tide me over and I'm taking time out now to find a new place to live and a new job,' he continued. 'I'm totally sorted.'

Shayleigh rolled her eyes. 'Darling, I want you to have your best life. Don't settle for middle of the road. You owe it to yourself to embrace freedom.'

Radagast pumped his fist. 'Yeah, listen to your mum. She's embraced universal love. You've got to integrate mind, body and soul to step onto a meaningful path. Don't get sucked back on to the treadmill of corporate repression.'

'There's nothing wrong with being employed. It pays the bills so you can do what you want the rest of the time.' It was on the tip of Noah's tongue to suggest Radagast try the treadmill of corporate life, but he couldn't think of a way to phrase it without upsetting his mother.

Shayleigh put her hands in the prayer position and adopted a pleading expression. 'We want to help you. Tonight, we're going to ask the universe to bless you with inspiration and spiritual enlightenment. Next week you can build on that at our "Finding Yourself" workshop.'

'If you are open, the universe will provide.' Radagast drew a huge circle with his arms – presumably this was to demonstrate to Noah what the universe was.

Noah closed his eyes and prayed for patience from a God he didn't believe in. He was not going to spend an evening chanting and banging gongs in the dark with strangers (even his mother was a stranger sometimes). As for spending a week doing it, that was out of the question.

An idea that had been a glimmer in the back of his mind suddenly crystallised into a tangible plan. All he had to do now was phrase it in such a way that he would be absolved of the necessity to bang gongs.

'I've already decided my path.' He channelled Radagast's

unwavering conviction. 'I'm going to explore my roots and take inspiration from the sea and nature. The road ahead is clear.'

'What do you mean by that?' Shayleigh folded her arms and sat back. Noah thought this unfair. She never questioned Radagast when he came out with similar bullshit.

'Sounds awesome,' said Radagast. He was obviously going to be easier to convince than Noah's mother.

Taking a steadying breath, Noah continued, 'The way to find myself is to rebuild from happy childhood memories, creating a platform to launch a new me.' He pumped his fist, imitating Radagast's earlier gesture, adding, 'If I start with my formative past, I'll be able to transmute that into a glowing future.'

Where was he getting this stuff from?

'You haven't said anything to us about this.' Suspicion clouded his mother's normally serene features.

'I wanted it to be crystal clear in my mind before I shared it with you,' said Noah, making it up as he went along. 'In my Christmas card from Uncle John he invited me to go and visit. Energy from the universe,' he mimicked Radagast's universe motion, 'is so much stronger near the power of the sea.'

Noah considered crossing his fingers, but rejected the notion as superstition. There were two things wrong with his statement. Firstly, it contravened his principles by articulating waffle he didn't believe in. Secondly, the Christmas card from his uncle had merely said 'it would be great to see you sometime', rather than issuing a specific invitation. But now was not the time for pedantry.

'Go you,' enthused Radagast.

'Your father's brother?' His mother's tone was close and clipped. She had never forgiven his father for the divorce, even after his death. His father's brother John was tarred with the same brush. There were limits to how far Zen and mindfulness could extend.

Noah changed tack quickly. 'I won't be staying with him. It's the spirit of the sea that's drawing me there.' Once you got into it, this mystic stuff was easy. Or had he spent too much time around his mother and her boyfriend lately?

His mother was still frowning. In desperation Noah added, 'I dreamt it's the right thing to do.'

She ignored this remark and circled back to the retreat. 'You could use the workshop to explore your idea and then go afterwards, provided you still think it's the right thing to do.' Her arms were folded.

'The universe is telling me to do it now.' Noah improvised, pumping the air with his fist a second time. His plan to get out of the gong-bashing session was not going well.

Just then, unexpected help came from Radagast.

'Shayleigh, babe. We mustn't stop him if his dreams are calling. If he goes now and the move feels wrong, he can come back in time to join our course.'

Shayleigh unfolded her arms, looking uncertainly from Noah to Radagast.

Sensing an unexpected victory Noah plunged in. 'Brilliant idea, Radagast. I'll go tomorrow. As soon as I get there I'll know if it's right and if it's not I'll come straight back for the workshop.' This time he did cross his fingers.

Chapter 3

Approaching his temporary new home, Noah's heart lifted when he saw the river Torridge shimmering in the distance, weak January sunlight reflecting off the surface of the water. The route had been straightforward and Noah had endured no unintentional detours on his way to Appledore. A record for him on such a long journey. A stress-free trip boded well for his month by the sea, he mused, before discarding the idea as too whimsical. Radagast's fanciful convictions must have rubbed off on him over the holidays. He had made his escape not a moment too soon.

Nearing the bottom of the hill the road became narrower with only glimpses of the estuary ahead. Finally, he turned the corner and a familiar vista spread out before him. A wide promenade alongside the estuary, stately buildings overlooking the quayside and green hills cradling the small village of Instow across the water. Some of the buildings had been spruced up and there were a couple of upmarket cafés he didn't recognise, but the feel of the place was as he remembered from his childhood.

Pulling up to the kerb, he got out of his car. The wind whipped around his ears and a fine spray of sea salt made him blink and pull up his hood. Leaning against the quayside railing he recalled two young boys, their legs dangling over the sea wall. Strings tied around bacon rind saved from breakfast stretched into the water. The memory of getting a bite and slowly drawing up a crab, then placing it in the waiting bucket of water made his toes tingle. The crabs were carefully returned to the sea before they strolled back to Uncle John's for tea.

They'd been a happy family then. Using his uncle's house as

a base, they walked along beaches, swam in the sea, ate ice cream, played crazy golf and visited amusement arcades. Noah had prowled the slot machines considering every option before pushing a two pence piece into a hungry maw. His brother James thrust all his coins into the first or second machine he came to and then tailed Noah, doling out advice and insisting that with a share of the remaining coins he would make a big win. Out of a desire for space to think, as well as altruism, Noah usually gave his brother some of his own change. James would soon be back, money spent, ready to join his brother's team again.

As the boys grew, holidays in Devon became less frequent and his father's lengthy business trips more prominent. The tension between his parents was often palpable and they finally separated when Noah was twelve and James fifteen. His father moved almost immediately to Australia with his new wife. Struggling with the break-up, his mother had become increasingly introspective, seeking alternative routes to happiness.

James shouldered more than his fair share of parenting in the three years after the divorce and the pain of his departure to join their father on the other side of the world still lurked in Noah's belly. His mother had then drifted even further from reality, her needs eclipsing Noah's. She was unable to provide the firm platform he craved to safeguard his fragile self-esteem.

Shaking away unwelcome memories, Noah walked briskly along the quay calling in at a small café and treating himself to hot chocolate and a flapjack. He took his treats outside sitting on one of the benches overlooking the water. Ferry journeys to the other shore had been another highlight of their holidays. James would stand on the seats for a better view or dangle his fingers in the water, while Noah held his mother's hand and screwed up his eyes against the wind. The images warmed him as much as the hot chocolate.

A heavy shower drove him back to the car. Pulling out his phone, he studied the directions to the studio which was to be his home for the next month. It was in Northam, a few minutes' drive away and promised splendid views over the sea. While staying there, he would allow himself time for introspection, relaxation and exploration.

'At the next junction, turn right.' Noah glanced at the arrow on his satnav to check which way he should turn. As always when driving somewhere new, he anticipated a stressful journey with several wrong turns. Things were going unusually well.

'Your destination is on the left.' He slowed to a crawl searching for Two Oaks House and a moment later pulled onto the drive. The studio, Acorn Nook, had been converted from the old garage. He let himself in using the key-safe as instructed. A small but functional bathroom was just inside the door; the rest of the compact downstairs space was occupied by a kitchenette and a large grey sofa. The promised view did not disappoint. Patio doors opened to deliver miles of beach and the Atlantic directly into his living space. Stairs led up to a mezzanine and the bedroom.

Ducking his head to avoid the sloping ceiling upstairs, he dropped his backpack next to the oak-framed bed and sat down. He could soak up the view without even getting out of bed in the morning. It was the perfect place to visualise his future.

'Mission Impossible' trilled from his phone and a familiar face appeared on the screen. Tanned with untidy hair, the same dark eyes as Noah and a grin full of mischief, it was James.

'Hey bro, how's it going? Are you in your new place yet?'

'I've just arrived.' Noah turned his phone around to give James a tour of Acorn Nook and its stunning views.

'It looks fantastic, apart from the weather, of course.' His brother laughed and Noah did too. Laughter was guaranteed on a call with James. 'We had great times on those beaches, didn't we? Do you think you'll stay?'

'It's too early to say. I'd like to, but I need time to get my head together before I decide. The job market's not great in this part of the world, so that's a problem unless I work from home.' Noah wasn't ready to make decisions on his new life and so he changed the subject. 'What's happening with you?'

James launched into an account of his life. Just home from a beach party (which is why he was calling so late), he was busy with the surf shop and had a new girlfriend who he claimed might be 'the one'. The regularity with which he fell in and out of love seemed alien to Noah, whose cautious nature extended to relationships. At the end of the call James promised to come and visit if Noah was still living in their old childhood haunt come the summer.

Noah tried to quell the warm glow at the thought of a visit from his brother. He had learnt from experience that James attacked everything with zeal and optimism, but practicalities often got in the way of action. He sat for a while taking in the view and reliving the vibrance of his brother's voice.

Noah had been living in Devon for a week, dividing his time between visiting old haunts, strolling along the beach and job-hunting. Jobs were thin on the ground, but he had half-heartedly applied for a couple of financial analyst positions. The beauty of the North Devon countryside made his desire to remain there stronger with every day that went by. He knew he couldn't spend too long pandering to indecisiveness, because the month's grace he had allowed himself was racing past. After that it would be a question of moving to wherever he could find a suitable job (Slough excepted).

His next task was one he had been putting off, but a couple of voicemails from his mother had spurred him into action. She wanted to know how things were going and whether he had seen his uncle yet. He needed to see Uncle John before he called her back to substantiate his story about the invitation.

His uncle sent Christmas and birthday cards every year, but that was the only contact they had shared for almost a decade. Despite this, John's colourful personality lived strong in Noah's mind. However, it was so long since their last conversation, he felt awkward about calling. Several times he had pulled the number up on his phone, but not dialled. He could not put the call off any longer.

'Noah, it's great to hear from you. Long time no speak.' Uncle John's booming voice brought the past rushing into the present. Images of a round, smiling face. Being thrown into the air and caught safely in burly arms. James's cries of 'higher, higher'.

Noah's concerns about being out of touch for so long faded like mist on the Devon hills.

'I'm in the area for a while and thought it would be nice to meet up,' he said.

John's reply was instant and heartfelt. 'Marvellous. It feels like only a couple of years since you were here with your dad (God rest his soul) and begging for ice cream on the beach. I can't believe how quickly time passes. Come over for lunch tomorrow and we'll catch up properly.'

'I'd like that.' His qualms about calling had been unnecessary. He should have known John would make him feel welcome.

'You know, of course, I'm not in Appledore anymore,' said John. 'I moved inland to Hatherleigh not long after I last saw you to start an antiques business. I'll show you around when you get here and then we can have lunch and a pint. The shop's closed on Wednesdays so I can indulge in a postprandial nap after you've gone.' His uncle's chuckle had not changed over the years and the joie de vivre vibrating down the phone reminded Noah so much of his absent brother, he needed a few moments to gather himself together after the call.

Parking in Hatherleigh's central car park the next day, Noah was enchanted by the sculpture of three farmers leaning over a railing observing a small band of sheep. The January sun warmed his back as he took time to admire the figures. There was something indefinable about being in Devon that gave him permission to stop and look, whether it was at the sea, a thatched cottage, the Dartmoor hills, or in this case an unexpected rural scene.

Permission to pause, admire, wonder or dream had been lacking in his years with Daisy. Life had been governed by schedules and tasks that drove him past the joys of life with barely a glance. He realised now he had endured, rather than embraced, the pace of life they had led and he was not sorry to have left that existence behind.

Strolling into the centre of the village, he scrutinised the thatched cottages, trying on the idea of living in one, but concluding that picturesque as they were, Hatherleigh was too far from the coast. On the high street, he browsed shop windows and examined the menu at the local café. Carrying on up the hill, Abacus Antiques jumped out from the next corner. A large man wearing a colourful waistcoat over an open-necked white shirt appeared in the doorway. His sleeves were rolled almost to the elbow, showing muscled forearms. Noah recognised John straight away, although his belly had grown and his hair had receded. Even if he hadn't, the booming voice would have given him away.

'If it isn't young Noah. What a treat. We've got some catching up to do, haven't we?'

'It's great to see you again.'

They shook hands then embraced before stepping into the dusky interior of Abacus Antiques. The shop went a surprisingly long way back from the high street and was stuffed to the gills. Antiques large and small ranged from old-fashioned dressers and large wooden cartwheels to art deco lampshades, carriage clocks and even postcards.

'This is where it's all at.' His uncle waved a meaty hand at his wares. 'I buy 'em low, sell 'em high – and have fun doing it. What's not to like?'

'It sounds great,' said Noah. 'It must make for interesting times uncovering all these treasures and then finding new owners for them.'

'I love it,' John asserted. 'Wouldn't want to do anything else.'

'Do you live near the shop?' asked Noah.

'My house is about a mile out of town. It's got great views and suits me just fine. You'll have to come over next time.'

Fascinated by the things on show, Noah explored the depths of the shop. Would an antiques business be right for him he wondered, even though he knew nothing about them? Probably not. Fingering each item in turn, he could easily have spent all afternoon examining the treasures and thinking his own thoughts, but John had other ideas.

'Time for lunch, laddie. There's a log fire and a pint of bitter calling.'

The Tally Ho! pub was warm and cosy with dark oak panelling and low beams. Farmers in tweed shirts and caps propped up the bar and the staff seemed to know everyone by name. Noah and John luxuriated in the best seats in the house: high-backed armchairs either side of the stone fireplace, where a glowing log burner pumped out its welcome and the pub's spaniel settled itself at Noah's feet.

By the time they had demolished burger and chips, followed by sticky toffee pudding, John was on his third pint. He waved it towards his nephew with a jovial 'cheers'.

Noah raised his orange juice in a return salute, enjoying being wrapped up in his uncle's reminiscences – tales of Noah and his brother running excitedly around Exmoor Zoo, surfing in the waves at Croyde and eating fish and chips on Appledore

Quay. John expounded at length on wild monkey impressions and tree climbing (James), a visit to A&E with a broken wrist (James) and sliding down a muddy bank wearing his new coat and bursting into tears afterwards (Noah).

Storytelling had always been a talent of his uncle's, aided by colourful embellishment at every turn. Noah marvelled that his uncle's seventy-year-old brain could recall family outings from more than two decades ago in so much detail, especially after several beers. He leaned back in his chair, the warmth settling over him due only in part to the burner in the tall stone fireplace. John, his cheeks flushed to almost the same colour as his nose, waved at the bar and ordered a whiskey. Noah requested coffee with a small pang of regret that he had to drive.

'So, you want to stay in the area then, young Noah?' There was approval in John's tone.

'I'd like to, but there's not many jobs to suit me in this part of the world.'

'You need to run your own business, lad,' John asserted. 'You can rent premises and get set up without worrying about big city prices and if you get your customer service right you'll be away.'

'I'm not sure what I'd do. A degree in maths and a few years' analysing data hasn't really set me up for running my own business.'

'Nonsense. You're a bright lad and if you can add up, you're already ahead of most people. Think about what you want to do and what you like doing, then away you go. What's the worst thing that can happen?'

I could lose all the equity from my flat, get into debt, have to live with the knowledge I've failed and be forced to attend a series of Radagast's self-discovery workshops. Noah cringed. But all he said was, 'there are risks.'

'A young lad like you should be taking risks.' John finished his whiskey, waving to the bar for another and expanded on why running your own business was the way to go.

Inspired by his uncle's conviction and passion, Noah spent the trip home striving to picture what he really wanted to do; ideas drifting like fog on a November morning, too nebulous for a plan but giving glimpses of an idyllic future. Paying more attention to his thoughts than the drive, Noah missed his way, suffering the usual cloud of frustration as he retraced his steps along winding country lanes.

The next morning, still searching for inspiration, Noah sat by the window drinking his coffee. Dark clouds raced across the deserted shore at Westward Ho! What had John said? He must do something different. He should be taking risks at his age. If he was going to make something of his life now was the time. Noah jumped up. The bracing wind and foaming shore would help solidify his ideas. Fresh air would be his catalyst.

Only a couple of dog walkers joined him braving the elements. They were prepared for the wind and rain. Noah, however, was wearing trainers and a padded hoodie. By the time he was back at Acorn Nook, they had soaked up almost his body weight in rainwater and salt spray. His ideas were still no more than misty concepts.

What did he want in life? Some things he already knew. To be near Appledore and the coast, independence, being his own boss and animals, or at least people who care about them. The practicality was that he had to earn enough to live on. Working at an animal shelter would only ever be a hobby, unless he won the lottery. What was the next best thing?

His sodden clothes tapped out a drip, drip, drip on the floor reminding him that if he planned to live in the area, he had some shopping to do. He put on a new selection of inadequate clothing and set off to buy an all-weather wardrobe. Inspiration would not come until he had mastered staying warm and dry.

Chapter 4

Snug in his new all-weather coat and walking boots Noah wound his way around the narrow alleyways of Appledore, munching on a sandwich. The old buildings seemed to lean over the pedestrian streets, giving the eclectic mix of homes, cafés, independent shops and galleries an intimate feel. It was a town whose charm and ambiance did not disappear with the tourists at the end of September, as it did in some holiday destinations. It had an enduring character of its own, even in the rain.

Still unsure of his future, his uncle's words resonated in Noah's head as he walked: *'You need to set up your own business, lad.'* Picturing the crowded interior of Abacus Antiques he wondered if a shop was the answer. What would he sell? There was nothing that inspired him.

About to turn off the narrow high street and walk down to the quay, he spotted an abandoned shop-front he hadn't noticed before. Something about it drew him closer. Low and dark, the mullioned windows were wreathed in dirt and cobwebs, but the front door was broad and solid. He felt a warmth emanating from the old building, at odds with its drab exterior. In one of the windows there was a dusty placard declaring the premises 'For Sale'. Noticing the name above the door he gasped.

'Noah's Ark.'

The shop had his name on it. He pictured Radagast nodding sagely and saying, 'It's your destiny, man.' Was the name a coincidence or a sign?

He peered through the windows, shading his eyes from the weak sunlight now prodding the alley and tried to make out what lay inside. A small counter faced the central front door, while shelving, still containing goods, stretched away to the right and the left. A square arch led through to further rooms at the back.

His heart pounded, as he pressed his face against the glass trying to make out every detail of the interior. It had obviously been a pet shop. The perfect business for him. He was experienced with animals and enjoyed dealing with people who loved them. Coping with the financial side of the business would be a breeze and the rest he could learn. The premises were on a corner at the far end of the pedestrianised main street, which ran parallel to the quay. An ideal location. A small alley led from the corner of the property down to the front and the estuary. He could be out of his door and on the quayside in less than half a minute. To the right and left of the shop streets banked by pretty, terraced houses stretched away from the water up the hill.

Sipping hot chocolate in a nearby café, Noah scrolled through everything he could find online about Noah's Ark. Firstly, he found an old website:

Appledore's best and only independent pet shop. Trading since 1989. For a friendly welcome, free advice and all your pet-related needs visit Noah's Ark on Market Street. Your one-stop shop for pet food, toys, cages, bedding, advice and much, much more.

The shop had been trading for over thirty years, so it must have been profitable or it wouldn't have lasted. Noah's Ark had sold everything pet related, except livestock, which Noah knew required a special licence. He then browsed the estate agent's details which showed a few dingy pictures of the shop, a courtyard at the back of the property and the two-bedroom flat upstairs. With a bit of negotiation, it would be affordable.

The more he thought about it, the more Noah convinced himself that running a pet shop would meet all his criteria: living near Appledore and the coast, independence, being his own boss, animals and people who care about them. Leaving the café, he bounded along the street heading for the estate agent's office.

Milton Estate Agents was manned by a lone youth, the owner being out on a viewing. Unfolding himself from behind the desk, his toned swagger and blond streaks declared he would rather be out on the surf than trapped in this small office. However, his eyes lit up and his casual attitude changed on gleaning Noah's interest was genuine.

'The property's an absolute bargain and in a prime location. It's amazing it's not been snapped up already.'

'It looks like it's been empty for quite some time,' Noah prompted.

'Looks can be deceiving,' shrugged the young man. 'The place took a while to come onto the market. It's in excellent condition inside and the current stock is available to purchase as part of the deal. It could be yours lock, stock and barrel within a few weeks.'

'I'll need to have a good look at the last three years' trading figures and the stock inventory, as well as inspecting the property.'

The agent's confident smile faltered for the first time, but soon returned. 'Old Greg who used to run it was pretty poorly towards the end, so the most recent figures aren't that great. Of course, with a new young owner,' he clapped Noah on the back, 'success would be guaranteed. You're perfect for the job.'

Surfer Dude explained that he was alone in the office today, but could show Noah around the following morning. They shook hands and Noah left with a sheaf of information, including the last three years' accounts. His body tingling with excitement, instead of going straight home he walked back to take another look at the shop. An old woman in fluffy blue slippers and an oversized coat was standing outside. Hands and nose pressed against the window, her hat pulled down over her face, she was oblivious to Noah's approach.

'Hello,' he said.

She glanced at him, eyes wide and scurried around the corner as fast as her osteoporosis stoop would allow. At least she can't be a prospective buyer, thought Noah with a shrug. He glanced up at the name plaque again. Noah's Ark. His shop. He pushed away all misgivings about profitability or the state of the building and pictured himself standing in the open doorway welcoming customers.

Continuing his research, he found the place had been empty for a year and the price reduced twice already. It was less expensive than the apartment he had sold in Slough and the two-bedroom flat above would provide him with somewhere to live.

He would spend every day with animal lovers and be his own boss. What's more, he would be in the centre of the town he loved and a stone's throw from the estuary. The cry of seagulls would trumpet his proximity to the sea and his commute would be descending the stairs. Sea air would fill his lungs. No more police sirens throughout the night, no more daily commute fraught with uncertainty about whether it would take twenty minutes or an hour and a half. No more lurking depression at the thought of being trapped in an office.

Noah had sold the idea to himself long before he had done his sums or even been inside the property. He needed to talk through this tantalising opportunity, but couldn't work out who to call. His mother and Radagast were not suitable contenders. Radagast, in typical Tigger mode, would pronounce any departure from the corporate world as a win and the property name a mystic omen of great significance. His mother would worry for his well-being and mental health, unless his business was selling tarot cards and crystals and he was meeting people who would 'enrich his soul'. Running his thoughts past James would involve revealing how unhappy he had been for longer than he cared to admit. He liked to match his brother's upbeat attitude when they chatted.

Now he had the glimmer of an alternative, the thought of returning to corporate life made it difficult to breathe. James would ask why Noah had stuck his old job for so long and that would be a difficult question to answer. Was it because he had been striving for a life social convention told him ought to aspire to?

In the end, he made two calls, firstly phoning his uncle, who he knew would be supportive, but would also give practical advice.

'Marvellous idea, my boy. I'm impressed you've made such a bold decision so quickly. If you want to stay around here (and who wouldn't) owning your own business is the way to go.' He could hear the delight in his uncle's voice. 'I've been running my place for ten years now and wouldn't change a second. If you're worried I can go through the numbers with you, before you commit.'

'I'm okay with the numbers, but a second opinion on the place itself would be great.' Noah didn't mention he was more likely to need help with words than numbers.

'With money from the flat in Slough and a mortgage I'll be able to buy the premises and contents "lock, stock and barrel", as the agent calls it. And I'll have a bit left over, for renovations, new stock and getting the business up and running.'

'There'll be lots to sort out,' warned John, 'website, insurance, accounts, suppliers, advertising and all the rest, but you're a bright lad, you'll soon get the hang of it. When do you want me over for a viewing?'

'Not just yet,' said Noah. 'I don't want to put you out unnecessarily. I'll have a look on my own tomorrow and if I still want to go ahead, I'll ask you to come for the second viewing early next week.'

Noah doubted a viewing would change his mind, but he wanted to inhale the place in peace before he allowed his uncle's big personality in there.

His second call was to Javier, who he hadn't spoken to since leaving Slough.

'What a pleasure.' There was no hint of reproach in Javier's voice for the lack of contact and after a brief update they were soon in discussion about Noah's Ark.

'You can turn your hand to anything, amigo.' Javier told him with conviction. 'You should do it. I haven't heard you this excited since we released that red kite back into the wild a couple of years ago. If you're passionate about something that's the best start you can have.'

The following morning, Noah hurried into town and the estate agents. Surfer Dude, who Noah now knew was called Aztec, grinned when he recognised his potential buyer and immediately re-launched into sales patter.

'Fantastic opportunity. Absolute bargain. Prime position on the high street. A great bonus to have the large courtyard behind. The stock alone's worth thousands.'

Noah filled in a few forms and when Surfer Dude realised his name was the same as that of the shop he slapped Noah on the back. 'Look at that. It's perfect for you.'

The dusty, half-empty shelves told their own story, but the sales space at the front was spacious and once the windows had been cleaned and the dim lighting upgraded it would be light and airy. There was a lockable door by the counter, which Aztec told him led to the flat above. The rear sales room, accessed through a square archway to the right of the counter, had two internal doors. One opening into a storeroom containing additional stock and the other a cloakroom. An external door lead into the private courtyard, at the back of which was a gate giving access to the street. A keypad provided secure entry.

A large aviary dominated one side of the outside space. Aztec informed him that Old Greg used to keep lovebirds in there, but they had been re-homed when the shop closed. The cage would be useful for storage until he got around to dismantling it. An outside staircase nestled against the side of the building on the side street, providing alternative access to the flat above.

They returned inside and Aztec flung open the door to the internal staircase.

'The flat's an absolute gem.' He took the stairs two at a time. 'There isn't a finer place in the whole of Appledore. No need to upgrade the kitchen or bathroom, you can move straight in.'

Noah walked slowly into the living area which overlooked the street through three mullioned sash windows. It contained a small but serviceable kitchen and a tired dining table. From the window on the right, over the kitchen sink, there were views down the narrow alley to the estuary. An unexpected bonus. If he got rid of the swirly carpet, which was sucking all joy from the place, it would be a great place to relax.

In the bathroom he eyed the avocado suite, matching tiles, epilepsy inducing lino and mouldering bobbled window. 'It's a bit dated.'

'Perfectly functional though.' The reply was accompanied by a huge grin. 'Come and see the main bedroom, it's really spacious and the spare room's not bad either.'

Noah followed the enthusiastic agent, finding his description of the bedrooms more accurate than that of the bathroom.

'And look what we have here.' Aztec flung open the external door with a flourish to reveal the stone staircase leading to the street below. 'There's separate access so you can let out the flat if you don't want to use it yourself. That's what the previous guy did. You could earn a fortune from a flat like this.'

Once the tour was complete and Aztec had exhausted his

repertoire of superlatives, he agreed to let Noah have some time on his own, provided he dropped the keys back at the office. His parting shot was, 'There's a couple of viewings scheduled for later this week, so you'll need to make a quick decision.'

Noah snorted and Aztec had the decency to blush.

Without a constant stream of words delivered at full volume, Noah could feel the heartbeat of the place. He took time to stand, eyes closed, and feel whether the place really was his new home. He trailed his fingers along walls uneven with age and felt the floorboards sloping up and down as he crossed the upstairs rooms. Opening the living room windows he inhaled salty air and the cry of seagulls. Returning to the ground floor, the atmosphere wrapped itself around him like a warm blanket. An embrace from a building that knew its new owner had arrived.

Returning to the estate agents, Noah struggled to relinquish the keys and their smooth, heavy fob from his grasp. In his mind Noah's Ark was already his.

Aztec's perfect teeth lit up his tanned face.

'Awesome isn't it? If you commit now, we'll take it off the market straight away.'

Noah took a deep breath and put as much uncertainty into his voice as possible. 'There's a lot of work to be done before it's viable. Even so, I'd like to arrange a second viewing. My uncle will be coming with me. He's been running a business in the area for a long time.'

Aztec looked disappointed once it became clear he would have to get the property past an old hand, as well as a gullible new arrival. He put on a brave face, insisting the viewing should take place as soon as possible to avoid the property being snapped up by the plethora of buyers he had champing at the bit.

With his negotiating hat on, Noah said he would check

availability with his uncle. He then expressed reservations about the price and whether any of the left-over stock was saleable.

Aztec's smile didn't waver, but his shoulders slumped. Noah wondered how often his sales-patter was swallowed whole.

Two visits later, one with John and a final visit on his own (he had firmly declined Aztec's offer to accompany him) and it was time to commit.

John had been thorough in his inspection; his main concerns being that the shop was at the far end, rather than in the middle, of the high street and that a couple of nearby properties were empty.

'You don't want to be at the dead end of town or you'll never get any business. It's footfall you need.' John had glared at the blank windows of the empty premises.

'There's a notice here,' said Noah, standing in front of the building opposite. 'A refill store's moving from Bideford in a couple of weeks. That should bring people to this end of town and there's refurbishment going on in the place a few doors down too. It looks like it might be a café. Any business could shut without warning in the current economic climate. It's as good a location as anywhere else.'

'You're justifying what you want to be true,' said John, patting Noah on the shoulder. 'The shop itself is a good size and if you want to make a go of it I'm sure you'll do well. The courtyard's a useful space too. If you take that big cage thing down, you'll have plenty of room for storage.' His tone became more thoughtful. 'Will you be selling animals too? Cute puppies in the window would bring in the punters.'

'There's strict legislation about the sale of live animals,' said Noah. 'Pet shops have been banned from selling dogs for years. It's to reduce puppy farming.'

'That's a shame.' John frowned.

Noah wasn't sure whether John thought puppy farms were

a shame or the fact that Noah couldn't display an eye-catching litter of pups in the window.

'I'll only be selling things like feed, beds, toys and that kind of stuff,' he replied. 'I've been reading about it and I'm not convinced about the ethics of selling livestock from a pet shop anyway.'

John had moved on from puppies and livestock and Noah's words were interrupted by a hopeful, 'How about a pint, while we talk things over?'

Two pints and a lifetime's worth of tips later, Noah left John chatting to an old friend in the pub. Returning to Acorn Nook, he got out his laptop to do a last review of the numbers and decide on his negotiation strategy.

A few weeks later, ready to make the final commitment, Noah turned his car onto the drive of his uncle's home, a shabby Victorian semi with bay windows that looked in need of a lick of paint or possibly complete replacement. The front lawn consisted of moss and bald patches and tufts of grass poked up between cracks in the tarmac drive. His uncle must be more of a businessman than a homemaker.

Gathering up a buff file crammed with papers, Noah wished he had the confidence to deal with the paperwork on his own. A grown man shouldn't need assistance ploughing through a few pages of text. He had tried going through it without help, but the stress of plunging every penny he possessed into a new business made the words swim on the densely packed pages. Still hovering by his car, he jumped at his uncle's booming voice.

'Don't shilly-shally, lad. Come on in.'

They settled themselves at the dining table in the front room. Shelves groaned with books on antiques, side tables teetered with magazines and used coffee mugs. Bric-a-brac filled every remaining surface and the place looked like it had not been dusted for some years.

Noah shifted in his seat, throat tight, palms sweaty. 'You said you could help me with the paperwork?'

'Not a problem.' John pulled the folder towards himself. 'All this paperwork will be a bit much with your dyslexia. We'll read through it together and make a note of any queries.'

Noah stared at his uncle. 'You know I have dyslexia?' He scoured his memory. Had he done something to give himself away?

'Of course.' John peered over the top of his glasses. 'Your father told me when you were a teenager. We think your grandfather had it too – undiagnosed, of course. It wasn't talked about back in the day. Your dad was sorry yours wasn't picked up earlier, although that's often the case with bright kids; they hide it and find ways around it for as long as possible.'

His uncle knew. His dad had discussed it with him. His grandfather had been a fellow sufferer. A man who had been a cabinet-maker of great skill, revered by all the family. A weight lifted from Noah's chest. Why had he fretted for two days before asking his uncle for assistance? So much unnecessary anguish.

'How's your reading now?' asked John, interrupting his thoughts.

'I can read well enough,' said Noah, 'I'm just slower than most people and it tires me out if there's a lot to plough through. All this,' he waved a hand at the myriad papers on the table, 'is overwhelming and I was worried about misinterpreting or missing something.'

'I'm glad you asked, it won't take us a jiffy.' John pushed his glasses up his nose and opened the folder. 'I see you've negotiated a good price,' he nodded approvingly at the first page.

Reviewing the purchase documents took a lot longer than a jiffy and as always was followed by a trip to the pub. Having been through everything with his uncle, Noah was comfortable with what he was signing up for. The papers had been organised into neat piles and annotated stickers marked the remaining points he needed to clarify. Leaving John to have a final whiskey at the pub, he set off for home. Preoccupied with his new business venture, Noah went wrong twice on the way home, but didn't even mind. What did he expect if he had bigger things to concentrate on?

Over the past few weeks, Surfer Dude had become surprisingly friendly and chatted enthusiastically with Noah about his reasons for moving to the area, plans for the business and his time working at Javier's animal sanctuary. He seemed almost ecstatic when Noah finally signed the purchase paperwork. It was as if he really cared.

With no chain, the final elements of the sale went smoothly and it was soon time for Noah to collect the keys from a beaming Aztec. He assured him without a hint of irony, 'You've bought the most awesome place on the planet, my friend. You're going to love it.'

Chapter 5

The keys were attached to a large wooden ball. It felt smooth, heavy and reassuring in the palm of Noah's hand. Putting the brass key, dulled with age, into the low oak door, he felt a well-oiled clunk and savoured a shiver of excitement as it turned. He had a business and a home by the sea. City life, pointless meetings, unheeded reports and mind-numbing spreadsheets were a thing of the past. No more being told what to do.

He traced his fingers down the panels in the front door, before pushing it open. Solid and imposing, it was almost worth buying the place for the front door alone. The interior was dim and dust motes floated in the February gloom. He paused on the threshold, his hand groping for the light-switch. The solid wooden counter from where he would make his first sale beckoned him to step behind it and take ownership.

Clang. There was a noise from the back of the shop. Peering nervously into the shadows, he renewed his fumblings for the light-switch. A rustle and the sound of metal against metal came from the dingy back-room.

'Who's there?' Noah's voice was higher and less self-assured than he would have liked. His armpits prickled. Clearing his dry throat, he channelled his uncle's booming tones, wishing John were standing beside him.

'Come on out. What are you doing in there?' The switch was nowhere to be found. He hesitated, loath to go further without knowing who or what was lurking in the dark. There was another rustle, then silence. His fingers finally found the switch, lower than he remembered. Neon strips threw a swathe of brightness right and left across the main area of the shop, some of it stretching beyond the square arch and into the room beyond.

Now there was only silence apart from Noah's breathing. Had the back door been left unlocked after one of his viewings? Noah inched forward holding both hands out in front as if to ward off evil spirits. Poking his head through the arch, he peered into the murky depths of the second, smaller room.

A huge metal cage glimmered in the corner. Something was in it and that something was alive.

Noah directed his phone torch at the cage, jumping when the light glinted off two dark eyes. The creature scuffled sideways along a perch and ruffled its feathers. His eyes now used to the dim light, Noah identified the interloper as a parrot. Neither the cage nor the parrot had been there when he viewed the premises.

Relieved that nothing more sinister had been the cause of his sweaty armpits and dry throat, he turned on the lights in the back-room and went to inspect his intruder. Larger than the African greys he was familiar with, its olive-green and emerald feathers and curved beak gave it a formidable appearance. A cardboard sign next to the cage announced: *My name is Harold. I am a kea. Please look after me.*

Fresh seed, water and even the remains of a slice of melon were in the cage. A bag of dried parrot food hung from a bird-stand that almost reached the ceiling. Next to it was a smaller portable stand. Harold had been deposited here very recently by someone who cared about him. There was no parrot on the inventory and the estate agent hadn't mentioned one. Noah scratched his head. The parrot scratched its head too.

'Hello,' Noah used the soft voice he had adopted when talking to Javier's parrots at the sanctuary. The bird appeared to be weighing him up but made no sound.

'What am I going to do with you?' Noah circled the cage a couple of times, then inspected the rest of the shop, relieved to find nothing else unexpected.

Observing him curiously, the parrot remained silent, its eyes following Noah as he walked around.

Pulling out his phone, Noah called Aztec at the estate agents.

'The place is yours, man. If there's a parrot there, it's yours too.'

'But it's not mine. Have you any idea who it belongs to?'

'Haven't got a Scooby. Listen, if it's in the shop it's yours. That's what the contract says.'

'I don't even want a parrot,' Noah insisted.

'I thought you loved them,' said Aztec. 'You used to work for free at that bird sanctuary didn't you?'

'I did, but that doesn't mean I want a parrot.'

'All pet shops need a parrot. Keep it. I've got to go, there's a customer here.'

Aztec had always been so chatty and interested in what Noah had to say. Commission now in his pocket, he seemed considerably less so.

Next he called the local police station. They had no record of a lost parrot, but promised to contact him if one was reported. His claims that a parrot couldn't actually be lost if it came complete with cage, a couple of stands and fresh food fell on deaf ears.

He called Javier and explained about the parrot and its missing owner.

'You've got a parrot. That's fantastic news.'

This was not the response Noah had expected. 'Be serious. I need to find out where he came from.'

'I'll put out some feelers,' said Javier. 'I've got loads of contacts in the bird scene. Kea are rare, so if someone's looking for him, I'll hear about it. You should count your blessings. There's no better companion than a parrot, although kea are a bit of a handful by all accounts.'

'He's not even mine. I don't know how to look after a parrot.'

'Everyone seems to think he's yours. As for not being able to look after him, that's rubbish. You're brilliant with birds. All animals, in fact. Whoever left that kea there chose the right person to look after him. You'll do a great job.'

Mystery unsolved, Noah turned to the parrot. 'You'll have to stay here for now. I need to move in.'

Moving in involved more trips between Acorn Nook and the shop than Noah had anticipated. He had been scouring Freecycle and local charity shops for essentials over the past couple of weeks, grateful for permission to store his treasures temporarily in the apartment. Together with the furniture still in storage from his old flat, he had everything he needed.

Throughout the day, Noah kept the parrot updated on what he was doing. What he was bringing in, how many more trips he had to make and how happy he was to be starting his new venture. Disappointed to receive no response, Noah was still glad to have someone to talk to. By the time his belongings were in and he could finally take a break, it was dark. Perched on a stool next to the parrot cage and eating take-away fish and chips out of a cardboard tray, he spoke his thoughts out loud.

'Well, Harold, I hope I've done the right thing. There's no going back now.' The enormity of the challenge ahead made it difficult to swallow his supper. Taking a pause from chewing, he poked a piece of fish through the bars of the cage. Harold shuffled up and down his perch a couple of times before bending forward and taking it with precision and care.

Not completely sure if he was speaking to the parrot or himself, Noah continued, 'I hope my new business works out. I can't imagine going back to office life, but that's what I'll have to do if I can't make a success of this.' He screwed up his fish and chip wrapper and placed it on the floor. He would need to buy a bin for the shop.

'Uncle John's very positive and James thinks it's the best

thing I've ever done – he would say that though. They both reckon it doesn't matter whether it works out or not, the important thing is giving it a go. That's easy for them to say,' he laughed. 'They're much more "have a go" people than I am.'

Pacing up and down in front of the cage, Noah was full of nervous energy despite an exhausting day.

'Radagast's another one who's all for it. He waffled on about my animal spirit and claims credit for unleashing it over Christmas. He even reckons he channelled visions of animals parading two by two and sent them to inspire me. The guy's such a fantasist. He's convinced his magical powers are the driving force behind so many weird and wonderful things. It's his own life he needs to sort out, in my opinion.'

Noah stopped in front of the cage. 'I'm sorry I've kept you locked in today. It's been full-on and the front door's been open most of the time. I'll let you out tomorrow if you promise to be good and stay on here,' he tapped the tall stand, complete with ladders, toys, a food bowl and a rope.

'It would be nice if I could keep you, but I'm sure someone'll claim you soon.' With no reply from Harold, Noah gave up any further attempt at conversation, but a kernel of warmth accompanied him up the stairs into his flat. He was not alone. Once the business was up and running he would have to make new friends, human friends, but first things first.

Before going to bed, Noah researched his new companion. He discovered that kea (*nestor notabilis*) are an endangered species from the Southern Alps of New Zealand and the only remaining mountain parrot in the world. Unlike many parrots, they don't talk, but they do make a wide variety of sounds.

Having only seen Harold's soft olive and emerald outer feathers, Noah read that observers are treated to a flash of orange from under a kea's wing and at the top of their tail when they fly. Making a mental note to look for this blaze of colour when he let Harold out in the morning, Noah then spent a while laughing at videos of the birds getting into mischief, damaging cars or delving into unattended backpacks in search of food and entertainment.

All the articles he read agreed that a kea's exceptional intelligence, need for stimulation and destructive tendencies meant they did not make good pets. It was going to be tricky coping with this unusual bird.

It took Noah a moment after he woke up to realise he was no longer in his rented studio but in the roomy flat above his new business. Above Noah's Ark. It was now up to him to make the pet shop work. Rather than feeling intimidated, he was thrilled at the thought. It would be a hard slog getting everything ready between now and opening day in three weeks' time, but he had a plan and was prepared to work day and night, if that was what it took.

Showered, dressed and armed with treats of fresh fruit and vegetables from the local store, he opened Harold's cage and offered him some lettuce. Stretching out from as far away as possible, Harold took the leaves, shuffling back to the far side of his perch to eat them. He showed no inclination to come out of his cage. Placing a selection of fruit and vegetables in a metal bowl, Noah left the bird to explore in his own time.

Opening his laptop, he studied the to-do list he had been compiling over the past couple of weeks. He had to clean, repaint and organise the shop, as well as order stock, set up a website and promote the new business. There was work to be done in the flat too. A plumber was coming to install a much-needed new bathroom (despite what Surfer Dude had said) and new carpets were arriving in a couple of days. Decorating the rest of the flat would have to wait.

He added a new item to the bottom of the list: *sort aviary*. Assuming no-one claimed Harold, the aviary in the courtyard would need to be furnished with sturdy perches and toys to create a safe place for the bird to fly and play. A perfectly placed small square window led from behind the parrot stand into the aviary. It would allow Harold to hop in and out as he pleased once the weather warmed up.

Uncle John came over several times in the following weeks, providing expertise, additional manpower and cheery company. Noah was grateful for the assistance and looked forward to him striding in mid-morning demanding 'a proper cuppa'. John filled the space, putting on country music at full volume and singing along. He interspersed the songs with his own brand of advice and instruction. Sometimes Noah found his company overwhelming, but John's ability to find a solution to any DIY problem was invaluable. Noah would not have managed to upgrade the light-fittings or secure shelves on the crumbling walls of the old building without his uncle's help.

Except when he was misbehaving, Harold retired to his cage and glowered from the top perch when John was there. Noah wasn't sure if it was the loud music, the shouting or simply Uncle John he didn't like. If the latter, the feeling was clearly mutual. John insisted the parrot had no useful purpose, took up valuable retail space and made a mess.

'You're a bloody nuisance, you are,' he would say, waggling a finger at the bird.

Harold hadn't helped his case. He had flown off with John's screwdriver more than once, destroyed a pair of his gloves and tipped over a tray full of screws, giving a triumphant 'keeaah' when they scattered across the floor. After the first couple of visits Noah locked him in his cage when John was there.

The days on which John helped out always ended in the same way. Hands on hips, he would survey their handiwork and announce, 'We deserve a pie and a pint now, don't you think, laddie?' This was clearly his favourite part of the day.

49

Initially aloof and uncommunicative, after a few days Harold started to hop from foot to foot when he saw Noah and before long climbed willingly onto his arm or shoulder. They soon developed a routine. First thing, Noah let Harold out. With a whoosh, he would circle the shop treating Noah to glimpses of the vibrant orange feathers underneath his wings and at the base of his spine, which were normally hidden by his emerald flight feathers. After that, Harold would run up and down the lowest rung of his perch, waiting for treats of fresh fruit and vegetables.

Aware that the powerful beak was capable of crushing a Brazil nut and could do serious damage to his finger, Noah cut long strips of fruit and was ready to withdraw his hand at any minute. However, Harold took his treats gently and before long Noah felt comfortable feeding him titbits as small as blueberries or even sunflower hearts with no fear of being nipped.

Harold spent most of the day on his stand where he could look out of the window and hop backwards and forwards into his cage. He quickly learnt to tap on the window to let Noah know if he wanted to go in or out of the aviary.

Noah's concern that Harold might soil the goods in the shop turned out to be unfounded. The bird had been trained to return to his cage to poop, making clearing up easy. Harold seemed to enjoy being in the part of the shop where Noah was working, so when they were alone Noah placed the small portable stand next to him and the parrot observed him from close quarters.

Chatting with Harold became as natural as talking to Javier had been, although Noah sometimes wondered if the amount of time he spent talking to Harold was unhealthy – despite its therapeutic value. Consulting Harold on where the new shelves should go and whether he should paint the wall behind the counter green rather than white helped Noah order his thoughts. Harold appeared uninterested in interior décor solutions.

At the end of three weeks working late into the evening, warm LEDs glowed from the ceiling and newly whitewashed walls reflected the light. The shop seemed brighter and more spacious than Noah could have ever imagined. The oak counter had been buffed to a soft sheen and in the evenings the gleaming mullioned windows reflected a pristine interior. A new bathroom had been installed upstairs and the bedrooms carpeted. Polished floorboards and a pattered rug had replaced sickly brown swirls in the living room. Furniture from the flat in Slough had reached its new home.

'It's the grand opening tomorrow,' said Noah, no longer self-conscious about chatting with Harold. 'I think we're as ready as we can be. I just hope the advertising, first-week discount and my home-made chocolate brownies lure customers in.'

Noah fished in his pocket at which Harold started to bob his head and hop from foot to foot.

'Here's your bedtime treat.' Noah proffered a shelled walnut and Harold took it gently from his fingers. Holding it in one claw and nibbling the edges, he looked as contented as Noah felt.

'Goodnight.' Noah turned to go.

Harold paused his chewing. 'Goodnight.'

Noah whipped around and stared. Kea didn't normally mimic human sounds in the way many other parrots did. Had he imagined it? Standing in front of the cage, he enunciated 'goodnight' several times, as if clarifying the pronunciation to a foreigner.

Harold demolished his walnut, eyeing Noah disparagingly.

We've said goodnight. Why are you repeating yourself?

The following morning, Noah was downstairs by the time the first fingers of dawn crept through the window. More excited about Harold having spoken for the first time, than he was about the inaugural opening of the shop, the first thing he did was stand in front of the cage saying, 'Good morning'. He even tried 'goodnight' in case this was the only word Harold knew. The bird gave him a scathing look.

Noah stopped and frowned. I'm spending too much time with only a parrot for company, if I'm attributing scathing looks to a bird, he thought. Shaking his head, he gave Harold breakfast and fussed round straightening items on shelves and wiping away imaginary dirt. Placing the brownies he had baked the previous evening on the pristine counter; Noah checked and rechecked his to-do list. Nine o'clock came around very slowly that morning.

Finally, he could turn over the gleaming sign in his window. The word 'Open', surrounded by paw-prints, beckoned to passers-by. A separate sign provided opening hours, letting people know the business was closed Wednesday afternoons and Sundays. On tiptoe he peered through the window in search of his first customer. There was no-one in sight. He fetched his new A-board, detailing special offers, and placed it outside.

With nothing more to do, he paced the shop. What if no-one came? He adjusted the position of the cake stand heaped with brownies and the jar of dog biscuits for canine companions. Every few minutes, he stuck his head out of the door.

Before long a small plump lady with a grey bob and no-nonsense manner pushed open the door and stepped inside.

'Hello, I'm Vera.'

'Hi, I'm Noah. How can I help?'

'Noah? What a coincidence!' she exclaimed, her face lighting up, giving her an air of boundless warmth.

'This shop's been called Noah's Ark as long as I can remember.'

Before Noah could get a word in, she continued.

'I own the refill store opposite. I called in to wish you good luck. It's lovely to see the pet shop restored to its former glory.'

Hiding his disappointment that it was not a real customer, but glad of her support, Noah replied, 'Thank you. I was going call in to say "hello" but haven't had a moment with getting everything ready.' He shuffled his feet and looked down. It was not preparations that had kept him from going to see his neighbour, but a worry that an outsider might not be welcome.

Vera seemed to read his thoughts. 'We're delighted to have you here. There's nothing worse than an empty shop on the high street. I should have popped in before, but I've been busy with my own relocation.'

Noah wondered who 'we' were and how Vera knew what other people thought, if her business had only just opened. Also, what did she know about the pet shop's 'former glory'?

He blurted out his most pressing question. 'Did you know the previous shopkeeper?'

'Not well, but I've been inside a few times over the years. Mr Gregory, Old Greg as everyone called him, was frail for quite some time before he died. Poor soul.'

She chatted away, explaining her business had relocated from premises in nearby Bideford, but that she had lived in Appledore all her life. She seemed to know everyone and provided him with a pen picture of several local business owners.

The details went into a jumble in Noah's mind. There was no way could he deal with this much information in one hit. He would write down anything useful as soon as she left; hoping she was the kind of person who repeated herself. He suspected she might be.

Vera picked up one of his business cards from the counter. 'Shall I get your details added to the Appledore business group? We get together about every six weeks to discuss local issues. It's a social thing too. We meet above the pub and most people stay on afterwards for a couple of drinks.'

'That would be great. I'd like to get to know more people and any help or advice is welcome.'

'I've invited Jemima and Alison too. They're from Brewberry, the new café,' she said.

'That's great. I saw it opens next week.'

'The menu looks delicious and it'll bring more business to this end of the street.' Before leaving she leant over the counter and lowered her voice, 'One more thing: you may want to update your A-board outside. It's special with an "I". An easy mistake to make when you're busy. I'll see you soon.' She gave a cheery wave and bustled out of the door.

Blushing and embarrassed, Noah corrected his mistake. He had written the A-board yesterday evening and thought everything was fine. Did Vera think he was incompetent? Why hadn't he checked his spellings more thoroughly?

His first customer interrupted his thoughts. She was a tall, slim woman with a careworn face even though she only looked in her mid-fifties. Short grey hair protruded from underneath her waxed green hat. After saying 'hello', she spent a while walking around the shop, including pausing to admire Harold. Noah hovered next to the counter, not wanting to pursue her, but doing his best to look attentive. Eventually, she came over with a couple of tins of cat food. Noah hoped she didn't notice his hands trembling as his first transaction went through.

'You've done a lovely job of sprucing the place up,' she said, taking her receipt.

'Thank you. I'm pleased with it.'

'I hope everything goes well for you.' A brief smile made her face look less drawn. Perhaps she was younger than he thought.

She was the first of many curious locals who left Noah with kind words and encouragement that morning. The support calmed his nerves and boosted his confidence.

The first week flew by. A steady stream of customers came in and out, some attracted by his opening week promotions, some out of curiosity and others, unashamedly, because they wanted a free chocolate brownie. Delighted with his initial success, Noah wanted to call and tell his Uncle John and James the good news, but held off in case sales didn't hold. He would look ridiculous if he crowed about his takings this week and they plummeted next week. He consoled himself with reporting to Harold.

'I know the first week isn't necessarily representative, but I can't help being pleased.' Harold raised the feathers on his neck and bent his head, tilting it to one side. Noah obediently reached up and scratched the bird's neck, receiving a muffled '*nice*' in appreciation.

'You've got quite a vocabulary, haven't you? "*Goodnight, hello, good morning, nice, yes please.*" Did no-one tell you kea aren't supposed to talk? You must be a lot smarter than most of your kind.' Harold stood up straight and fluffed his feathers. Sometimes Noah was sure he understood every word. Giving Harold one last scratch he headed upstairs to bed.

Noah was awake and sitting on the side of the bed with his feet on the chilly floor, before he realised he had even moved. It was three o'clock. Every muscle taut, his ears strained for unfamiliar sounds. The rain hammered down outside and there was a steady pouring sound from the broken guttering on the building opposite. Getting up to peer out of the window, he saw only a dark, empty street. The security light had not come on. He scoured the street until a shiver prompted him to get back under the covers. He had heard and seen nothing unusual, but nevertheless lay for a while with his eyes open. Had it been a dream that disturbed him?

The next morning, Noah inspected his shop more thoroughly than usual, looking for a sign something had been disturbed. He found nothing.

'Did you see anyone here last night?' he asked Harold, unlocking the back door to check the courtyard. Harold ignored him. Closing the door, Noah went over to the cage. 'I'm sorry. I haven't even said "hello" yet, never mind let you out or given you breakfast.' He opened the cage and brought a couple of juicy grapes out of his pocket.

'Good morning, Harold.'

'Good morning, Noah.'

Noah dropped the grapes, all thoughts of intruders driven from his mind. 'How did you learn my name?'

Harold hopped to the floor, retrieved a grape and flew up to his stand.

'Say Noah for me.'

Silence. Noah tried again. 'Good morning, Harold.'

Harold chewed his grapes.

You only say good morning once each day, not every few minutes on demand.

Having been ignored for several minutes, Noah gave up, checked today's to-do list and started his pre-opening duties. Every so often he glanced over at Harold, delighted that the bird knew his name. Noticing Vera had arrived at the Refill Store, he went across the street to tell her about the leaking gutter and ask if there had been any recent trouble with break-ins.

The Refill Store had a much more modern feel than his own premises, with large windows across the front, high ceilings and smooth walls inside. The far wall was lined with commercial dispensers where customers could fill their own containers with rice, beans, lentils, pasta and much more. Large jars of spices and herbs sat on shelves behind the counter. Vera weighed these out as necessary. Eco cleaning and hygiene products were also on sale together with environmentally friendly brushes, cloths, containers and gifts. Canvas prints showing spectacular scenery adorned the bits of the walls that were not covered by shelving.

Vera assured him that the area was normally low in crime. 'You could ask the question at the business owners' meeting on Thursday,' she suggested. 'See if anyone else has had trouble lately.'

'I'll do that.' Noah glanced at his watch, 'I'd better get back to the shop, I need to open up.'

'Noah,' Vera gave an overly bright smile, then fiddled with the pearl necklace adorning her pink jumper. 'I hope you don't mind me mentioning it, but you've made another little mistake on the board outside your shop. I used to be a teacher you see. I can't help noticing these things.'

Noah blushed and glanced over his shoulder at the board. It looked fine to him.

Vera was blushing too now. 'I shouldn't have said anything.'

There was an awkward silence while Noah's tongue stuck to the roof of his mouth. He wanted Vera's help. It didn't look good if the first thing prospective customers saw were misspellings. 'It's fine. I er, don't mind,' he mumbled.

'I'm such a busybody. It's a wonder anyone puts up with me. I need to remember I'm not a teacher anymore.' Vera seemed more embarrassed than he was.

'I'm not good at spelling,' he blurted, heart racing. It was out. 'I've never been good at it.' He waited for the look of surprise and pity, but it didn't come.

Vera nodded and held his gaze. 'Are you dyslexic, dear? It's very common. About one in every five people, but you probably know that.'

Her matter-of-fact tone helped decrease his pulse rate. 'I've seen various statistics, but you never know what's true.'

'It often runs in families,' Vera stated confidently.

How did she know so much, wondered Noah, saying, 'I found out only the other day that my grandfather had dyslexia. I had no idea.' The words started tumbling out. 'Mine wasn't picked up until quite late. I spent most of primary school languishing in the bottom set, bored because everything we did was so obvious and at the same time feeling stupid because I couldn't read or write properly.'

'You poor thing. I guess you managed to cover it up a lot of the time because you're such a bright lad.'

'I'm not that bright,' Noah muttered looking down.

'Rubbish.' Vera waited until he looked up again. 'I've met and taught enough people to know you're an intelligent and capable young man. Don't underestimate yourself because you had a hard time at school.'

'I do find it difficult to discuss,' he confessed, feeling lighter at the admission. 'People seem to treat me differently if they think I can't spell, so I try and hide it. Sometimes people even speak to me more slowly when they find out; as if I'm some sort of idiot.'

'That's just ignorance!' Vera banged a fist on her serving counter. 'You should be proud of what you've achieved, despite not having had it easy. Doubly proud.'

Noah's shoulders straightened. 'Thank you, I do know I'm not stupid. Feel free to let me know any time you notice I've misspelt something.'

'You're sure you don't want me to keep my pedantism to myself?' she laughed.

'Not at all, in fact as a thank you, why don't you come over Sunday morning for cake and coffee?' Noah had shocked himself with the invitation, but Vera's reply was immediate.

'I'd be delighted. Sundays can be a bit quiet sometimes.' A flicker of sadness touched her face.

It had not occurred to Noah that this cheerful and busy woman would ever struggle with being alone. Should he mention the emotion he had seen in her face, or would she prefer him to pretend he hadn't noticed? While he was still wondering what to say, she scribbled one word on a piece of paper and handed it over. 'On your board – it's weather, not whether.'

'I'll sort it straight away,' he took the paper. 'Ten o'clock Sunday then?'

'Perfect,' she beamed. 'I'll see you soon.'

He left the shop, his shoulders back and his head held high. A few minutes later, he had updated his A-board to read: *New in – all weather coats for your dogs. Sizes S, M, L.'*

Thinking back to his school days, Noah remembered his burning desire to learn and contribute in class and his frustration at being unable to read questions or write answers, even though it was stuff he knew. He had found himself lumped with the children doing the least interesting activities and with whom he had nothing in common. Books with mono-dimensional characters and facile storylines were all he was allowed. The ones with interesting covers and the ones his friends talked about were denied him. Excluded from a whole swathe of interest and development, he had retreated into himself and lost confidence in his abilities.

Things improved at senior school, where he was moved into the top set because of his mathematical ability and making friends became easier within a peer group of bright children. The school identified his dyslexia when he was twelve, just after his father left, informing his parents and providing targeted help.

His mother, distracted by and reeling from her recent marriage break-up, resorted to alternative therapies. She placed fluorite crystals around the house to awaken his third eye and arranged for a course of acupuncture to balance his energy and focus his thoughts. His father, absorbed by his new relationship and forthcoming move to Australia, told him not to worry and that everything would be alright in the long run. After a few months, Noah's reading improved to adequate levels, testament, said his mother, to the power of crystals. During the course of a brief phone call, his father declared, 'I knew it wasn't really a problem.' Noah kept his feelings of inadequacy to himself.

The business owners' meeting was taking place this evening. Having changed into a smart shirt and newly washed jeans, Noah put a pen and notebook in his bag. Vera had assured him the meeting would be useful and he was looking forward to getting to know a few people and spending an evening in company rather than on his own. However, the thought of walking into a room full of people he didn't know had him searching for excuses not to go. He supposed he would know Vera and the owners of the new café, Brewberry. He had called in to introduce himself a few days ago. Jemima and Alison had been delighted to meet their new neighbour, insisting he have a hot chocolate and a syrupy flapjack on the house.

There was a knock at the door. Noah opened it to find Vera wearing a long beige puffa coat against the chill and her usual red cloche hat.

'I thought it would be nice for us to go together. It can be a bit intimidating to walk into a group where you don't know anyone.' The corners of her eyes creased as her lips broke into a smile. 'I know that's how I felt the first time.'

'Thank you. That's very kind. I'll grab my coat.' Noah couldn't imagine Vera ever feeling intimidated. She walked with such confidence he had assumed that was how she felt. Perhaps he should try a more confident stride himself?

The room above the pub was panelled to half-way up the walls and had wide wooden floorboards. Lamps around the room gave out a soft glow and dark curtains were pulled across the windows to keep out draughts. Several small tables had been put together to make one long table in the middle, around which a few people were sitting. The rest of the group were crowded at a dresser where there were urns of tea and coffee as well as a box of assorted biscuits. Vera introduced Noah to the chairman, Aaron Chalmers, a tall, skinny man with a weathered face and grey hair pulled back into a ponytail. Noah repeated the name to himself a few times and wrote it down as soon as they were sitting at the table. Remembering names was another of his failings.

'A very warm welcome to our new members,' said Aaron. 'Noah Wood owns Noah's Ark, the pet shop at the end of Market Street, and Jemima and Alison Gardener have just opened the new café, Brewberry, a couple of doors along from Noah.' He waved towards each of them as he said their names. 'We wish them success with their new businesses.'

'Hear, hear,' said a man, who Noah recognised as the owner of the fish and chip shop. 'The last thing we want is empty properties on the high street.'

Aaron then asked them to introduce themselves.

Bright and bubbly Jemima spoke for herself and her more reserved partner, Alison. She furnished everyone with far more rambling detail than was necessary, including describing the small restaurant they used to run in Reading. Hoping for more social hours and to be near the coast, they had moved to Appledore. She then produced a large tin of flapjacks and handed them around.

Wishing he had thought to bring something to share, Noah explained his move also came from a desire to live nearer the sea and change his lifestyle. He did not mention Daisy, his mother, Radagast or even his childhood holidays in Devon. The information seemed too personal for this group of unknown businessmen and women. He did say that his uncle lived in the area, soon establishing that several of the attendees already knew his larger than life relative. Later in the meeting, Noah brought up his worries about security. Aaron advised that crime rates in the area were low, but several people suggested he invest in CCTV.

After the meeting Noah walked home alone, as Vera lived at the opposite end of town. He took a detour to stroll along the quay, admiring the lights twinkling across the estuary and the sound of the water lapping gently at the sea wall. The salty smell of seaweed pervaded the air. He sat on a bench and inhaled rippling calm and starlight. The moon was a small sliver in the sky. Times like this were the reason he had moved to Devon. Eventually, the chill March air and the need to give his parrot some company sent him back to the flat.

Putting Harold on his stand, Noah scratched the parrot's neck. Normally, he spent a couple of hours with Harold after the shop closed, but there hadn't been time this evening. It was now late and the comfort of his sofa was calling. Hoping the bird wouldn't destroy anything in his flat, Noah offered his wrist asking, 'Would you like to keep me company in my living room?'

There was no hesitation on Harold's part. Noah picked up the small portable stand and they went upstairs together. Harold kept very still, as if afraid Noah might change his mind. Surprised how comforting he found the bird's company, Noah told himself he must start getting out and about and meeting people now the shop was up and running.

The companionable new arrangement became a regular occurrence with parrot and young man spending their evenings together. Harold was free to perch on his stand, Noah's shoulder or the table until it was time for bed and he was returned to his cage downstairs. If Noah had been out during the evening, he would return to a cacophony of 'Hello Noah's' until he either relented and took Harold upstairs, or mounted the stairs alone, followed by a high-pitched 'keaaahh' of dismay.

Chapter 6

It was at the end of his second week that Sunshine Girl first brightened Noah's day. He had just served Mrs Chalice, someone he already viewed as a regular, noticing that the circles under her eyes were more pronounced than usual. She always had a weary air, but this morning her whole face looked grey. Loading tins of cat food into her trolley, Noah worried about her dragging it up the steep hill, although he guessed she was only a similar age to his mother.

'Are you sure you wouldn't like me to deliver your tins? I've started a delivery service on Wednesday afternoons. It'd be no trouble to add you to my round.'

Blue eyes smiled and Mrs Chalice looked much younger for a moment. 'I like to get out when I can and buying cat food is a good excuse. I always feel better after some fresh air.

'I do too,' said Noah, adding 'and sea air is the best.'

'We are blessed living here,' she agreed.

Feeling brave, Noah asked a question he had been wondering about since her first visit. 'How many cats do you have, Mrs Chalice?'

'I don't have any, dear,' she tipped her head to one side and smiled. 'This is for the hedgehogs.' Noah held the door as she trundled her plaid trolley onto the street, bowing her head at the March drizzle.

He was still holding the door when a petite girl, cheeks glistening with raindrops, stepped inside. Her smile lit up the room like a thousand candles. She gave the impression she smiled a lot. Throwing back her hood uncovering long blond hair, she sent a shower of raindrops through the air. Noah could see she had clear blue eyes and a smattering of freckles on her nose. He wondered if her personality was as vibrant as her smile and her mango-coloured coat.

In a soft and melodious voice Sunshine Girl said, 'Hi, I'm looking for a new cat collar. Pink would be great, but any colour will do. Can you help?'

What a sexy voice. Noah realised his mouth was open and closed it with a snap. A blush crept up his neck.

'Of course.' Struggling to maintain eye contact, he opted for leading the way into the back-room where a selection of collars, leads and harnesses were kept. Seemingly oblivious to his discomfort, the girl chatted easily.

'Buffy's a year old now. She's grown so quickly lately. I guess all kittens do.' The warmth in her chuckle told Noah she was a true animal lover.

'I didn't know this shop was here, but my friend told me about it, so I thought I'd call in. Have you been open long?'

'Just over a month,' croaked Noah. Why couldn't he think of anything witty or interesting to say?

'Noah's Ark is a great name for a pet shop. What made you think of it?'

'It came with the name,' said Noah, wondering if he should tell her his name was Noah and ask hers. Would that be too familiar, after all, she was only a customer? Opting for a safe topic, he cleared his throat and took her through the pros and cons of the various collars on display. Comfortable covering detail, his blush subsided and he found he could now make eye contact.

Having chosen a collar, Sunshine Girl continued to chatter, telling him she taught art at a local secondary school and had been living in nearby Northam for three years. She seemed very taken with Harold, who fluffed his feathers and strutted.

All too soon Noah's sunny customer was ready make her purchase and leave. A swift wave of her card sent the payment through and with a radiant smile and a swish of golden hair she left the shop.

Harold had observed the events with interest.

The girl is pretty. Noah's blushes mean he thinks so too. 'Handsome Harold' she called me. Clearly a discerning young lady.

Harold chewed his claw.

A cat lover though. There's always a downside.

He preened a couple of wing feathers.

Why had Noah let the card payment go through so smoothly, missing an easy opportunity to keep her chatting?

Noah stared at the door wondering what he could have done to get Sunshine Girl to stay longer.

In preparation for Vera's visit on Sunday, Noah vacuumed and tidied the flat. He had even bought a cafetière and ground coffee. He couldn't offer instant coffee when he'd made a special invitation and Vera had been so helpful. Apart from Uncle John, she would be the first guest to visit his flat even though he had lived there for over a month.

When Vera arrived, she breezed in through the door wearing a belted raincoat (much smarter than her usual puffer coat) and carrying a small handbag. Hatless today, her grey bob swung neatly around her jawline. Noah noticed she had put on lipstick. Did she view coffee with him as an occasion worthy of lipstick? He felt honoured and a little embarrassed.

'Something smells delicious,' said Vera, lifting her nose into the air.

'I made brownies.' Noah had slid from cheerful anticipation to tongue-tied in seconds. In his mind's eye her raincoat transformed into a lab-coat and her handbag into a clipboard. He envisaged her marching through his flat, mouth turned down in disapproval taking note of things which were not in order. Was his invitation a huge mistake?

'Brownies are my favourite,' she trilled, taking off her rain-mac and draping it over her arm, revealing a fluffy red jumper and grey slacks. 'It's nice to have time to chat,' she continued. 'Whenever I'm in the shop a customer comes in before we can have a proper conversation. It'll be lovely to get to know each other better.' Her smile was warm and open.

Noah nodded and looked at his feet. He couldn't reconcile his brief vision of a disapproving Vera in formal attire, with the bright and homely woman standing in front of him.

'Come up to the flat, then we can sit and talk in comfort.' Noah led the way. He would feel better once he was making coffee and cutting up the freshly baked brownies. It helped to do something when he was nervous.

Vera paused at the top of the stairs. 'What a bright and airy place you have. Are all the rooms so spacious?' she exclaimed, craning her neck from one end of the room to the other and then in the direction of the closed doors leading to the bedrooms and bathroom.

Sensing she was keen to explore the whole flat, Noah felt obliged to offer, 'Would you like to have a look around?'

'Only if you're sure,' she said, throwing her coat over the sofa and looking expectant. 'I find it so interesting looking around other people's houses.'

Noah wasn't sure his two-bedroom flat qualified as a house, but Vera declared it charming. He was glad he had tidied before she came.

Vera chatted openly over coffee, telling Noah she had lived in Appledore for most of her life. After retiring early from teaching she had opened a refill store in Bideford. Her husband had died following a heart attack a year ago and she was still adjusting to life on her own, but had plenty of friends. She found driving at night difficult these days and when the premises opposite the pet shop became vacant, she had jumped at the chance to relocate her business to within walking distance of her home.

Putting her second empty coffee cup on the table, Vera

squared her shoulders. 'I remember you saying you'd like to get to know some more people. Well, I've had a great idea.'

'Yeees.' Noah suspected he wasn't going to like her idea. She was looking too bright and keen.

'I don't know why I didn't think of it before, but I'm in a book club and thought you might like to join us. Everyone's very friendly and you wouldn't be the only man there . . .' Her voice tailed off when she saw the look on Noah's face.

He was speechless. Why was Vera suggesting he join a book club after their discussion about his dyslexia?

She laughed. Noah didn't and her face became more serious.

'You don't have to read any books; you just need to enjoy them. Several people use audiobooks. I assumed that's what you'd do.'

'Isn't that cheating?' He remembered listening to audiobooks as a child, sometimes listening to them several times, before trying to read them. Despite this, he always felt a twinge of guilt when saying he had read a book which he had only listened to.

'It's a *book club*, not a reading club and anyway it's more about having a glass of wine or a beer and enjoying the social. Give it a go. If it doesn't float your boat, there's no obligation to come again.'

Vera looked so pleased at this opportunity for Noah to expand his social life, he didn't feel he could say no without sounding rude. 'I'll give it a try,' he offered and was rewarded with a beaming smile and a pat on the arm.

'Wonderful. We're meeting next Wednesday, so there's plenty of time to listen to the book before then.' She wrote the details on a piece of paper and picked up her coat.

'I'm glad we've got to know each other a bit better and I think you'll love book club.'

'I, um, yes.' Noah wasn't so sure. Would the other members be as relaxed and friendly as Vera?

Her familiar trill of, 'I'll see you soon,' rang out and she was gone.

Looking down at the note she had left, he read '*The Authenticity Project* by Clare Pooley'. It didn't sound like his kind of book, but then it was so long since he had read anything, it was difficult to tell. He Googled it. At least he would know what he was facing. The reviews told him the book began with a lonely artist who believed that most people aren't honest with each other about their feelings. The artist writes his own truths in a notebook and leaves it in his local café. Other characters find the book and add their own truths and through the notebook a disparate group of individuals get to know and support each other. Noah downloaded the book, shuddering at the thought of a stranger reading things he might write about his inner doubts and fears.

A couple of days later, shortly before closing time, Sunshine Girl bounced into Noah's store again. His heart raced. She had come back. And so soon.

With a cheery wave and a 'hello', she went straight into the back-room and spent several minutes telling Harold how handsome and clever he was. Noah hovered a few feet away, regaling her with an array of facts about kea.

'The collective noun for kea is a "circus",' he said. 'Probably because they behave like such clowns. Despite that they're the most intelligent parrots on the planet and can even recognise colours and shapes.'

Harold tossed his head and gave a 'keeaah'.

'I think he thinks he's cleverer than that,' said the girl.

'He's got quite a high opinion of himself,' Noah agreed.

Sunshine Girl laughed, her hair glinting as she tilted her head backwards. She laughed a lot.

To Noah's disappointment she bought a couple of tins of cat food and left soon after. But why had she come all this way when she could have bought the tins at her local corner store? Was it because she liked Harold? How could he get to know her better?

A sliver of moonlight lit the bedroom. Noah opened his eyes and lay still, ears straining for unfamiliar sounds. It was the second time this week something had woken him and tonight he had an uneasy feeling the disturbance came from the shop below. Leaping out of bed he peered out of the window into the dark and uninformative street. A lone stooped figure shuffled round the corner, too elderly and infirm to be a burglar. Putting on slippers and a dressing-gown he tiptoed down the stairs, pausing at the bottom to listen once again. Nothing. He leapt out from the stairwell turning on the lights, his heart racing.

'Who's there?'

Silence greeted him apart from Harold fluffing his feathers at the sudden brightness. Noah patrolled the shop and then the courtyard. Returning inside, he noticed droplets of water on the floor near Harold's cage. Had Harold been flicking his water around or had an intruder jogged the cage? Why would someone come into the premises and then leave again without a trace? How could they have got in? Noah opened the door to Harold's cage and reached in to scratch his neck. 'Was someone here?' he asked.

'Nice,' said Harold, adjusting his neck to help Noah reach exactly the right place.

Taking comfort from the warmth and softness under his fingers, Noah let his heartbeat return to normal and then headed back to bed.

The CCTV Noah had ordered arrived the following day. He heaved a sigh of relief and called his uncle, who had offered to help with installation.

'I'll come over early on Sunday,' John boomed. 'The Seagate do a great roast lunch. We can go there afterwards. My treat.'

'I should be treating you,' Noah protested. 'You're coming over to help me.'

'Helping you is a pleasure, young Noah and it'll be great to see the shop now it's up and running. By the way,' he asked, 'did you ever get rid of that parrot that was foisted on you?'

'I never heard from the estate agent again and the police said no-one has reported a parrot missing. As he came with the "please look after me" sign, everyone seems to think he's my responsibility. Even Javier with all his contacts couldn't find anyone who's missing a kea.'

'You could always sell the bad-tempered bugger.'

'I couldn't do that,' Noah replied hastily. 'I've grown fond of him. Anyway, kea are on the endangered list, so I'd need his paperwork and a permit to sell him.'

The casual suggestion of selling Harold sent a chill down Noah's spine. He had come to rely on the parrot for company and as a sounding board for his ideas. Harold made him laugh too. His mannerisms or the words he chose often had Noah convinced that his companion understood a lot more than the average parrot.

John thumped his tools down with a grunt. Harold flapped his wings, giving a loud screech. Noah had locked him in his cage to prevent any more damage to his uncle's belongings. John scowled, then marched over and stood, legs apart, facing the disgruntled parrot.

'So, you're still here then, reject.'

Harold glared at him through narrowed eyes.

'Uncle John's here to help me install CCTV, so we can make sure the shop is safe from intruders,' explained Noah.

John guffawed. 'What are you talking to him for? He can't

understand a word.'

Harold turned his head to look at Noah, who paused before speaking. He was sure Harold was waiting to find out whether he would agree with his uncle. Whether Noah would downgrade him from friend and confidante to caged bird. Unwilling to be disloyal to Harold and not wanting to enter into a debate with his uncle, Noah settled for, 'I'm not sure how much he can understand, but I've got into the habit of keeping him up to date with what's going on.'

'He's a parrot for God's sake. You need to get out more.' John threw his arm around Noah's shoulders. 'Come on. Let's get this CCTV installed and then we'll go for lunch.'

Harold turned his back and pooped.

With John's help, the security cameras were soon in and working. Noah had ordered two for the main shop area, which covered the shelves to the right and left of his counter. In the back-room there was one camera. John positioned it so Noah could keep an eye on his stock and the majority of Harold's cage from his laptop, while he was at the counter serving customers. It wasn't possible to cover the whole room, despite trying a number of angles.

'Do you think I should have ordered two cameras for the back-room?' asked Noah frowning at the view on his laptop.

'I think we've positioned it as best we can,' said John. 'You can always add another camera later if you find you need one.'

'I did want to be able to see the door,' said Noah, although John had a point about protecting his stock.

'If someone comes through the door and into the store they'll be caught on camera. That's the whole point, laddie, to see what they're doing when they're in the shop, not to watch them opening the door. Come on, it's lunchtime now.'

Noah locked up and they set off for lunch. He would go with John's recommendation for now.

An imposing 17th century pub and hotel, the Seagate overlooked the Torridge estuary. Now the better weather was here, a collection of small crafts were moored at the river mouth and the *clink clink* of rigging against masts accompanied the short walk from Noah's premises. A few people were sitting at the tables outside the pub, but John ushered Noah into the muted cream and green interior, where they sat at an oak table by the window. When lunch arrived, the beef was tender and pink in the middle, the roast potatoes crunchy, the vegetables plentiful and gravy oozed thick and shiny over the top. There was barely room on the plate for the Yorkshire pudding.

'This is the life,' said John, and Noah nodded in agreement, his mouth too full to speak.

'How's business coming along, laddie?'

Noah swallowed. 'Good, considering it's early days. With me, Vera and the new café, our end of the high street's quite busy now. My Wednesday delivery service is getting popular too.'

'I knew you'd make a success of it,' boomed John.

'How's the antiques business?' asked Noah spearing a roast potato.

'Never better.' John took a draught from his pint. 'I'm an old hand now. I pick up something at a house clearance or car boot for a song and sell it on for three times what I paid. It's easy money.'

'If I get to the point where I earn a decent living, I'll be happy,' said Noah, envying his uncle's confidence.

'You're doing great.' John raised his empty glass. 'Let's have another pint to celebrate.'

'Celebrate what?'

'Good businesses and friendship,' said John. 'What'll you have?'

'Just a coffee for me.' Noah shifted in his seat before plunging on. 'Perhaps we should both have a coffee? After all, you've got to drive home.'

'Nonsense. I'm fine. If you can't relax over Sunday lunch, when can you?'

Noah didn't have an answer to that.

Chapter 7

Noah eased his back, which was sore from standing all day. He was looking forward to some down-time with Harold. Before he could close up for the day, the doorbell tinkled and Sunshine Girl burst in, her face glowing from the March wind.

'Hi. How can I help you?' The hint of a blush crept up Noah's neck. The pain in his back vanished.

'I've come to say hello to Harold, of course,' she laughed making her way towards the cage. 'And I thought I'd treat Buffy to a new toy.'

Noah hurried after her, pleased to notice she stood a respectful distance from the cage. Her chin jutted forwards underneath pursed red lips and an upturned nose. Golden hair tumbled over her shoulders.

'Is that a new mirror you've got?' she asked Harold.

He banged the mirror then leapt onto it dangling from one foot before returning to his perch. Fluffing his feathers and raising a claw, he tilted his head to its cutest angle.

A sure-fire way to get a reaction from admirers.

'He's so cute when he does that claw thing,' the girl exclaimed.

'I think it means he likes you,' Noah replied. Harold definitely reacted differently to this girl than to other customers. 'Would you like to give him a few grapes?'

'I'd love that,' she dazzled the space with her smile. 'I'm Aurora by the way.'

Harold preened at his reflection in the mirror.

I knew it. Aurora. Sunshine Girl.

'That's an unusual name. Where does it come from?'

'My dad was into Roman mythology and wanted me to have

the name of a goddess. The only one he and mum could agree on was Aurora – the goddess of sunrise.'

'It's very apt,' said Noah, the blush creeping higher up his neck. How could he explain the way she lit up the space around her? To stop himself saying anything embarrassing he muttered, 'I'll get those grapes.' Racing upstairs to his fridge, his heart pounded and not just from the effort of ascending the stairs. Returning to the shop, he realised he had not told the girl his own name.

'My name's Noah by the way. Not as exotic as yours.'

'But perfect for the shop you've bought. Did the name inspire you to buy it?'

'I'm sure I'd have bought it anyway, but the name did help convince me it was the right thing to do. Although now I often find myself just calling it "The Ark".'

He opened his palm to show Aurora a handful of glistening black grapes. 'I'll show you how to offer the grapes to Harold if you're certain you want to do this. His beak's a bit intimidating.'

'That doesn't worry me, I can tell he's a sweetie.'

Harold hopped from foot to foot.

'He is very gentle but keep your hand steady.' Had he gone mad? He had never allowed any customer to feed his parrot. What would happen if she got bitten and sued him? What if she never came into the shop again?

While Noah went through disaster scenarios in his head, Aurora took a grape and moving slowly offered it to Harold. She giggled with delight when he took it delicately from her fingers. By the time Noah had run through a myriad of potential disaster scenarios, she had fed Harold several grapes and was scratching his neck – the parrot had climbed onto his stand and put his head down.

'I can't believe he's letting you scratch his neck. It was about a week before he let me do that,' laughed Noah.

'He's adorable.'

They moved on to choosing a suitable toy for Aurora's cat, then returned to the front room and the counter, where they were out of Harold's view.

Despite normally remaining by his cage when there were customers in the shop he flew over to Noah's shoulder; shaking his head, when once again his owner let the sales transaction go through smoothly instead of feigning a failed signal and extending the opportunity for conversation.

With a swish of golden hair Aurora headed for the door. Noah wracked his brains for something to keep the conversation going but drew a blank.

It was time to intervene. Taking a lungful of air Harold gave his best and loudest wolf-whistle *(political correctness be damned)*.

Aurora whipped around, hand still on the door.

'That wasn't me!' Dark crimson raced from Noah's toes to his scalp. Any hope of this girl liking him was gone.

'I'm so sorry. He's never done that before.' Was it possible to teach a parrot etiquette?

His heart lifted when Aurora chuckled. 'I'll take it as a compliment this time.' Giving Harold a stern look, she said, 'Behave yourself and I'll come back and feed you more grapes on Saturday.'

Harold rewarded her with his cutest head tilt and a 'thank you'.

She's quite charming for a cat lover.

Aurora's words went round and round in Noah's head: 'I'll come back and feed you more grapes on Saturday.' Only four days until he would see her again. He struggled to keep his mind on cashing up. It kept drifting to a smiling girl with red lips and golden hair. Eventually, cashing up was complete and it was time to go up to the flat for supper.

'Let's have dinner,' said Noah, holding out a hand to Harold so he could step onto it.

'Let's have dinner,' repeated Harold making Noah laugh.

'You're picking up phrases quickly now. I wish you wouldn't imitate the doorbell though; I keep thinking someone is there, but actually it's you.' He gave Harold an affectionate scratch.

'Let's have dinner.' Harold reminded him.

Noah rustled up salmon pasta, removing some of the salmon for Harold before adding cream. He enjoyed cooking with the bird on his shoulder. Making something delicious from fresh ingredients had always been his therapy and helped him relax after a busy day. Cooking with the parrot for company made it fun and there were never any complaints about 'the mess'. He put Harold's salmon in a dish on the perch and sat down to eat his own supper.

'I'm off to my first book club with Vera this evening,' he informed Harold. 'I need to get going.'

'I'll see you soon,' trilled Harold in a perfect imitation of Vera's voice.

Noah laughed. 'Vera's helping me get out and meet people.'

He didn't expect to see any of Daisy's friends again and had not been good at keeping in touch with his old university pals. His life had been too full and it hadn't been a priority. Although he had Harold, John, Vera and calls with his family for company, he did need more. An image of Aurora's smiling face came to mind. He wondered if she would be interested in hearing about the book club. It was a talking point and would show he had some sort of social life.

He had listened to the novel twice through and made notes on his thoughts. With Julian and Monika as his favourite characters, he was ready to discuss the plot, but not ready to reveal his own 'authentic' thoughts – not all of them anyway. He folded the notes and tucked them into his pocket, then put on his smartest jumper and smoothed down his hair. Taking a deep breath and trying to picture Vera's face, rather than a room full of strangers, he set off.

'I needn't have worried about book club,' Noah informed Harold when he arrived home. 'I remembered loads about the book and didn't even need my notes. It was incredible how much people opened up about their own lives, just on the back of discussing a book.'

Some people seemed to find it so easy to talk about their worries and fears. He would never be able to do that. A couple of people had tried writing their own 'authentic truths' in a notebook, wanting to know whether what they wrote would differ from the reality they put forward to others. Both had admitted that they found it easier to write their truths than voice them out loud.

'It's amazing what an impact reading one novel can have,' he told Harold. 'Next month's book doesn't sound like my kind of thing though. It's some children's book from over a hundred years ago. Vera chose it, but I've no idea why.' Noah shrugged, unlocked the cage and offered his hand to Harold.

'Let's go upstairs. You've been alone all evening.'

'Alone,' said Harold in a forlorn voice.

Noah scratched his neck. 'You're a lucky bird. Don't go getting all morose just because I've been out for a couple of hours.'

Turning on the lamp, he settled onto the sofa with Harold, glad of the companionship even though he had been with people all evening. Having been in company made him feel more rather than less lonely when he got back home.

His phone rang and Noah grinned as James's voice brightened the quiet room.

'Hey bro, how's it going?'

Pleased he had more to report than the weather, number of customers and latest solitary beach walk, Noah described the evening at book club and Sunday with his uncle.

'I've got such great memories of Uncle John,' reminisced James. 'Do you remember that time he let me have a go at driving his Land Rover across the field? We nearly ended up in the stream at the bottom. And what about when Mum and Dad went for a night out and he let us stay up till midnight playing Monopoly? We had to dive into bed and pretend to be asleep when we heard their car on the drive. He was the best.'

'I remember the Land Rover incident,' said Noah, 'I thought we were going to die. I'm scarred for life by your under-age driving.' They both laughed.

Noah continued, 'I was quite relieved when he wouldn't let me have a go, even though I pretended I wanted to drive.'

'You'd never have reached the pedals,' James said, pragmatically.

'True, but I wasn't as brave as you either.'

'You've got qualities that are much more worthy than bravado.' James's voice was more serious than usual. 'You're caring and sensible for a start. Anyway, where does brave end and reckless begin?'

'Talking of reckless,' said Noah, not sure how to respond to his brother's compliments and choosing to gloss over them, 'I'm worried about Uncle John. He seems to drink a lot. On Sunday he had three pints before driving home, so was definitely over the limit. I think he would have had more without much encouragement.'

'He's always been a drinker and he's not your responsibility. I wouldn't worry about it. What can you do anyway?' James's voice was light and unconcerned.

'What about other people on the roads?' John was their uncle. Didn't that mean they had some sort of responsibility?

'He must be nearly seventy, I don't think you're going to change him.'

Frustrated that James was so dismissive, Noah let the subject drop. Perhaps Uncle John's behaviour bothered him more than James because he had seen it for himself.

'Have you spoken to Mum lately?' asked James, suddenly

changing tack. 'She hasn't been answering her phone.'

'We had a chat last week. She was going on a silent retreat with Radagast. You're probably not allowed phones while you realign your chakras, or whatever they're doing.'

'She's such a fruitcake,' said James. 'I think it makes her happy though.'

'I hope she can afford it. I know she's got her freelance editing job, but I'm not sure how much she's even working now. It's all about Radagast. She's either attending or running some wacky course every other week. And surely, she shouldn't simply cut off communication. What about her clients?'

'Maybe they actually make money from the events they run? Radagast's got a lot of followers on social media. Have you seen him on TikTok?'

'TikTok,' snorted Noah. 'Life's too short.' James roared with laughter.

The rest of the call passed with anecdotes from James's life, which seemed as full as ever. The surf shop he owned was busy with late summer trade and when he wasn't working his life seemed to be a round of parties, beach, sports and fun. The last girlfriend had not, it turned out, been 'the one' and James was single again, but didn't seem remotely concerned by his bachelor status.

Noah had never been able to compete with the speed at which his brother led life, but it warmed his heart to hear about it.

The following morning, still carrying a residue of warmth from the call with his brother, Noah was singing to himself when his first customer of the day arrived. It was hedgehog lady, Mrs Chalice.

'You sound happy,' she said.

'I love it here.' Noah embraced his off-tune singing. He felt comfortable with Mrs Chalice and she seemed to like him.

'That's wonderful. I'm glad to hear it. And you're doing a great job with the shop.' She smiled and her complexion looked less grey than usual.

Noah stood tall and put his shoulders back. His customers wanting him to make a success of Noah's Ark meant a lot.

'That's kind of you,' he beamed.

Mrs Chalice picked up her usual hedgehog food, but instead of leaving straight away she placed a brown paper bag on the counter. 'I've brought a lettuce heart for Harold. I hope that's alright?'

'He loves lettuce. Do you want to wait while I feed it to him?'

'Don't worry. You've got customers waiting. I just . . .' she paused seeming to lose her train of thought, '. . . I just thought it would be nice for him to have a treat.' She walked away, her plaid shopping trolley trundling behind.

Noah turned to his next customer, a portly man with the rough reddened hands of a farmer and a flat cap pulled forward so that it looked as if it were resting on his bristling eyebrows. 'How can I help you, Mr Wainwright?'

'It's a shame,' he said, looking out of the window after Mrs Chalice and shaking his head.

'A shame?' Noah looked enquiringly at his customer.

'A real shame.' Mr Wainwright nodded, agreeing with himself.

Noah waited but no more information was forthcoming. Mr Wainwright continued to nod his head and purse his lips.

It wasn't any of Noah's business, but Mrs Chalice was one of his regulars and he liked her. Was there any way he could help? 'I'm afraid I don't know the story.'

'Weeell,' the pause for dramatic effect went on far too long.

'Yes?'

'It bain't really 'er you see. It's 'er sister. Poor auld soul.'

'Right.' Noah nodded encouragingly.

'Aye. Terrible. Just one thing after t'other.'

Noah searched for a way to say 'get on with it' without sounding rude, eventually settling for, 'What happened?'

''Ee died you see.'

'Her sister died?' Had Mr Wainwright said he or she?

The man peered at Noah as if he were an idiot. ''Er old man.'

What was he talking about? Noah opted for repetition. 'Her old man.'

'You've got it.' Wainwright wagged an approving finger.

'And Mrs Chalice?' prompted Noah.

'A good woman that. Always puts others first, yer know.'

'She does seem very nice.'

'Mad as a box of frogs, of course.' Mr Wainwright heaved a world-weary sigh. 'Getting worse too, by all accounts.'

Who was mad? What was the sigh all about? 'Mrs Chalice seems quite sensible,' Noah said as politely as possible.

After way longer than the actual facts shared merited, Noah gleaned that Mrs Chalice looked after her sister, who had dementia. It was the sister's husband who had died and the only time Mrs Chalice got out of the house was when an outside carer came in or her daughter took over caring responsibilities.

Noah stared thoughtfully after the rambling Mr Wainwright, as he left the store. He had imagined Mrs Chalice's sole responsibility lay in feeding hedgehogs, but now knew she carried a much heavier burden. One which would undoubtedly increase as time passed. He wondered what the full story behind Mrs Chalice was but hadn't had another hour to find it out. Getting information out of Mr Wainwright had been like squeezing the dregs out of a tube of toothpaste. Each squeeze gave a little and then the paste retreated back into the tube, requiring further extraction efforts.

Aurora turned up at the shop again on Saturday morning as promised, but the shop was frustratingly busy. Noah wanted to shoo his customers out and have the peace to chat with her, but couldn't think of a pretext on which to do it. She hung around for a while bobbing from foot to foot and turning in circles in front of Harold. Her laughter rang around the shop when he mimicked her. Twice Noah forgot where he was up to in ringing up sale articles, because he was too busy watching Aurora and Harold on the CCTV. After about twenty minutes with no sign of a quiet spell she waved to Noah, saying, 'I have to go now.'

She hadn't bought anything. Had she come in specifically to see him? His heart raced at the thought. Galvanised into action by her retreating figure, he called out, 'It's quieter at the end of the day.'

'Next Saturday then,' she said, turning around and giving him a thumbs up.

Next Saturday! That was a week away. It was a struggle to stop himself from abandoning his customer and leaping after her. The rest of the day dragged by.

'Good morning, Harold. Look what I've got for you.' Noah held up a slice of pomegranate, sticky red juice dripping down his wrist.

'Good morning, Noah.' The parrot danced from foot to foot. 'Yum, yum.'

Harold held the treat carefully in his claw and began to lift pomegranate seeds from their skin, one by one. Noah was about to fetch fresh water and clean the juice off his hand when he stiffened and frowned at the bottom of the cage. On the floor was a cherry stone. Could a customer have given a cherry to Harold without Noah noticing?

He had put up a notice asking customers not to feed Harold. Most of them were wary of his powerful beak and wouldn't have tried anyway. The stone couldn't be from yesterday; he had cleaned out the cage after the shop closed. Pacing around, he searched for other unexpected debris or a sign that someone had been there. Harold chewed his breakfast with unruffled enjoyment.

Examining the CCTV footage from the previous evening, Noah peered at the dingy grey images. They showed nothing until about two in the morning, when he glimpsed a shadow by the corner of Harold's cage. He replayed the image over and over. Even though the dark blur only flickered into view for a second, he was sure it was a person. If he had only got a second camera for the back-room he would have had a clear view.

He checked the rear door, which was behind Harold's stand and could not be seen on camera. There was no sign of damage or forced entry. Nothing apart from one shadowy, almost ghostly, smudge on his camera footage.

Noah went outside and inspected the courtyard but found no hint of a disturbance there either. His hands were clammy despite it being a warm day. The lock on the front door had been changed when he moved in, but he had not bothered with the back door. It was something he shouldn't have skimped on. Harold was the most valuable thing in his shop. His value on the black market would be huge, but more importantly the bird was his friend and confidante. He would call a locksmith today.

Returning to the shop he found two customers standing outside peering through the window. He had been so busy puzzling over the mysterious intruder he had forgotten to open up.

Red faced and apologising, Noah told them he had been on the phone handling a delivery enquiry. He didn't want to publicise the fact there had been an intruder.

That evening, Noah finished restocking the shelves and added a couple more items to tomorrow's to-do list, knowing not to rely on his memory. Walking over to Harold, he offered his arm.

'Come on, old chap.'

Harold, who had been about to step onto it, retracted his leg and glared.

Old chap? Bloody cheek. I'm in my prime.

Noah put his arm back by his side.

'Sometimes I don't know what's going on in your head.' What had he done to offend the bird? He wandered over to the front door checking it was locked, then tried offering his arm again. 'Let's have dinner.'

Harold considered for a moment.

Dinner was always delicious.

'Let's have dinner,' he said, stepping onto Noah's hand but with a more aloof air than usual.

Climbing the stairs, Noah clutched Harold's small portable stand in one fist, feeling the comforting weight of the bird resting on his other. Putting the stand next to the sofa he set about preparing supper; quality time for both of them. Noah took comfort in the rhythmic chopping and neat piles of identically sized vegetables while Harold, perched on his shoulder, enjoyed regular titbits of sweet pepper, mangetout and cashew nut. Swishing the stir-fry round in his wok, Noah added hot noodles to his fried vegetables, nuts and sauce.

'You're not allowed the sauce, it's too salty,' Noah informed Harold, setting him on his stand and putting some cashews and a couple of plain noodles in his bowl. They were demolished with gusto, apart from the bits that ended up around the bottom of the stand and on the rug. Uncle John was right, parrots are messy.

At ten o'clock, Noah turned off the TV, picking up Harold so he could return him to the cage downstairs. As he tucked his fingers between ruffled neck feathers, he felt the warmth of soft skin and the latest spiky, keratin-coated pins coming through, ready to burst into new plumage. Harold nuzzled into him.

'I can't lose you,' Noah murmured. He put Harold back on the perch next to the sofa. 'You'll have to stay up here tonight, just in case.'

He re-checked all the doors downstairs, then locked the

door at the bottom of the stairs – something he didn't normally do. Returning to the flat, he found Harold sitting innocently on his perch by the sofa, but in the kitchen the scene was less than tranquil: a box of teabags was scattered across the room. Shreds of cardboard were flung far and wide. Most of the teabags had been ripped apart. A fine coating of tea leaves covered the worksurface, floor and sink.

Noah had been gone less than five minutes.

'Was that you Harold?' Noah demanded. Harold ignored him. Muttering, Noah rescued the teabags that were still whole and cleared up.

Waggling one of the remaining unscathed teabags at Harold he asked, 'Why did you do that?'

Harold fluffed his feathers and looked serene.

'You'd better behave tonight. If I hear you causing trouble you'll be straight back downstairs in your cage, intruders or not.' He knew he would not carry out his threat of returning the parrot to the shop that night, even if his belongings got damaged, but he couldn't leave Harold roaming free in his flat every night. Despite being ready for bed, Noah opened his laptop and scrolled through adverts, balancing the urgency of his need and the specifics of what he wanted. Eventually he found a second-hand parrot cage, which was close enough for him to collect after work tomorrow. There were many things in the flat that would not survive if chewed by Harold, but until he had resolved the intruder problem his companion would have to stay upstairs overnight.

Noah gritted his teeth and slammed his hands against the steering wheel. Why did the day he had to get away promptly have to coincide with his sense of direction playing tricks on him? Benefitting from the double advantages of fewer roads to choose from and less traffic on those roads, he had been navigating his way around Devon with relatively few unplanned diversions. Today was not one of those days.

Delivering his Wednesday orders, Noah put up with savage spikes of rain soaking him at every stop, while his windscreen wipers struggled to maintain visibility on the narrow country lanes. Water droplets dripped from his hair onto his neck, then ran down his back distracting him as he scrutinised the winding road and high hedges ahead. Down Farm was definitely not at the postcode he had been given and there was no mobile signal to call them. Despite delivering to the farm twice previously, coming from the opposite direction this time nothing looked familiar. He sighed. There was nothing else for it, he would have to drive back to the main road (providing he could find it) and come in on his normal route.

'You are useless,' he muttered to himself, refusing to pull over and ask a dog walker for directions. He probably wouldn't be able to follow them anyway, he told himself. Full of lefts and rights, local dialect and arm waving. He gripped the steering wheel, mulling over his inadequacies and trampling any positive thoughts that dared intrude.

He found the farm eventually, relieved to make the delivery and get on with his day. Chatting with the owner and meeting her new puppy had soothed his frayed nerves and he was ready for the next task.

Distributing orders had taken over an hour longer than it should and his satnav informed him his next destination was two hours each way (without detours). Seizing the opportunity to punish himself further, he decided to use the time to listen to classic children's literature from 1913. What had Vera been thinking, choosing some dated drear that was more than a century old for her book club choice? He clicked 'play', glared at his satnav and set off to fetch Harold's new cage.

The cage was awkward rather than heavy and Noah wobbled precariously on the stairs, while heaving it up to his living room.

Putting it down with a grunt, he straightened himself up, before springing back downstairs singing Cream's 'I'm so glad, I'm glad, I'm glad, I'm glad.' Returning with the cage legs, he collected Harold and spent a productive twenty minutes attaching the legs to the cage, making sure it was level. By the time it was ready Harold was also singing 'I'm so glad.'

Noah laughed and stroked the bird's beak. 'You'll be sleeping safely up here until the locksmith's put that new lock on the back door. I'm not going to risk losing you.' He tapped the cage and gave Harold an accusatory stare. 'I'm also not going to risk losing the rest of my teabags.'

'I'm glad,' sung Harold, looking virtuous.

Inspired by his day, Noah poured out his thoughts to his companion. 'At lunchtime I felt so dismal, but now I feel great and it's all thanks to Vera's book club choice. I'd never heard of *Pollyanna* before, but it's helped me snap out of my usual self-critical state and look at the positives; just like the little girl does in the book.' He shook his head. 'I think most of my problems are in my own head. Is it simply mind over matter to solve them? What do you think?'

Harold nodded.

'If you spot me being all negative remind me to play the "glad game" won't you?' he told the parrot. 'Whenever anything is getting me down, I have to re-set and think of something about the situation that makes me glad. It's that simple.'

Harold gave Noah's finger a gentle nip. 'Let's have dinner.'

Chapter 8

Inspired by *Pollyanna*, Noah had spent the last couple of days finding things to be glad about, surprising himself with how easy it was. Today he was glad it was a sunny day and that he had found the time for a brisk walk along the quay before opening. He was also glad it was Easter Saturday, the day Aurora had said she would call in. Customers responded to Noah's chatty mood several of them buying little extras, aided by his cheerful recommendations.

But locking the door at five o'clock, a cloud descended. Aurora hadn't shown up. His new-found 'glad' approach struggled under a crush of disappointment. Why would she call in anyway? It had just been a throw-away comment, not an appointment to keep. He sloped over to Harold's cage.

'It's just you and me old chap.'

Harold picked up a piece of lettuce, threw it on the floor and turned his back.

Haven't we already been through this 'old' business?

'Now I've offended you,' said Noah morosely. He picked up a broom and started to sweep around Harold's cage. Hearing a tap at the door, he gave a tut of annoyance. Would he be able to rustle up a convincing smile for his tardy customer?

Spotting a familiar mango-coloured shape through the window, his back straightened and his head lifted like a puppet whose strings had just been pulled. A warm flush crept up his neck as he fumbled with the lock.

Aurora burst into the shop. 'I'm so sorry I'm late. I got held up.'

'No problem,' said Noah. All irritation had vanished. 'I only locked up a second ago and I've no plans for this evening anyway.'

'That's lucky,' said Aurora, hurrying over to Harold and grinning at Noah. 'I'd better say "hello" to my favourite bird before I do anything else.'

Petite and perky, she danced in front of the cage. 'Hello, handsome.' Harold mimicked her dance and laughter filled the room.

'Hello Sunshine.' Harold raised a claw and tilted his head. Noah shuddered at the thought Aurora might guess he had been talking to his parrot about her.

'How cute. He knows me.' Aurora's eyes were wide with delight. She fished in her pocket. 'I've got a treat for you.'

Noah gave a sigh of relief and was grateful Harold monopolised Aurora's attention for the first few minutes of her visit. It gave him time to gather his thoughts.

'Here we are. I've brought blueberries today,' she trilled.

Harold climbed down to his lowest perch and took the blueberries one at a time, holding each one in his claw and savouring every bite. Mesmerised by Aurora's slim fingers topped with fingernails which were almost the same colour as the fruit, Noah followed her every move while trying to look as though he was not staring. By the time Harold had finished his treats, Noah's self-conscious flush at being so close to this attractive woman had receded. He made her laugh with a couple of slickly delivered and amusing customer anecdotes – the very same anecdotes he had practised on Harold earlier in the day.

After a while, Noah had run out of stories and Aurora had bought her cat food.

'I suppose I'd better get home now,' she said, a tinge of regret in her voice.

Harold clanged his mirror and gave a loud 'keeaah'.

'Bye Harold.' Aurora gave him a wave and took a step towards the door.

'Carpe diem,' shrieked Harold, landing on Noah's shoulder

with a thump.

'Calm down Harold. What are you talking about?' Put off his stride by Harold's antics, formality and Noah's blush returned.

'It was nice to see you, do call in anytime,' he stammered. Aurora had her hand on the door handle.

'It was nice to see you too.' She paused as if waiting for the gap to be filled.

Noah's throat seized up.

Harold flapped his wings.

For goodness' sake, how difficult is it?

Taking matters into his own claw and in his best imitation of Noah's voice he said, 'Let's have dinner.'

Noah looked at his feet, while Aurora giggled and smiled hopefully. 'He's so funny, isn't he?'

Noah said nothing and her hopeful look waned.

Harold tried again, louder this time, 'Let's have dinner.' He hopped over to Aurora's shoulder.

Do I have to drag you people upstairs and cook myself?

Tearing his gaze away from the floor, Noah plunged in. 'That's a good idea. I enjoy cooking.' Overcome by his own bravery, he then stuttered, 'That is, um . . . only if you want to. I mean . . . you don't have to.'

Harold flew back to Noah landing on his head and pulling his hair.

While Noah fought off his attacker Aurora laughed and gave her broadest sunshine smile.

'That sounds lovely. My fridge is bare and I'm starving.'

Noah froze. How had that happened? He had not intended to invite Aurora over right now. Not tonight. The flat needed to be pristine, special ingredients purchased, at least one practice run at what he was going to cook. Impromptu, it would be a fiasco.

Aurora looked at him expectantly. Noah's heart pounded.

The flat wasn't even tidy. What pretext could he find to leave her in the shop while he ran upstairs and put things in order? Disaster scenarios, including Aurora storming out because she deemed the flat too messy or because his food was inedible, raced through his head. Trapped by his own careless comment, Noah resigned himself to failure.

'Great. Come on up.'

Harold stopped pulling Noah's hair and settled quietly on his shoulder.

Well, that was more difficult than it needed to be.

Sitting on a corner of the kitchen work-surface, Aurora swung her legs and sipped a glass of red wine. Harold sat on her arm chewing a slab of red pepper. Having found cooked chicken, a few vegetables and cheese in the fridge, together with a pack of wraps, Noah was frying quesadilla. A green salad, yoghurt dip and tomato salsa sat in cheerful yellow bowls on the table.

'How come you're such an amazing cook? With no notice and just what you've got lurking in the fridge you've rustled up a feast. I'm impressed.'

Busy with his hands and doing something well within his comfort zone, Noah met her eyes and grinned. 'I've always enjoyed cooking. It's therapeutic. Preparing the ingredients, creating things as I go and seeing it all come together. It's my go-to activity when I'm stressed. My substitute for meditation.'

Aurora laughed. 'My substitute for meditation is eating chocolate. Your idea sounds much healthier.'

Noah grinned. She had a way of making him feel good.

Supper lived up to expectations and Aurora didn't seem to notice Noah sweeping his papers off the dining table, removing the coats from the back of the sofa or kicking a basket of washing into the spare room. In fact, she declared the flat homely and welcoming.

After supper, she made Noah's heart flip over, saying, 'You must come round to my place next time.'

'That would be fantastic,' he answered. Their evening had been relaxed and easy. Why had he been so worried?

'It's nice to meet someone who's so easy to talk to and happy with the simple things in life. Is next Friday OK?'

Noah glowed. He was easy to talk to. He hadn't even known it was a good thing to be happy with the simple things in life.

'Yes please,' shrieked Harold jumping from foot to foot and bobbing his head.

'I'm sorry, Harold, you're not invited. I'd love to come though,' he grinned at Aurora.

Harold flew onto Aurora's shoulder and nuzzled her cheek. 'Hello Sunshine,' he said, leaning in to have his neck scratched, twisting it around to make sure her fingers found exactly the right spot.

'Does he understand what we're saying?' said Aurora tilting her head and wrinkling her nose.

'I think he picks up on mood and body language,' said Noah, thinking how adorable she looked. 'Although sometimes it feels as though he understands everything.'

'You can come another time maybe,' said Aurora, giving Harold a final scratch, 'but you will have to be nice to Buffy.'

Another time! Noah's heart leapt. She was already thinking in terms of inviting him over more than once. His heart was still pounding, minutes after she had gone and it was no effort at all to think 'glad' thoughts.

Bursting to share his delight, Noah thought of his brother. It was eight in the morning in Brisbane; he could call. But what if Aurora changed her mind and he never saw her again? James would think him a fool if he declared his feelings for her and nothing came of it.

He settled on a tentative message.

Let me know when you are free for a chat. All is well here. N.

There was no immediate reply, but Noah went to bed feeling better for having taken a small step towards sharing his news, without having risked sharing something that may not actually be news.

With the Easter holidays in full swing, The Ark was benefitting from the rush that came with tourist season. Noah was amazed by the number of people who came on holiday with their pets having forgotten dog beds, leads, bowls or even food. To encourage holiday browsers to make impulse purchases, he had set up a stand with gifts and luxury items near the door and refreshed his window display. He also stocked a new line in hand-crafted doggy treats, which Jemima and Alison had created. The treats had become so successful they were thinking of expanding the range to cat treats.

Having become an avid fan of Brewberry's hot chocolate, on most days Noah put his 'Back in 5 minutes!' sign on the door and nipped along to the café. Lately, business was so brisk his opportunities to get hot chocolate were restricted. He would need to hire an assistant before the busy summer season arrived and had already made a note to ask for advice about employing staff at the next business owners' meeting.

Today was the day he was going to Aurora's for supper. Ironing his shirt and trousers before breakfast, shivers of excitement and anxiety raced through Noah in equal measure. He hung his pressed clothes over a chair next to the orange and yellow tulips he had bought, still in their cellophane wrapping. Did the invitation mean Aurora fancied him? Were they going to be more than just friends? Noah shook his head. He was getting ahead of himself. When James had called a couple of days ago, Noah had got cold feet about mentioning Aurora, so instead deflected attention on to what James was doing. He didn't want to talk about her while he was still unsure about the status of their relationship.

Despite his nerves, he was saved from spending the whole day dwelling on disaster scenarios, because the shop was too busy to allow for daydreaming – although he did work through a few potential catastrophes in quieter moments.

'Thank you. That'll be twenty pounds and ninety-nine pence. Just tap your card over the machine.' Noah pointed to his card reader and handed over a Noah's Ark carrier bag with a smile.

The next customer moved up to the counter.

'Apologies for the wait. How can I help?' There were six people standing in line and more browsing the shelves. He reminded himself to be 'glad' that business was so brisk. The thought did not remove all his stress at keeping customers waiting but helped a little. The line inched forward and more people joined the back of the queue. The door opened with a tinkle as it clipped the bell fixed above. Noah glanced up from wrapping a dog bowl.

An elderly woman in an oversized raincoat shuffled in. Noah hoped she wouldn't require too much one-on-one attention. He had no time for that today. Seeming to know where she was going, she headed for the back-room. She was the kind of person who would be looking for a toy for her cat. He returned his focus to the current transaction.

'It's a good quality, heavy bowl and won't slip around when your dog is eating,' he said with a smile.

After a while, the queue subsided. Taking a gulp of water Noah checked his CCTV to see how many customers were still browsing. He had forgotten about the old woman who had shuffled in earlier, until he spotted her in front of Harold's stand, reaching up as if offering him something to eat. Harold bent his head towards her. Noah leapt from behind the counter and rushed to where she was standing.

'Don't!' he shouted.

The woman jumped and dropped what she was holding.

95

Realising how rude he had sounded (she was a customer after all), Noah apologised.

'I'm sorry, I didn't mean to make you jump. He's on a special diet and I'd hate anyone to get bitten, so I can't let customers feed him.' Noah waved at the sign he had put up making this very request. 'He's not vicious, but he does have a strong beak,' he added. Noah didn't want his bird fed anything harmful. He had caught one misguided woman trying to feed him chocolate, not realising it's as toxic to parrots as it is to dogs.

The elderly woman shrank back into her oversized coat.

Bringing out his best service smile, Noah said softly, 'Can I help you?'

Without speaking the woman returned to the main body of the shop, her slippered feet scuffling in the now silent space. Where had he seen her before? Noah had almost grasped the memory when the door burst open and a young woman with long, dark plaits and a bejewelled septum ring dashed in.

'There you are! I've been looking all over for you.' She marched up to the woman. 'Good job I spotted you. I was in a right tizz.' She turned to Noah, clutching her quarry by the elbow. 'I'm so sorry, I turned my back for one minute and she'd vanished. I hope she wasn't being a nuisance.'

'Not at all,' reassured Noah.

'It's dementia.' The young woman's shoulders sagged a little. 'She doesn't realise how dangerous it is for her to be out and about on her own.' Turning back to the woman she said, 'You mustn't sneak off like that – you'll give me a heart attack.' She hastily guided the woman out of the shop with a cheery wave.

Worried about Harold, Noah checked the floor to see what the woman been trying to feed him. On the floor he found a piece of broccoli and breathed a sigh of relief. It was a healthy treat and one of Harold's favourites. Reaching up, he gave Harold's beak a rub.

'You shouldn't take food from people you don't know,' he

admonished, pocketing the vegetable and turning back to attend to customers.

'Broccoli,' said Harold sounding disappointed.

The short drive to Aurora's flat was straightforward. With no need for his contingency time, Noah arrived so early he couldn't knock on the door just yet. He had twenty minutes to kill. He spent them pacing the neighbouring streets, imagining everything that could go wrong. Was a bunch of tulips the right thing to bring? What if she had hay fever and the flowers made her sneeze? He had a brief mental image of Aurora sneezing, her eyes streaming, asking him to put the flowers back in his car. Should he have brought wine as well as flowers? Aurora had not brought anything when he had cooked dinner, but that had been impromptu. He looked around for a corner shop where he could buy wine but couldn't see one. What if the evening were punctuated by awkward silences? What would they talk about? So preoccupied was he with worrying, he didn't notice the time passing until it was already seven o'clock. He was supposed be at Aurora's by now.

Jogging back up the street Noah stopped on the corner to Google his route. He was sure it was right then left, but he had been sure of his route on other occasions and gone the wrong way. Tulips sagging in his hand and a sheen of perspiration coating his brow, it was nearly ten past seven when Noah rang the doorbell.

The intercom crackled into life. 'Come in. I'm number two on the right.'

Aurora was smiling at the open door to her flat by the time he stepped into the entrance hall.

'Hi Noah. What beautiful flowers. I love tulips and you've even got them in my favourite colours.'

'They reminded me of your mango coat and your bubbly personality.' She didn't seem annoyed that he was late.

'That's such a lovely compliment,' she laughed, beckoning him in. 'I love the way you make me feel good. And well done for arriving late. I was still in the shower at seven, hoping you weren't standing outside. We had a staff meeting after school and it went on ages longer than normal. There was no way I could sneak off.'

Following her inside, he stepped across the hallway and into a bright, spacious room. At the near end was a small kitchen overlooking the road, an island separated it from the lounge area. At the far end a sofa faced patio doors leading onto decking, and a small patch of grass surrounded by shrubs and trees.

'The tulips will look lovely in this.' Aurora produced a dark green jug and filled it with water.

Noah relaxed a little. The flowers and his arrival time had both been a hit. Perhaps the evening would go well after all.

'Thank you for inviting me,' he said formally.

'My pleasure.' She began chatting and didn't seem to notice his anxiety. 'I'm so disorganised I haven't even unpacked the shopping.' Waving a hand at the bulging shopping bag on the island, she looked delighted rather than worried by her lack of preparation. 'It's a good job you're such a great cook; that means you can help.' She started taking things out of the bag.

A small black cat jumped onto the work-surface. 'This is Buffy.' Aurora picked up the cat. 'You're not supposed to be on here,' she said, kissing the top of the cat's head and putting her on the floor. Buffy permitted Noah a brief stroke before strolling over to the sofa, clawing a brightly coloured cushion and making herself comfortable.

Noah turned his attention to supper, selecting ingredients for a stir-fry from the freshly purchased vegetables and chicken, then delving into the fridge and store cupboard to see what else was available. With a knife in his hand and a chopping board under his fingers, he was in his element. He wondered if Aurora would prefer a knife sharpener to flowers next time.

Aurora was in charge of making strawberry mousse and opening the wine. Cooking had been the ideal icebreaker and by the time Noah remembered his concerns about conversation not flowing, it was almost time to return home.

Aurora finished her wine. 'What a lovely evening. You can cook for me any time you like.' She grinned, her clear blue eyes looking directly into his.

Noah's chest swelled at the 'anytime you like' from this beautiful young woman. Everything had been so easy, even their next date was fixed (assuming it was a date). He hadn't quite nailed the answer to that one.

Finding they both loved walking, a hike over the cliffs at Baggy Point had been arranged for Sunday. Only two days until their next encounter and they had a favourite pastime in common. He really should spend less time worrying. Aurora always seemed so relaxed; how did she do it?

'How are you so positive and chilled all the time? I wish I could be more like that.' The words were out of his mouth. He had intended to think them, but had spoken them instead.

'Oh, loads of therapy and hiding myself away when I have a bad day,' said Aurora without a shred of embarrassment.

Was it normal to admit to therapy? It didn't seem to worry Aurora. 'How come the therapy?'

'Doesn't everyone need therapy?' she replied with a shrug.

'Um. I don't think so.'

'Sorry, I'm being flippant. It's the negative side of trying to seem cheerful all the time; sometimes I give flippant answers to important or relevant questions.' A more serious expression came over her features.

'I went through a low patch when I was studying for my teaching degree. I had a relationship break-up and then let everything get on top of me. The uni were really supportive and got me counselling. I got back on track and learnt coping strategies for whenever things get too much.' She pulled her hair back off her face. 'Everyone has anxieties and insecurities you know, no matter how confident they appear on the outside.'

'I suppose.' Noah processed her words. Maybe confidence really was about faking it until you make it. That was what James said.

Aurora interrupted his thoughts. 'You're so measured and calm, I can't imagine you having anxieties.'

Noah laughed – he leaned back into the sofa and roared. The kind of laugh James would have been proud of. Aurora's expression switched between a polite smile and a light frown. Noah thought he should explain.

'I'm sorry. That's just so funny. I'm the most anxious person going and you think I'm measured and calm. I must be better at putting on a front than I thought.'

'What sort of things are you anxious about?'

'Everything, given the chance.' Noah laughed again. 'This evening for example.' He listed the things he had worried about while pacing the roads around her flat and how his fears had even made him late, before turning out to be completely unfounded.

It was Aurora's turn to laugh. 'That's brilliant and now you need never worry about any of those things again.' Her face became serious. 'It's great we can be so honest with each other. That's important you know. Life's about wanting to be with someone despite their faults, not because you think they don't have any.'

Wanting to be with someone. Noah's heart beat more quickly. Did Aurora want to be with him despite his faults? He hoped so. 'I do have a tendency to try to hide my deficiencies,' he admitted, 'but you're right, a relationship has to be built on honesty.'

'It does. I can tell you're an honest kind of guy and that's important to me.' Aurora edged closer to him and looked into

100

his eyes.

He leaned forward and stroked her cheek. Her head tilted upwards. It was an invitation. He took it.

Noah's step was light and springy and he sang along to the radio, while checking the shelves and sweeping up around Harold's cage.

'Aurora's great,' he informed Harold. 'I think she likes me as much as I like her. No wait. I know she likes me as much as I like her,' he corrected. 'I've promised her I'm going to spend less time worrying about life and more time enjoying it.'

'I'm glad,' said Harold.

Noah leaned over and gave Harold a scratch. 'How lucky I am. A parrot for a best friend and a beautiful girlfriend.'

Harold gave a wolf whistle.

Noah stopped scratching his neck. 'Wolf whistles are not permitted.'

Harold put up one claw and gave his cutest head tilt. 'Sunshine.'

'You know who I'm talking about, don't you? She likes you too. And I think it might have taken us longer to get together without your help.' Noah wasn't sure if Harold was nodding his head in agreement or because he wanted another scratch.

There was plenty of time before opening this morning, so Noah flicked through the CCTV from the previous night, even though nothing had woken him. He stiffened and scrolled back. Someone was there. At one o'clock there was a smudge near Harold's cage. Could it be someone's arm? He studied the next few minutes of footage frame by frame. For one moment a figure stepped into full view and then was gone. A cold chill ran down Noah's spine. An unknown person had been in the shop again. He had been upstairs, asleep and oblivious.

Harold was still sleeping in Noah's living room overnight, as the locksmith could not come until next Wednesday. He hadn't been in danger, but Noah couldn't have intruders wandering around his property. Should he get a whole new back door? This one had glass panels, so wasn't as secure as a solid one would be. How had the intruder got through the keypad on the back gate? Had they been planning to steal Harold, but were foiled because he wasn't there? Noah went over to the cage and inspected it for signs of anything unusual. Taking Harold from his perch he placed him on his shoulder and the bird nuzzled his cheek, while Noah mulled over what his night-time visitor could possibly want (nothing had been stolen). The cold hand of fear clutched his guts when he imagined finding Harold missing.

There had been something familiar about the grainy figure on the screen. He watched it through again but couldn't put his finger on it. Berating himself for not doing it weeks ago, he Googled how to change the code on his keypad, something he had put off time and time again. Fifteen minutes later it was done; a much easier task than he had anticipated.

There was a knock at the door. Noah jumped and checked his watch. It was nine o'clock. Hurrying over he saw Jemima from Brewberry through the window. He turned over the open sign while unlocking the door.

'Hi Noah, I've brought some fresh doggy treats.' Stepping inside, she reached a hand tentatively towards Harold who moved his head away.

'He's not sure about me yet, is he?' She removed her hand. 'Isn't he normally on his stand while the shop's open?'

Noah explained about the intruder and how he had felt the need to be reassured by Harold's weight on his shoulder. 'I'll put him on his stand in a minute.'

'That's worrying. How many times have you had an intruder now?'

'It's difficult to say, this is only the second time I've caught someone on CCTV. Let me show you the figure, there's something familiar about it. Maybe you'll recognise who it is.'

Jemima peered at the images on his laptop and shook her head. 'I don't think I've seen that person before, but it's hard to tell.'

'You can't see the face at all with that hat they're wearing.' Noah stepped away from the screen. 'Thanks for looking anyway. Sharing my worries has made me feel better and at least Harold and the shop are fine.'

'You're always so positive,' smiled Jemima, 'looking on the bright side even with something this serious going on.'

'I'm working on being less of a worrier. Maybe I'm actually making progress.'

'I'd say so.' Jemima grinned and headed for the door. 'I'll drop you in a hot chocolate later – that'll help you chill out.'

Remembering his promise to Aurora about being more positive, Noah gave himself a mental pat on the back. Not only had he been upbeat in the face of adversity, Jemima had noticed and complimented him on it.

His phone pinged, interrupting his self-congratulation.

Hey bro, how's things?

Noah tapped out his reply immediately. *Really great! And you?*

Really great hey? That sounds like something special. Is it a girl?

How did he know? Noah had only typed *'really great'*. Was that so out of character? At least it prevented any more agonising about when he should tell James about Aurora.

Maybe ☺

His phone rang immediately, James's tanned and smiling face appearing on the screen, his untidy hair looking like he had come straight from the beach.

'That's fantastic. Tell me all.'

Noah laughed. 'Nah. You don't really want to know.'

'Stop messing about and spill the beans. Look at your grinning face. This is someone special. I can tell.'

'I'll have to be quick, the shop's open. If a customer comes in, I'll call you back later.'

'Stop waffling and get on with it,' said James.

The shop remained quiet for the next few minutes so Noah filled his brother in on meeting Aurora, Harold's interventions and the time they had spent together.

'And we're seeing each other tomorrow for a walk.' Noah tried to repress a mawkish grin but failed.

'I'm happy for you, bro, she sounds great.'

The doorbell tinkled.

'I need to go,' Noah said.

'Okay, speak soon,' said James. 'By the way, Mum said she's coming to see you. Did you know?'

'What?' Noah stared at James's droll expression.

'I guess that's a "no" then? See ya.' James hung up, cutting off his own laughter.

Was James joking? He'd have to call his mum later. There was no time now. He turned to the customer who was already at the counter explaining that her elderly dog needed to lose weight. Two more customers came into the shop while Noah was still in conversation about senior dog food and freshly cooked vegetables. Calling his mother went completely out of his head.

Noah and Aurora had walked the ten miles, from Baggy Point around the cliff tops and along the beach from Putsborough to Woollacombe, making their way back to the National Trust car park where they had started. The April weather had been kind, with a clear blue sky adorned with streaks of white cloud, although the wind on top of the cliffs had almost whipped Aurora off her feet. The sun glinted on the water and early season surfers were out in the waves.

'I think we need to reward ourselves with a cup of tea and some cake before we head back,' said Aurora. Noah agreed and within a few minutes they were in the local café chatting over tea and a thick and sticky slab of carrot cake.

'What a wonderful way to spend Sunday afternoon. The views were amazing. I think I might have taken about a hundred photos. The company wasn't bad either.' Aurora giggled.

'Not bad at all,' he agreed.

Noah had taken one photo, making sure it included the two of them, the grassy hilltop they were standing on and the sparkling Morte Bay in the distance. He had sent it to his brother, captioning it with 'Having a really great day!'

Wanting their perfect day to last as long as possible, Noah invited Aurora back to his flat for supper. He had all the necessary ingredients for a salmon, tarragon and mascarpone pasta and a bottle of wine in the fridge – just in case.

Walking up the narrow alley to The Ark, Noah put his arm around Aurora. She leant into him, her head on his shoulder. Less than four months ago he had walked away from the life he knew, not knowing where it would take him. Today had been more than he could ever have hoped for. Until . . .

'Surprise! We've come to see you for your birthday.'

Noah's arm dropped from around Aurora's waist.

A short middle-aged woman with turquoise hair, a green tie-died handkerchief dress and magenta mohair bolero was descending on them. Bangles jingled on her wrist as she threw her arms around Noah's neck.

'Mum. What are you doing here?'

Aurora frowned. 'Your birthday?'

Shayleigh stepped back examining the pair of them. 'And who's this? You didn't tell us you were seeing someone.' She turned to Aurora. 'We're so happy to meet you, dear.'

'Yo, dude. Get that golden aura of lurve. A-ma-zing.' With the sweep of an arm, Radagast outlined the aura he was referring to.

Noah had been so startled to see his mother he had not even

105

noticed Radagast, who was also wearing some sort of green tie-died garment. It looked similar to an Arabic dish-dash without the shemagh scarf. There would be no blending in with the locals.

Noah couldn't move. A carcass in a butcher's cold room would have been better able to counter this unannounced salvo. Although his body was frozen, his thoughts were not. They whirled into overdrive. Was his life about to be ruined? Was it already ruined? He had to remove Aurora from any further contact with his mother and Radagast – at least until their relationship was better established. Where were holes in the ground when you needed them? Why had he not told Aurora more about his family? After all their discussions about honesty, here was subterfuge by omission. Not only that, he hadn't even told her it was his birthday. That hadn't been subterfuge, it was because he didn't want it to sound like he expected a present or special treatment. Everything was a disaster. His mouth opened and closed but no sound came out.

'Hi, I'm Aurora. You must be Noah's mum. You've both got the same beautiful dark brown eyes.' Aurora abandoned the petrified Noah and stepped forward to shake hands with his mother.

'I'm Shayleigh. It's lovely to meet you. You're so perfect together,' she cooed scooping Aurora into her arms.

Please let me be abducted by aliens now. Noah was still rooted to the spot.

Radagast was kissing Aurora's hand and bowing to her. 'You're a Virgo, I can tell.'

Noah closed his eyes. *No please!*

'The harmony and energy between you two is beautiful to behold.' Another sweeping gesture was performed.

'That's a lovely thing to say, but actually I'm a Leo,' said Aurora.

'Taurus and Leo.' Radagast's eyes opened wide in horror.

106

'That's a challenging partnership. What do you think Shayleigh?'

'I see only love,' she trilled.

They were not an apparition which was going to vanish. Noah had to stop the conversation right now. He grabbed his mum's arm.

'Let's all go in. I'll show you around and we can have a cup of tea.' Why hadn't he phoned his mum yesterday after James warned him? What an idiot. Was there an easy way to let Aurora know that he didn't mind if she escaped and went home? That he would prefer it.

He released his mum to fumble with the lock. By the time he had the door open his mum and Aurora were arm in arm. He could hear her asking, 'So tell me how you two met.'

Radagast had gone straight through to the corner with Harold's cage. Noah hurried after him. 'He can be a bit unpredictable. Let me open the cage and bring him out.'

Prizing Radagast's fingers away from the cage door, he put in his hand to collect Harold. In the background, his mum was still questioning Aurora. Noah wasn't sure whether it was worse to hear what she was saying and be forewarned or remain in blissful ignorance.

'This is Radagast. He's a . . . friend.' Noah informed Harold. He couldn't bring himself to call Radagast his mother's boyfriend and hadn't come up with a suitable alternative.

Radagast's face was now inches from Harold's. 'That is one special bird. Totally magnificent. A shaman in a former life, there's no doubt about it.' Radagast put his hands together in the prayer position and gave a low bow.

'Namaste my brother. We have much to discuss.'

Harold bobbed his head in reply.

Radagast looked around, as if searching for something. 'Dude, no bird this exceptional should be alone. To fulfil his passage on this earth he needs a mate. Reincarnation won't happen unless he's passed on his seed.'

Noah was glad Aurora wasn't within earshot. He almost laughed, realising he had found something to be 'glad' about in this cringe-worthy situation. Maybe he was getting better at seeing the positives.

'He's got me for company. I'll have to do. Anyway, kea are endangered, there's no way I could get another one.'

Harold hopped onto Radagast's shoulder and pulled companionably at his beaded dreadlocks.

'The bird recognises one of his own.' Radagast laid a hand on his breastbone and closed his eyes in apparent ecstasy. Opening his eyes again, he looked at Noah. 'Did I tell you my spirit animal is a bird? A bird of paradise.'

'You didn't,' said Noah. A bird with emphasis on its elaborate plumage was not a bad shout for Radagast.

'Namaste,' said Harold. Normally silent in the presence of strangers, he was obviously taken by Radagast.

'My brother, we will work on your spiritual vocabulary, while we are here.' Radagast lifted his hand to his shoulder and Harold stepped willingly onto it.

'No swear words,' said Noah, not sure what Radagast was talking about.

He was rewarded with the first frown he had ever seen on the man's handsome face. 'Dude, I spread only love.'

A new worry struck Noah. What did 'while we're here' mean? Were they planning to stay in the flat? 'What are your plans now you're here?' he asked.

'We go with the flow,' said Radagast unhelpfully with an expansive wave of his hands. Harold fluttered his wings to keep on balance.

Did the man never give a straight answer?

Radagast nodded slowly, looking around. 'I appreciate why you moved here now. The place has fantastic vibes. Respect.' He high-fived Noah, then turned back to Harold.

'Let's have dinner.' The parrot was obviously done with

spiritual vocabulary.

'Awesome,' said Radagast.

'Awesome,' said Harold.

Noah's supplies did not stretch to dinner for four so they ordered pizza. Much to his relief, once supper was over, Radagast and his mother returned to their camper van. Escorting Aurora downstairs Noah wondered whether he should apologise for his family or try and pretend they were normal.

'I've had a lovely evening.' Her expression was genuine and open. 'Your mum's so nice and easy to talk to and Radagast is amazing. Fascinating. I've never met anyone like him.'

'I'm sure you haven't,' said Noah, trying to sound neutral. 'I hope you didn't find them too . . .' – how could he describe them? – ' . . . overwhelming.'

'They're great and it was lovely of them to come all this way for your birthday.'

Noah looked at his feet. 'I'm sorry I hadn't told you it was my birthday. I didn't want you to feel obliged to buy a card or anything.' Was Aurora replaying their discussion about being honest? Did she think him deceitful? He still hadn't told her about his dyslexia. Would his failings put her off?

Seeming oblivious to his inner turmoil, she continued, 'I love birthdays. It was great we got to celebrate with your family and such a fun evening.' She gave him an impish grin. 'How did you turn out to be so normal?'

'I think it's a bit of a reaction,' he laughed. 'My dad was a pretty serious type, maybe that's where it's from. James is more like Mum or my uncle John, chatty and full of life.'

Aurora put a hand on his arm. 'Do you know your face always lights up when you talk about James? I guess you miss him a lot.'

Noah had to swallow a lump in his throat before he could

reply. 'I do. He's the best. I miss Dad too, but I've come to terms with that one.'

Aurora encircled him in her arms and rested her cheek against his chest. He inhaled the scent of mango and coconut and basked in the feeling of her warm body. The ache of missing family members abated.

Chapter 9

Noah was in blissful ignorance that his mum and Aurora had swapped phone numbers the previous evening. The first he knew about it was when his mother trilled, 'Hurry up. Aurora's meeting us at eight o'clock. We mustn't leave her sitting in the pub on her own.'

'Aurora? She's coming tonight?' Fork frozen in mid-air, Noah stared at his mother.

'Of course. She's part of the family now. We've been messaging all day. She's joining us for the live music at The Beaver.'

Noah cringed. What had his mother been saying to his girlfriend? She had never been close to Daisy. Why was she all over Aurora when Noah hardly knew her himself? Was Aurora as horrified as he was?

'Come on, eat up.' His mother waved towards the fork in his hand, which had still not made its way to his mouth.

Descending stone steps into the cosy traditional pub with Shayleigh and Radagast, Noah craned his neck looking for Aurora. Perhaps she had decided not to come? He couldn't decide if that was a good or a bad thing. They walked past the crowded bar and up a few steps where a wall of windows provided stunning views over the estuary. Aurora waved to them from a table near the back of the room. If he was lucky, the music would start in a few minutes, reducing the opportunity for conversation. His relationship with her was less than two weeks old, too soon to subject her to more of the bizarre ideas of his mother and Radagast.

Shayleigh, wearing jeans and a relatively conventional top

slipped into the seat next to Aurora. They were deep in conversation almost immediately. Disappointed by the seating arrangements, Noah sat next to Radagast who was also wearing jeans and looking almost normal for a change (apart from unnecessary reflective sunglasses and being the only person in the pub with dreadlocks).

He turned to Noah. 'There's an exquisite intimacy between you and Aurora. I was worried because of your opposing star signs, but fear not, I've discovered it won't be an issue.'

Noah shifted uncomfortably in his seat. Did Radagast have to be so weird?

'I can see from your face you've been worried about it too, dude. I was up most of last night researching how the sun and Venus affect your star signs and their relative positions on your actual birth dates. There are no barriers to you two becoming one beautiful soul and living in harmony.'

'You're getting ahead of yourself. We hardly know each other.' Noah studied the table and wished anew that he was sitting next to Aurora.

Radagast ignored his protests. 'Once you two have embraced honesty, trust and open communication, you'll enjoy unparalleled sensuality, sexual connection and love.'

Cheeks colouring, Noah glanced over at Aurora praying she couldn't overhear and was relieved to see she was engrossed in conversation with his mother. He hoped their discussion was about something normal.

He looked back at Radagast who added, 'And yet more good news: your Devon family will swell before the year is out.'

Noah was not going to discuss his sex life, or lack of it. The man was a menace. 'Whatever.' He shrugged.

What could he say to divert Radagast? Anything would do. He plunged in with, 'You spent a lot of time with Harold today. How are you getting on?'

Radagast's face lit up. 'The only person I have a deeper

112

connection with is your mother.' He turned towards Shayleigh, doe eyed, before returning to the subject of Harold. 'That bird is among the most awesome creatures on the planet. It's no wonder we are in tune. Brothers.'

Was there no limit to the size of this guy's head?

'Mostly we commune in silence through a meeting of minds, but I have challenged him with physical and verbal learning too. Daily growth is critical for an animal of supreme intelligence.'

Relieved Radagast had been so easily diverted, Noah seized on the subject of training parrots. 'Absolutely. All parrots need the stimulation of learning. I try to play games or teach him something new every day.'

'His education needs to be physical as well as spiritual,' agreed Radagast. 'As per Friedman, the ABCs of behaviour analysis – Antecedent, Behaviour and Consequence are a great foundation for learning.'

Noah stared. How did he know this stuff?

Radagast continued to discourse on the technicalities of training, stimulating and empowering parrots for the next half hour. Noah couldn't help but be impressed. Radagast already knew at least as much as he did about parrots. But then the guy always immersed himself in his latest passion, using his boundless energy and intelligence to absorb information.

The music limited conversation for the rest of the evening. A blessing as far as Noah was concerned. Shayleigh then signed them all up for a quiz on Thursday, to which Aurora cheerfully agreed.

On getting home, Noah messaged her to say she shouldn't feel obliged to come unless she really wanted to. Aurora replied that she was looking forward to it and would see them all on Thursday. She added that she had enjoyed chatting with his mother, which he took to mean that the conversation hadn't been too embarrassing.

The quiz night was surprisingly successful. Noah had to miss his business owners' meeting, but Shayleigh insisted family time was more important. Their team 'The Sun Gods' (name chosen by Radagast) won by a clear margin. Aurora amazed them all with her knowledge of sport, shrugging as she informed them, 'I have three brothers, I can't help it.'

Radagast excelled in every round. There was no subject where he didn't seem to have in-depth knowledge. Noah supposed he would be a CEO by now, had he decided to focus his abilities in the corporate world.

Noah smashed the food round, and his mother stunned them with her ability to recognise faces in the photographic round – a talent she had not passed on to Noah.

Laughing together on the walk home, Noah noticed he had stopped worrying about what Aurora thought of his mum and Radagast's eccentricities. The evening had been full of jokes and laughter. Even Radagast hadn't been too irritating.

After spending a week in Appledore, Shayleigh and Radagast left to run a woodland retreat in Cornwall. Despite a worrying start, Radagast's wild predictions and some embarrassing moments, Noah had enjoyed their visit, although he couldn't wait to have Aurora to himself again.

'We came to say goodbye,' said Shayleigh, looking ethereal in long turquoise robes. 'We need to be at the campsite by lunchtime to get everything set up. What are your plans for the rest of the day?' She clasped Noah's hands in her own. It felt oddly comforting.

'I've lots of admin to catch up on. It's been a busy week.'

'And then?' She gave him a knowing look.

'Aurora's coming round for supper,' he admitted.

'It's wonderful you've found each other.' She squeezed his hands. 'Radagast and I have been visualising golden auras around the pair of you. You are destined to be together.'

'Calm down, Mum. We've only been seeing each other for a couple of weeks.'

'But when you've been intimate with someone in a former life, that's irrelevant,' she insisted.

Radagast, who had been communing with Harold, came over beaming. He had obviously heard Shayleigh's last remark. 'Your mum's right. You have met in many previous lives, giving rise to numerous progeny.'

A blush rising across his cheeks, Noah was thankful Aurora was not there. He took a purposeful step towards the door.

'It's been lovely to see you. Have a great time at the retreat.' A sigh of relief escaped him as he closed the door behind them. Aurora had seemed unphased by their company, but enough was enough.

Later that week, his Wednesday delivery round finished, Noah was on the way to John's antiques store in Hatherleigh. He glared at the voice emanating from his dashboard. The road ahead did not look inviting. Should he trust the satnav or his intuition? His intuition was normally wrong. Hands tense and leaning forward over the steering wheel he inched down the lane. It got progressively narrower until vegetation was scraping both sides of the car. Rounding the next bend a sign brought him to a halt. A sign that would have been more helpful at the top of the lane, rather than half-way down. '*Unsuitable for motor vehicles.*' He could have told them that.

He inched backwards until he reached a gateway where he could turn around, wheels spinning on the muddy ground. Why had he not been blessed with an unerring sense of direction? The satnav was still encouraging him to venture back down the unsuitable lane. He sighed and got out his map. Taking deep breaths and muttering 'you can do this', he traced a finger along the main road, trying to work out his exact location.

He had promised his uncle he would help transfer some

antiques from the shop to his barn. Despite having left in plenty of time, he was running late. Heading back to the main road, Noah's head was full of negativity. It wasn't as if he hadn't been to Hatherleigh before. Why wasn't he competent like everyone else? His plummeting self-worth didn't rally, even when he spotted a sign for the small town where his uncle lived. His satnav had only just forgiven him for abandoning the farm track.

John appeared as soon as Noah pulled up outside Abacus Antiques. 'My boy, good to see you. Come in.'

'I'm sorry I'm late. The satnav took me down some impassable track.' Noah tried to sound light-hearted.

John guffawed. 'There's a lot of those around here. I've been down quite a few myself. Come and have a brew, or something stronger if you like. It won't take long to shift this stuff.'

Noah declined a tot of whisky, but did feel better after a cup of tea. Filling in a chortling John on some of the more embarrassing moments from his mother and Radagast's visit, Noah realised his uncle was not in the least bit bothered by him being a few minutes late. Not everyone was as draconian as Daisy.

'Sounds like Aurora coped well with the unexpected family onslaught. She's a bit of a smasher, isn't she,' said John.

Noah blushed. 'She is pretty special.'

'Good on you, lad.' John took a nip from his hip flask and stood up.

'Let's get on then. I need help getting some of the heavier items to my storage barn. After that we'll have to rearrange the shop a bit, so it doesn't look too empty. I've got a dealer coming up from London next week and he's taking most of my stock.'

'How come a dealer's taking most of your stock?' asked Noah.

'Everything from down here in the west country is a bargain

for these London dealers. They can't snap it up fast enough. I'll soon pick up some more stuff though. I've got my sources.' He tapped the side of his nose.

Noah envied his uncle's perpetual optimism. Was it mind over matter or had John created his perfect life?

They loaded up the van and drove it out to John's barn, which was perched on a hill in a grassy field several miles away. After that Noah helped rearrange the remaining antiques in the shop.

'Well done, lad. I couldn't have managed without you.' John moved an art-deco lamp into the window display and stepped back. 'Do you fancy joining me for supper at the Tally Ho! They've got a steak night on this evening.'

'I can't tonight,' said Noah. 'I left the shop in a bit of a hurry, so I've got things to sort out and Harold's been on his own all day. I need to get back and give him some company.'

John snorted. 'You've got to get back for a parrot? I've never heard the like. Your girlfriend won't like playing second fiddle to another bird.' He chuckled, delighted at his own witticism.

Noah gave a polite smile. He couldn't explain his bond with Harold and he sincerely hoped his uncle would never refer to Aurora as a 'bird' to her face. What was it with his relatives?

'I'm afraid I need to go,' he insisted. Harold was his responsibility. 'Parrots can't be left alone for long periods without becoming anxious. In severe cases they even pluck out their feathers and get depressed.'

'That parrot's nothing but a bloody nuisance,' said John, rolling his eyes, but after another few minutes of cajoling waved Noah off with a cheery, 'See you soon, laddie.'

Noah was glad he had insisted on getting back to the flat. He needed some down-time and hopping from foot to foot on his shoulder while he prepared supper, Harold was the perfect companion. Once the vegetables were chopped, Noah settled

117

his bird on the stand with a piece of broccoli. He had learnt that allowing the bird to eat whilst on his shoulder resulted in very messy clothing.

'I hope your day hasn't been too boring,' said Noah, getting a handful of cooked chicken out of the fridge and adding it to the pan. 'I'm glad I could help out John today though; he's done so much for me.'

'Bloody nuisance,' said Harold.

Noah glanced sharply at Harold. 'Yes, I am talking about Uncle John. It's a mystery why you two don't like each other. Perhaps two such big personalities will always clash in a small space, or are you both vying for my attention?'

Harold flew over and landed on Noah's shoulder, leaning down towards the pan. 'Chicken.'

Noah handed over a piece of tender meat and put Harold back on his perch. It would be fascinating to know just how much his feathered companion understood.

After supper Noah checked the day's takings and then turned to his post. There was the usual selection of junk mail and bills together with a large brown envelope, addressed by hand.

He slit the envelope along the top. A personalised card with a picture of Harold and Aurora on the front fell out.

Dear Noah,

This is a belated birthday gift for you. I have been wracking my brains and found the perfect present.

Here is your taster copy. I've set up an annual subscription, so one will drop through your letterbox every month. I hope you think of me every time it arrives ☺.

Lots of love – Aurora xxx

Reaching into the oversized envelope, he pulled out a magazine. Across the top in bold letters, it stated, *'Parrots',* below was a photograph of a brightly coloured scarlet macaw. Opening it at random Noah's heart sank. So many words. There were photos too, but this was a magazine for enthusiasts, not children and was full of tightly packed text. The words swam in front of his eyes and he put his hands over his face.

He should have told Aurora about his dyslexia. There was no excuse; not after they had promised to be honest and open with each other. How could he explain that her thoughtful gift was a millstone around his neck? Would he have to pore over it every month and pretend to be delighted to avoid hurting her feelings?

Slumped on the sofa, Noah mulled over his unpalatable options and cursed the fact that he had not already told Aurora about his disability. He had fretted needlessly about Vera and John finding out. Neither of them thought any worse of him because of it. Was it now too late to tell Aurora?

Harold landed on his shoulder and nuzzled his cheek. Softly he sang, 'I'm glad, I'm glad.'

Noah lifted his head and buried his fingers in Harold's soft feathers. He re-read the note. Aurora wanted him to think of her every month for at least a year and she had signed off the note *'lots of love xxx.'* He took a deep breath. Harold was right, these were things to be 'glad' about.

He pulled the magazine towards him and opened it at a random page. A plethora of words surrounded a photo of a splendid, crested cockatoo. Tracing his finger along each line and muttering the sentences out loud, he started to read.

The article, on avian enrichment, contained useful ideas on providing stimulation for Harold. It even suggested taking parrots on outings, which Noah thought was a great idea, especially as Aurora had said Harold could visit her flat next time Noah came over. It had taken a while, but having read the article, he could call Aurora with genuine enthusiasm.

'The magazine's fab. I've got some great ideas on

enrichment activities for Harold.'

Aurora squealed with delight. 'I'm glad you loved it. I was so excited when I came up with the idea. I bought you last month's copy so I could send it with my little note and next month's copy should arrive in the post in about a week.'

Noah crushed a momentary desire to confess his dismay on receiving the magazine. He couldn't bring himself to spoil Aurora's pleasure at having chosen the perfect gift. The next half hour passed exchanging updates and arranging to have dinner at her flat on Saturday night. Aurora remembered her promise that Harold could accompany him and she laughed when he told her the magazine article had said it was good for parrots go on outings.

After the call, Noah leant back into the sofa letting his thoughts drift. Was Aurora as keen on him as he was on her? She had given him a whole year's subscription to the magazine and said she hoped it would remind him of her. That was a great sign. How would it feel to have been together a whole year?

A ripping sound jolted him out of his reverie. Harold was wantonly shredding the magazine, his strong beak making short work of several pages at a time. The splendid cockatoo had been demolished.

'Hey! That was a useful article.' Noah snatched the torn remains and held it above his head.

'What do you think you're doing?' Harold was not often destructive and Noah was normally sanguine in the face of his misdemeanours. This time, however, he was incensed by the heedless damage to a gift from Aurora – although a tiny part of him was relieved he had a valid excuse for not reading the rest of the magazine.

Harold flew up to the curtain rail and glowered.

I did you a favour. No-one wants to look at a preening cockatoo. And how does sorting red and blue tiddlywinks into separate piles show intelligence anyway?

He didn't come down for the rest of the evening.

Eventually, at bedtime, Noah persuaded him onto his hand so he could take him to the large cage downstairs. Harold was sleeping there again now that the locksmith had put a new lock on the back door.

The following morning, Noah took extra time to fuss over Harold and feed him treats.

'I'm sorry I shouted last night. Were you bored because I was ignoring you?'

Harold didn't reply but gave Noah's ear a friendly nibble and hopped over to the window, indicating he would like to go out.

Before Noah could open it, there was a rat-a-tat at the door. A smiling face framed by a neat grey bob peered through the front window.

'I know it's not opening time yet,' chirped Vera, 'but I wanted to check you're coming to book club tonight and I also need to have a look at what you have in your eco range.'

'I loved *Pollyanna* and I'll definitely be at book club,' Noah reassured her. 'What do you need to know about my eco range?'

'I've had a few customers ask about things like biodegradable poo bags and eco-friendly dog toys. I always direct them over here, but it would be useful to see exactly what you stock.'

'Sure. Give me a moment to open the window for Harold. I don't want to fall out with him again.'

'Fall out? That doesn't sound like you.' Vera raised an eyebrow.

'It's a long story, but I was reading a magazine yesterday evening and all of a sudden Harold started ripping it up.'

Bit by bit the whole story came out, with Noah explaining how he had failed to tell Aurora about his dyslexia and now compounded the issue by saying how great the magazine subscription was.

'You're going to have to come clean.' Hands on hips and lips pursed, Vera looked quite fierce.

'What if she ditches me because I've lied?' Did Vera think badly of him?

'Of course she won't ditch you, although she might wish you'd told her earlier. It's important she knows because of the associated issues you've got.'

Associated issues?

This was worse than he thought. There were other things wrong with him. Things even he wasn't aware of. 'What do you mean?' He wasn't sure he wanted to hear the answer.

Vera's tone softened. 'It's a common misconception that dyslexia only affects the ability to read and write. It affects a whole host of things including memory, self-esteem, organisation, concentration and sense of direction. These things vary by individual. If you're in a relationship you both need to understand all the differences in the way your brains work. That way you'll prevent misunderstandings.'

Noah stared at Vera, not knowing which of the many questions racing through his mind to start with. He honed-in on the one that stressed him most.

'Sense of direction? What do you mean?' All his life it had been a mystery to him how other people remembered routes and he didn't. Often, he couldn't even follow his satnav to a destination without an unplanned detour. Was it his dyslexia rather than incompetence that was responsible for his struggles to travel from A to B without getting lost? And what about memory, self-esteem, organisation and concentration as well. He struggled with them all.

Harold landed on Noah's shoulder.

'We've got a few minutes,' she said. 'Let's have a cup of tea and talk about it.'

Noah nodded, looking shell-shocked.

'You let Harold out and I'll pop upstairs and make tea. I

know my way around your flat.' Vera headed to Noah's kitchen, while he let Harold into the aviary and processed Vera's revelation. Did everything he struggled with stem from his dyslexia? A glimmer of light flickered at the end of his tunnel of recriminations.

He sipped his tea, nose wrinkling at the sweetness of the brew. 'Is there sugar in this?'

'You need sugar, it helps with shock.'

There was no point in arguing.

'How do you know so much about dyslexia?'

'I told you I used to be a teacher, but I didn't mention I was an SEN specialising in dyslexia. It's something I've studied extensively.'

By the time Vera had explained everything and Noah had drunk his tea, a whole world of understanding had opened up. His low self-esteem stemmed from lack of support during early education and his poor sense of direction was a common issue for people with dyslexia. Short-term memory including remembering tasks, directions and names was also an area where dyslexia typically caused issues.

The skills he lacked stemmed not from incompetence, but from the disability he assumed he had overcome when he learnt to read and write.

'I can't believe no-one ever explained the wider ramifications to you.' Vera pressed his hand between hers. 'You've done brilliantly. As well as learning to read and write, you've developed a whole raft of coping strategies to manage your life. Do you ever congratulate yourself on that?'

'Um, not really.' Noah wondered if it would be rude to withdraw his fingers from hers. He didn't like being on the receiving end of sympathy. But perhaps it was empathy? He flexed his fingers and Vera let go of his hand.

'Think about all the coping mechanisms you already use:

making lists, writing down names, setting reminders, using your satnav. You've achieved so much. Be kind to yourself and give credit where it's due.'

'I'll try.' He studied the countertop.

'We can have another chat whenever you like,' said Vera. 'You need time to process all of this. And don't forget,' she added, 'you need to explain everything to Aurora when you see her on Saturday.'

In the quiet after she had gone Noah heard a light tapping. Harold was still outside. Opening the window, he offered his wrist to the bird saying, 'Well, that's given me food for thought.' Remembering it was book club tonight, he added, 'I'm "glad" Vera explained all this to me. It really helps.'

'I'm glad,' repeated Harold.

At book club that evening, Noah was not the only person who had reconsidered their attitudes and tried to incorporate the 'glad game' into their daily life after reading *Pollyanna*. In the face of admissions from others, he found himself revealing his tendency to focus on the negative and how thinking positively had a tangible impact on his mood and levels of anxiety. It had been easy to talk about his feelings in the context of the book and in a space where other people were doing the same. Also, he was not the only one who admitted to the negative spirals their brains could manufacture. Even though it was only his second time meeting the other members of the group, he was amazed how comfortable he felt opening up.

Their next book was *The Midnight Library* by Matt Haig. It followed the journey of Nora Seed who through a magical library was given the chance to explore the lives she could have had, had she made different life choices. Noah considered himself too logical to enjoy a book with magic in it, but the previous two choices had surprised him, so he was determined to start the book with an open mind.

Chapter 10

Noah had cleaned Harold's stand and purchased (from his own shop) a grey and white cat carrier, in which he planned to transport Harold to Aurora's. Everything was ready for their visit. Today was also the day he planned to tell her about his dyslexia. Potential conversations with Aurora had been running through his head all week, interspersed with incidents from the past where his dyslexia had made Daisy find him wanting. Would his disability put Aurora off? His stomach lurched at the thought.

He placed the cat carrier on his dining-room table, where Harold was pottering around playing with a teaspoon.

'In you get, Harold.' Noah opened the mesh door and put some grapes inside. 'This is just for the journey, once we get there you'll be able to come out.' Harold rolled his eyes and backed away.

Picking up one of the grapes, Noah wafted it under Harold's nose. The parrot glanced sideways at the stark plastic interior of the box, the whites of his eyes glistening, his body rigid.

'Come on. Don't be scared.'

Harold fluttered over to the sofa, standing tall and swivelling his head from side to side.

'If you don't get in you can't come.' Noah made to clamp his hands around the recalcitrant bird.

Harold zoomed out of reach onto the rail above the window. A slimy green and white blob slid down the curtain. They were due at Aurora's in twenty minutes. Contingency time was slipping away.

Things went from bad to worse with Harold determined not to be caught and Noah increasingly stressed about being late.

Hiding the cat carrier in his bedroom, Noah battled to lure Harold down from his lofty perch, offering pomegranate, banana and even Frosties. Frosties were strictly not allowed, although Harold had discovered the delights of them one morning when Noah was not paying attention.

Harold was not to be tempted. Trying to swoop down and snatch Frosties while still on the wing he knocked the box out of Noah's hand and all over the carpet. Crawling round on his hands and knees with a dustpan and brush, Noah muttered words he was normally careful not to repeat in front of Harold.

He messaged Aurora explaining they were going to be late.

Flapping and skidding round the room Harold managed to smash a glass and knock a second batch of Frosties onto the floor. He had now retired to the shower rail.

'I'm going without you,' stormed Noah, torn between frustration that he was late for Aurora and guilt at the parrot's distress. Why hadn't he simply picked Harold up as normal and then produced the cat carrier? They would be there by now.

He put on his coat, picked up a bottle of wine from the counter and headed down the stairs. What could he do? Leaving Harold in the flat wasn't an option. Not in this mood, he would destroy everything he could get his beak on. To Noah's relief, the parrot landed on his shoulder just as he reached the ground floor.

'Let's have dinner.' Harold fluffed out his feathers.

'I can't be won over that easily. You're staying here.' Noah walked towards Harold's cage.

Harold nuzzled his neck. 'I love you, Noah.'

Stopping in his tracks, Noah's heart melted and his anger vanished. Harold had never said 'I love you' before. How could he leave him on his own now? Moving slowly, he clasped his hands around the bird's body taking care to hold the wings securely.

'I love you too, Harold, but perhaps I should rename you

126

Machiavelli?' He rubbed his nose against Harold's beak. 'Where did you learn "I love you"? You certainly know how to pick your moments for maximum effect.'

Keeping a firm hold, Noah took Harold up to his bedroom, retrieved the cat carrier from under his bed and put the now struggling bird inside. Harold leapt round his prison making plaintiff 'keeaahs' all the way to Aurora's.

Half an hour late, cat carrier in one hand, Harold's stand in the other and a bottle of wine tucked precariously under his arm, Noah pressed the doorbell.

Aurora opened the door, smiling and sunny as ever in yellow- and white-striped dungarees. 'You've had a stressful time then,' she sympathised, taking the carrier and the wine.

'I did consider selling Harold to the highest bidder,' laughed Noah, 'but he won me over in the nick of time.'

'I know you'd never sell him, no matter how naughty he was,' she said, giving Noah a kiss. 'The chicken bake has only just gone in the oven, so we've plenty of time to settle Harold and relax before dinner.'

Squawking at top volume and leaping at the wire mesh on the front of the carrier, Harold was making it known he wanted to be released. As soon as the carrier door opened, he shot out and flew around the room three times before landing on his stand. He had just calmed down and was munching on a piece of apple, when Aurora's cat, Buffy, stalked across the room.

Harold dropped his treat and hunched over to peer at the cat. Feathers fluffed at right angles, he looked twice his normal size. Buffy glared at the intruder, fur on end, tail rigid. Hissing, she prowled around the stand. Harold swivelled to watch her every move.

'Come on, you.' Aurora scooped up the cat and stroking her, walked over to the sofa. Settled on the high back, Buffy licked a paw, shooting disgruntled glances at both her owner and the intruder.

'They'll get used to each other,' Aurora said airily.

Noah wasn't so sure, but Buffy did purr loudly with appreciation when he scratched behind her ears. Harold glared.

There was no room for a dining table in Aurora's compact living room, so they ate supper on their laps on the sofa, looking out over the garden. Harold and Buffy ignored each other and all was calm.

Noah had hoped Aurora's suggestion that he bring Harold was because she wanted him to stay the night, but when he declined a second glass of wine because he was driving, she did not demur. His disappointment was tempered by the fact that she frequently referred to 'next time' and 'another day'.

Leaning back into large, soft cushions, he slipped an arm around her shoulders. Now was the perfect time to explain about his dyslexia. Vera would be impressed he had got around to it so promptly. He swallowed a couple of times and leaned forward to take a sip of coke. His throat felt unnaturally dry.

'Thanks for supper, the chicken was delicious,' he croaked trying to remember the planned segue into his tricky topic.

'It's a favourite of mine,' said Aurora 'and I've got plenty left for lunch.' The dish containing the remains had been placed on top of the tall fridge to keep it out of Buffy's reach – chicken was a favourite of hers. Aurora leaned into Noah, their bodies melting together. He bent to kiss her, feathering kisses down her neck and murmuring endearments. A warm glow raced through his body as their lips met.

He must not be distracted. He had to get the dyslexia conversation out of the way. Unable to give their kisses the attention they deserved, he shifted in his seat and moved away.

'What is it?' Aurora looked puzzled and not a little disappointed.

'Nothing . . . well . . .' He would have to get on with it. 'There's something I want to talk to you about.' He had practiced his opener several times, earlier in the day. Everything would be fine.

'It's connected to the magazine you got me. The article I mentioned last week was really interesting. I've already bought Harold a foraging toy and we're working on new training commands.'

Aurora nodded. 'I'm glad I chose the right thing.' She looked puzzled at Noah's sudden change of tack.

Noah took a deep breath. He could do this. 'The magazine's great, there's one thing though . . .'

There was an almighty crash at the other end of the room. Noah and Aurora leapt off the sofa and turned to look. Harold was on top of the fridge-freezer, a tell-tale piece of juicy chicken dripping from his beak. His eyes were rolling and he had backed into the corner. The roasting dish and its contents were strewn over the kitchen floor. A soggy fur-ball streaked down the hall and into Aurora's bedroom, leaving greasy and bloody paw-prints in its wake.

'Buffy!' Aurora rushed after her cat.

Noah surveyed the glass, carrot, peppers, chicken and greasy residue, which adorned not only the floor, but the cupboards, wall and fridge.

Harold flew to his perch, chicken firmly clamped in his beak.

The cat was remarkably easy to win over. One strip of chicken and they were best buddies.

Noah had dealt with most of the debris by the time Aurora came back, a disgruntled-looking Buffy in her arms. Her yellow and white dungarees were covered in grease, blood and splodges of food.

'She's cut her paw, but it's stopped bleeding, so I don't think it's too bad. She wasn't very happy about me trying to get the worst of the gravy off her fur, but I think she'll be able to clean up the rest.'

'I hope she's okay.' Noah could hardly bring himself to look at Aurora. 'I'm so sorry. It didn't occur to me Harold would try and steal the chicken. I've no idea how he knocked something so heavy onto the floor.'

Aurora was clearly preoccupied with the cat and not listening.

'I'm going to lock Buffy in the bathroom for a while; she's still covered in grease. I don't want it all over the flat. And I need to get changed and clean up my bedroom.' She turned around and went back down the corridor.

By the time Aurora returned Harold was squawking in the cat carrier and Noah had his coat on. The earlier ambiance had vanished.

'I think I'd better go now?' It was half statement, half question.

At that moment Buffy re-appeared having escaped from the bathroom. She jumped on the sofa and vomited up what looked suspiciously like most of a chicken breast.

'I guess so.' Aurora picked up a cloth and advanced on the sofa. 'Would you let yourself out?'

Noah stared at the ceiling. Most of the night had been given over to fretting about the incident at Aurora's and checking to see if he had any messages from her. The seagulls were already awake and dawn was creeping over the horizon. He plumped his pillow and turned over. Did she hold him responsible for the injury to Buffy and the mess in her kitchen (and bedroom and bathroom and living room)? He should have taken Harold's small cage and kept him in it for that first visit, or paid more attention to what the bird was up to. Instead, he had thought only of himself. Noah sighed and turned over. Sleep was not going to come. Throwing the covers aside he got out of bed.

Harold lifted a claw and bobbed his head as soon as Noah appeared downstairs. 'Good morning.'

'I'm still cross with you.' Noah made a show of scowling and

130

dumped a handful of treats in Harold's bowl, rather than feeding them to him one by one.

A kilo of feathered friend arrived on his shoulder with a bump and nuzzled his ear.

'I love you.'

Noah smiled despite himself. 'You're not going to get around me that easily. Just because it worked yesterday, doesn't mean a couple of cute words gives you carte blanche to behave however you like.'

Harold gave a loud and familiar purr.

'And don't try and blame Buffy.'

Noah shooed Harold onto his perch and did some unnecessary cleaning and tidying in the shop, before going for a walk. He had messaged Aurora to ask if she wanted to join him for a Sunday stroll, but she had replied that she was busy. There was no mention of meeting up anytime soon. Or ever.

Even the stunning vista and fresh air of Westward Ho! didn't cheer him up today. Kicking his way along the shoreline, he called James.

'Give her a couple of days. I piss girlfriends off all the time but they always forgive me.' James never stayed in a relationship for more than a few months.

'Always?'

'Well, mostly.' James laughed. 'It depends how badly I've behaved. But this was a complete accident. You've contacted her since. You've apologised. You're totally in the clear.'

'You get away with things I couldn't. It's the Mr Charming gene that I didn't inherit.'

'I'm no more charming than you, it's self-belief you're lacking. You're a fantastic person and everyone loves you. You need to believe it.'

'Yeah, yeah.' James was always so positive about everything, including his brother. Had he only called James to hear how great he was? Probably not. He was never convinced by James's accolades anyway.

'What happened to that "glad game" thing you talked about?' James asked.

Noah sighed. He should never have mentioned his resolution to find something to be glad about every day. Hoisted by his own petard he scratched around for something he could be glad about. It had been easy when Aurora filled his life with sunshine. The pause in the conversation went on too long and James filled it.

'You must be glad to have such an awesome brother?' James was trying to joke him out of his mood. But he did have a point.

'I am glad; even though my awesome brother is big headed.' James laughed and Noah joined in. 'I'm glad I've got the pet shop too and that I live in a beautiful place by the sea.' The soft sandy beach was almost deserted now Noah was a couple of miles from the town. For company he had sand dunes to one side and rolling waves to the other.

'I've got so many great memories from our childhood there,' said James. 'I envy you your new life.'

'Envy me?' Noah snorted. 'You've got it all. Sun, sea, sand, surf, loads of friends.'

'The only thing I've got that you haven't is year-round sun. You get the soft refreshing rain instead.' James laughed again. 'I'm wet when I'm surfing, so there's not much difference.'

Grateful to his brother for trying to make him feel better, Noah didn't argue. Instead, they exchanged more memories of holidays in Devon. By the end of the call Noah's dark cloud had lifted a little.

'I feel better now. Thanks,' he told James 'And I *am* glad to have such an awesome bro.'

'Ditto,' James replied.

On Monday there were still no new messages from Aurora. Noah's mood slumped again and his chit-chat with customers lacked its usual enthusiasm. During a mid-morning lull and fed up with the negative thoughts swirling through his head, Noah put his 'Back in 5 minutes!' sign on the door and headed to Brewberry for a pick me up.

'Eat in or take-away?' asked Jemima.

'Eat in, why not,' said Noah. It was drizzling outside and the street was quiet. He settled himself on a stool at the counter. The café had a pleasant buzz and smelt of ground coffee and warm scones. What better place to get a bit of TLC?

Jemima appeared in front of him with a steaming mug of hot chocolate, topped with cream and marshmallows. She put a brownie next to it.

'I only ordered a standard hot chocolate,' said Noah checking his pockets for change.

'You look like you need the bells and whistles version today. The extras are on the house.' After a pause Jemima said, 'Do you want to talk about it?'

'Not today.' His short reply sounded rude, so he added, 'How are the new cat treats coming along?'

'We should have our first batch ready for you later this week.' Jemima pulled a wry face. 'Do you know, we make more profit on the dog treats than we do on cake.'

'Well, I prefer your cake,' said Noah and they both laughed.

As soon as Noah left the warmth of the café, gloom settled over him once more. He had been away from the shop for an unheard-of twenty minutes and hoped he wouldn't have to deal with any irate customers. That would only add to his misery.

Fortunately, the only person waiting outside his shop was Uncle John.

'Noah, my boy, there you are. Vera said you'd be back any minute, but I'd almost given up.'

'I'm sorry, I popped to the café. I didn't know you were coming.' John had never called in unannounced. What had prompted this visit?

133

'I was in the area and thought I'd call in.' He peered at Noah. 'You're looking a bit glum. What is it?'

Noah recounted the incident with the parrot, the cat and the chicken and how he thought he might have scuppered his chances with Aurora.

'A catch like you,' John boomed. 'Not a chance. She'll be back. You're worrying over nothing.'

For the first time, Noah found his uncle's optimism irritating. Not wanting to reveal the detail of Daisy's damning letter from the previous year, which still preyed on his mind, he knew he wasn't the catch James and John thought he was. Unwilling to discuss his failings, he also couldn't bring himself to say, 'You're probably right, everything will be fine.'

Saved from answering by the arrival of a couple of customers, Noah was busy for the next few minutes. John wandered around the shop and told Harold what he thought of him.

A booming 'Look at all this mess. You're a bloody nuisance you are,' drifted from the back of the shop.

Noah smiled politely at his customers and made a mental note to ask John not to swear when customers were on the premises. It wasn't a great idea to swear in front of Harold, customers or not. You never knew when he was going to latch on to a word or phrase. He'd already picked up 'bloody'. What next?

Once the shop was empty John reappeared at the counter. 'I see you've had a new lock fitted on the back door. No more intruders since then I guess?'

'No. I changed the keycode on the gate too. I've been checking the CCTV and seen nothing suspicious, so whoever it was must have come in the back way. Thanks again for your help with the installation.'

'No trouble, my boy. No trouble.' John patted him on the shoulder, then started to wander around the shop again, seeming distracted. He came back to the counter. 'I'll be off now, but if I could use your facilities that would be splendid. The old bladder's not what it was.'

Noah grimaced at John's retreating back. Had his uncle downed a couple of pints (or something even stronger) with breakfast or was it tea filling up his bladder? Was it any of Noah's business? His uncle had always been the one in charge. James seemed to think it wasn't Noah's problem, but he couldn't help worrying.

The afternoon was marred by a visit from the postman who brought the next edition of *Parrots* magazine, reminding Noah of the sorry state of his fledgling relationship. The baleful yellow-rimmed eye of a hyacinth macaw reproached him from the front cover. As soon as the shop was empty, he dashed upstairs, throwing the magazine on the sofa. At least he wouldn't have to look at it all day now. No longer being glared at from the front cover of a magazine, he found it easier to concentrate on his sales.

Noah glanced at his watch; only another hour to go. The effort of dealing with customers had been more wearing than usual, especially the looking cheerful part. An elderly woman shuffled in, a voluminous hood covering her face, an old-fashioned handbag over her arm. Noticing her slippered feet, Noah realised she was the frail and confused lady who had been in before. She must have eluded her young carer again. At that moment, the doorbell tinkled and Uncle John strode into the shop for the second time that day.

'Hello again, young lad. How's it going?' John was carrying a couple of brown paper bags and looking very pleased with himself.

'Good, thanks.' Did John want to drag him to the pub as soon as the shop closed? Not tonight, surely. Noah wanted to wallow in his own misfortune. He wasn't even sure he could be bothered to cook.

'Have you heard from that young lady of yours yet?'

'No.' Noah looked at his shoes and longed for solitude.

'Well, I'm sure you'll hear from her soon,' John said briskly, thumping his bags on the counter. Noah could smell whiskey on his breath and steeled himself to decline an invitation.

'I've brought something to cheer you up and something to help you woo your young lady back.' He beamed and waved a meaty hand at the packages.

'You didn't need to do that,' stammered Noah, a lump forming in his throat.

'It's my pleasure. There's a bottle of wine for you. I know you're partial to a good red and there's something special for you to give to Aurora. A pal of mine makes the best hand-made truffles in Devon and I've got you a box. Take 'em round and tell her you're sorry for the trouble that bloody parrot caused.'

It was not the right moment to take his uncle to task for swearing.

'One taste of those chocolates and all will be forgiven. I guarantee.' John beamed.

Feeling guilty for assuming John only wanted a companion for a visit to the pub and touched by his unexpected thoughtfulness, Noah gave him a hug.

'Thanks for looking out for me. I'm lucky to have family nearby.'

'Anytime, my boy. Anytime.' John patted him on the arm, his eyes welling up.

'I'll be off now.' His voice sounded gruffer than usual.

Noah watched him leave. His uncle lifted a hand to his face, as if to wipe away a tear.

The sound of Harold chuckling made Noah glance at his CCTV. The old woman who had come in earlier was bobbing from one foot to another in front of Harold's cage. Harold was bobbing back, obviously enjoying the company. Was she trying to feed Harold again?

He walked into the back-room. Not wanting to startle her, Noah spoke softly and from a distance. 'Hello. Can I help you?'

She pointed at Harold and laughed, increasing the speed of her movements. Harold also increased his speed. They made a joyful pair.

What should he do? He couldn't send her outside without a carer. Leaving her to entertain Harold, he peered into the street. A couple strolled hand in hand, a woman with a pushchair was chatting on the phone and an elderly man was walking his dog. None of them looked like the carer with pigtails. Noah ventured to the corner. He didn't want to leave the old woman alone with Harold, even though she seemed harmless. She had tried to feed him last time and although it had only been broccoli, it could easily have been something harmful.

A matronly looking woman appeared from the direction of the quay. Eyes wide, mouth in a tight line, she scurried towards him.

He took a chance, 'Excuse me, are you looking for an old lady wearing slippers?'

The woman's hand flew to her chest. 'Have you found her? I've been frantic. It's nearly half an hour since she gave me the slip. I was just about to call the police.'

'Don't worry,' Noah was almost as relieved as the carer. 'She's in my shop, just here.' Thank goodness the old woman was no longer his responsibility.

'Do you know how worried I've been?' Hands on hips, a sheen of sweat on her forehead and upper lip, the carer stood in front of her charge.

Blue-slipper-woman blinked and backed away.

'I don't think she meant to worry you,' said Noah, uncomfortable at the carer's aggressive tone.

'I've been worried sick,' she snapped, transferring her hostility onto him. 'If I take my eyes off her for one moment, she's gone.'

'It is the second time she's wandered in here,' he said. 'Why don't you give me the number of the home where she's a resident, then if it happens again I can call?'

The carer's eyes narrowed and she looked away. Seizing slipper-woman's arm, she looked back up at Noah, suddenly all smiles. 'It's no bother. No need to inform anyone. It won't happen again.' She ushered her charge out of the shop.

Noah guessed she was worried about getting into trouble, but if the old woman came in his shop again, he would insist on getting a contact number. He knew people with dementia respond well to animals, but he couldn't have her roaming round The Ark while people were frantically searching for her. He needed a way to let them know where she was. Pleased it was time to close up for the day, he locked the door and set about his evening chores.

Slicing the chilli and garlic, Noah's knife clacked against the board. He chopped longer than was necessary, until his ingredients were almost a pulp. The rhythmic movement made him feel better. Perhaps his uncle was right and all was not lost with Aurora. But perhaps his uncle was wrong. He threw the mushy pulp into a hot pan together with some pak-choi then turned over his teriyaki salmon, basting it with extra marinade. Harold observed every move from his shoulder.

'I know you didn't mean to cause any trouble or smash the dish,' Noah told him. 'I shouldn't have been so cross, but I'm worried about the cat and that Aurora might not want to see me again.' He checked his phone again for messages. Nothing.

'Whatever happens, I'm glad I've got you.' Reaching up he rubbed Harold's beak. 'It was kind of John to bring those chocolates. I'll take them round tomorrow.'

'Bloody nuisance,' said Harold.

'No swearing,' Noah wagged a finger in front of Harold.

'And you need to cut Uncle John some slack. He's a great guy.'

Settled on the sofa, Noah shared his supper. Salmon and pak-choi, free from salt, soy and chilli, had been fried in a separate pan for his companion. At least he didn't have to cook for one. That would accentuate his loneliness.

Putting his empty plate on the coffee table, he reached for the magazine, which had contributed to his gloom earlier in the day. He would read one article. That would be something to talk to Aurora about.

After spending longer than necessary admiring the hyacinth macaw on the front cover, Noah couldn't put off finding an article to read any longer. Turning to the index page he looked for something he could face reading. He scanned the list of contents: breeding red-tailed amazons, nest adoption for hyacinth macaws (hence the photo on the front), evaluating parrot seed mix. His heart sank, nothing was inspiring him.

Then he spotted the perfect article. 'Parrot expert Doctor Donovan Little discusses kea in captivity'. Noah had found very little information on captive kea, because their intelligence and destructive tendencies mean they do not make suitable pets. He rummaged eagerly through the magazine to find the article. The page was dominated by a photograph of a magnificent looking kea called Freya. She was part of Doctor Little's private collection. The parrot in the photo had a narrower head than Harold and her plumage looked brown and olive rather than olive and glossy green, but that could have been the lighting. He started to read.

Doctor Donovan Little, renowned aviculturist and ornithologist born in Edinburgh in 1957, first became interested in parrots when he was gifted a pair of lorikeets for his eighth birthday. Psittacine culture soon became his passion. He published his first article at age twelve and his first book at nineteen. Subsequently, Doctor Little spent many years studying and working with conservationists in Bolivia and Brazil before returning to the

UK to oversee breeding programmes of endangered psittacine and, where appropriate, their subsequent release into the wild.

He owns a small private collection of parrots, most of which were intercepted as part of operations to clamp down on the smuggling of endangered birds. His five-year-old kea, Freya . . .

Harold landed with a thump in the middle of the page.

'Get off. I'm reading that.' Noah flapped his hand to shoo Harold off the magazine. It had no effect. Harold simply jumped over his hand and back onto the photo of Freya. Fluffing up all his feathers he hopped from foot-to-foot shouting 'keeaah, keeaah.'

'Calm down will you.' Noah chuckled as Harold bestowed fervent kisses on the pictured bird, then continued to dance, bobbing his head furiously.

'Have you never seen another kea before?' Noah sat back, enjoying Harold's display. After a few minutes his expression became more serious. Did Harold need a companion of the same species? He could give his bird company and toys and teach him things to keep his brain active, but that wasn't the same as having a mate. Why had the necessity of Harold having company of his own kind not struck him before; especially when being with Aurora had made him so happy?

Performing some sort of ritual dance Harold was now making sharp chuckling noises. Suddenly, he flew off to his stand. Noah wondered if it was all over, but the parrot returned with a grape which he placed next to the photo of Freya. He then re-commenced his dance.

Forgetting the anxieties about his own love life, Noah videoed the strange behaviour and sent it to Aurora.

I think Harold's in love! What shall I do?

He tried scooping Harold off the magazine and closing it, but the bird became quite frantic, flying in circles then pulling at the pages trying to get to his beloved inside. Noah opened up the magazine again. Before long, the photo was scuffed with claw-marks and disfigured with mashed grape. Harold had pounded his offering against Freya's photographic beak, making clear his frustration at the lack of response.

Noah could empathise. He was equally frustrated by Aurora's lack of response to his video. She had not even looked at the message. Was she asleep or deliberately ignoring him? His mood dipped again, if she was ignoring the video, a box of chocolates probably wouldn't have the desired effect.

Harold stood in the middle of the article, his head drooping and his feathers no longer fluffed. He looked how Noah felt.

It wasn't until the following lunchtime that Noah's phone buzzed with the message he had been waiting for.

Poor Harold, how is he? Are you free for a call? Ax

'It's Aurora,' he announced to Harold, who was slumped on his perch, eyes dull.

'I'm so sorry about the other night,' he blurted. 'I should have kept better watch over Harold. In fact, I shouldn't have brought him round at all. Is Buffy okay? Can you ever forgive me?'

Aurora laughed. 'There's nothing to forgive. Accidents happen. I'm sorry if I was a bit of a grouch, but I was worried about Buffy and that was my favourite casserole dish.'

'Oh no, I'll buy you another one. Where was it from? How can I make it up to you?' gabbled Noah.

'Honestly, don't worry.'

'But I do. And I've bought you chocolates. Well, John did, but they're from me and I thought . . .'

Aurora butted in, 'It's all okay. Stop fretting. Now, tell me what's going on with Harold. I'm on my lunch hour and haven't got long.'

Noah explained Harold's animated reaction to the kea in the magazine and how depressed he had seemed since. 'He hasn't eaten or spoken. He's not playing with his toys. I'm worried he'll pine away if he carries on like this.'

'I'll come over this evening and we'll see if we can cheer him up together.'

'That's great. Thank you.' At least only one of us will be pining if Aurora comes, thought Noah.

Aurora arrived that evening to find a small feathery shape hunched on the table next to the magazine. Every so often it bestowed a desultory kiss onto what was left of Freya's photograph. He had never looked so dejected. Even his inquiring black eyes were dull and unfocussed. Normally delighted to see Aurora, Harold showed no interest in her caresses or her treats.

'He's totally in love,' said Noah. 'Kea aren't designed to live alone. I feel so guilty. Why didn't it occur to me before how lonely he might be?'

'Stop beating yourself up. You've only ever done your best for him.'

'What if he doesn't recover? What can I do?'

'We'll work something out, I promise.'

Despite his worry, Noah was cheered by Aurora's 'we'll work something out.' He was not alone in this.

Aurora smoothed out the tattered page. 'Doctor Dolittle,' she snorted. 'That's hilarious.'

'Dolittle? What do you mean?'

'Doctor Donovan Little. Surely everyone calls him Doctor Dolittle. He's Mr Wildlife with the perfect name.' She was giggling. 'Don't tell me that hadn't occurred to you?' Pulling the article towards her, she moved a limp Harold onto her shoulder. Noah watched the emotions crossing her face as she flicked her way through the soggy text. Everything seemed to be back to normal between them.

She looked up. 'What a fascinating guy.'

'Yeah.' How had she read the whole article already?

Aurora cradled Harold under her chin. 'You poor thing. You've got it bad haven't you.' She scratched his neck and kissed his head. Harold lay back against her, still and listless.

'I could buy another parrot,' said Noah, making mugs of tea. 'I'd never be able to get a kea, but maybe I could find an African grey. They're very intelligent, so one might be good company for Harold.'

'I think he's made up his mind which parrot he wants to be with,' said Aurora, still cuddling the lovesick bird.

'I can't write to one of the most eminent parrot specialists in the country and say, "*Can I have your parrot please?*".'

'Could you write and say something different.' Aurora turned and looked at him, her face pale.

'He's famous. I don't have any contact details. What would I say? There's nothing I can do.' Noah's voice was shrill and anxious.

'You can't not try, just because it might not work. This is for Harold. I know you'd do anything for him. We must get Harold and Freya together somehow.' Aurora placed a comforting hand on his arm. 'Do you want to ask if Harold can go and live with Freya and Doctor Dolittle? That's more likely to work than asking if you can have his parrot. Could you bear to be without Harold?' She stroked the lovesick bird's wing with the back of her finger.

Noah reached over and ruffled his neck. Aurora could see the muscle in his jaw clenching and his eyes filling with tears. It was several minutes before he wiped his face with a sleeve. 'He's my best friend, even though I've only known him a few months.' Squaring his shoulders, he said, 'I want what's best for Harold. Let's write a letter now.'

'Are you sure? Do you want to wait a few days?' asked Aurora.

'I want to do it now, but . . .' Noah paused, '. . . I'm not very good at writing.' Was now the time for his great reveal?

'I guess it's tricky with your dyslexia. Why don't we compose the letter together and I'll type it into your laptop.'

Noah gaped. 'How do you know about my dyslexia?'

'Your mum mentioned it, although she said your reading's good now. Everyone's got things they're good at and things they're not so good at.'

Noah's mouth hung open. How could Aurora be so calm about something that had given him sleepless nights? She was talking as if dyslexia were perfectly normal. Once again, all those hours worrying for nothing.

'What's wrong? I'm sorry, I didn't mean to take over, I just wanted to help.' She looked away biting her lip.

Noah laughed and lifted her chin. 'I can't tell you how much I've fretted over telling you I have dyslexia. And now I find you already know. I thought you'd think I was stupid or something. Then in my head it became a big deal and I got all anxious about telling you.'

Aurora put Harold gently onto the table and leaned over to give Noah a hug. 'It's just one of the quirks that makes you You. Why would I think of it as anything else?'

'I don't know,' Noah mumbled into her hair.

Aurora disentangled herself and looked directly at him. 'I really like you, Noah. I like you for what you are and who you are. You're smart, gentle, kind and honest. You don't need to pretend to be anything else.'

'I like you too. A lot.' He pulled her towards him again.

It was some time before she said, 'We ought to make a start on the letter if we're going to do it today.'

Noah glanced at Harold. He remained exactly where Aurora had placed him on the table; head bowed, beak resting on his chest. Lifting him onto his shoulder and caressing his soft feathers, Noah said, 'He needs company more than I need him. We have to try.'

Aurora read the article out loud to Noah, so he knew its full contents, then found an email address for the doctor on LinkedIn.

Noah insisted the letter should be written as though it were from Harold. He wanted to emphasise that the strange request was for the benefit of the parrot and not its owner. It was a couple of hours before they were finally satisfied with the wording.

Dear Doctor Little,

My name is Harold. I am a handsome and exceptionally intelligent kea, currently in the keeping of a young man called Noah Wood. This evening, we chanced on your article in Parrots magazine. An article which shed a whole new perspective on our lives.

Before I move on to the purpose of this correspondence, I think it is important to tell you a little more about us. We live in a pet shop in Devon and have known each other for almost three months. My acquisition is a long and strange story, which is for another day.

Noah gives me as much attention and freedom as possible and I move between a selection of stands and my aviary during the day. I spend most evenings with Noah, helping him cook, entertaining him with tricks, socialising or just relaxing. Thanks to Noah, I benefit from an epicurean diet, although he is careful to keep sugar and salt to a minimum. Despite our acquaintance being short, we are the best of friends.

Until today, we assumed I was doomed to a bachelor life. On catching sight of Freya, everything changed in an instant. I can no longer calmly contemplate a life of solitude. Two such perfect examples of nestor notabilis will only be whole if they are one.

Noah understands that my life needs the richness only a psittacine partner can bring and although my absence would leave a parrot-shaped hole in his life, he does not want to stand in the way of my happiness. My wellbeing is his only concern and he is confident that an avian expert such as yourself could give me an ideal home.

145

I understand that formalities must be taken care of and a face-to-face meeting will be necessary before a decision can be made. In the meantime, we are at your disposal to answer any questions. We would like to meet at a time and place convenient to you, to discuss this matter further.

A few photos are attached so you can see my fine physique for yourself, together with a video demonstrating my uncompromising adoration for La Belle Freya. Watching the video will dispel any lingering doubts you may have concerning this unusual request.

The hearts and minds of two beautiful kea are in your hands. I entreat you, allow me to live in your home with my only love, Freya.

Yours sincerely,
Harold

Noah pressed '*send*' and closed the lid of his laptop. He had a pain low in his belly and a lump in his throat, but knew he was doing the right thing. Harold's happiness was what mattered most. Taking a deep breath he turned to Aurora, 'Thanks for your help. We've just got to wait and see now.'

'The letter's brilliant. He can't fail to see how much you care and how important it is for Harold and Freya to be together.'

Noah gave an imitation of a smile. Speaking was difficult. Digging his fingernails into his palms he managed, 'I'm glad we tried.'

He must be getting better at the 'glad game'.

Pushing himself up, he said, 'It's late, you need to get home.'

Aurora got off the sofa too. She was standing very close.

'Unless I stay and go home in the morning.'

Her scent filled his nostrils. He could feel her, even though they were not quite touching. His heart hammered against his ribcage.

She put her arms around him. 'That's a very selfless thing you've just done. I know you're sad and sad people need to be hugged.'

Their lovemaking was tender. Aurora trying to take away the pain in Noah's heart. Noah rising and falling on a seesaw of emotion, discovering that happiness and melancholy can co-exist, even when both are big enough to fill the body on their own.

Chapter 11

Memories of waking up next to Aurora suffused Noah with warmth. Smiling at the message on his phone, it felt almost impossible to wait until evening to see her again, but they both had to work. Leaving after a last lingering kiss, she had promised to see him later. He sighed and went back to his pre-opening chores. The world doesn't stop and let you get off, just because you're in love.

The morning inched slowly by, even though the shop was busy. Noah scanned his phone between customers looking for messages from Aurora, a hollow forming in his belly when no new ones arrived, although he knew she must be busy teaching. He had pushed all thoughts of Doctor Donavan Little to the back of his mind. The guy would probably never reply anyway.

With an effort he brought his attention back to a fussy middle-aged lady sporting bright green fingernails and matching glasses. Nodding as she explained her query, he patiently explained the difference between normal and senior dog food. The doorbell chimed. He glanced over to see who had come into the shop. It was the stooped woman with dementia once again. Without her carer. Shuffling past the counter, she headed straight for the back-room and Harold's cage. As he was in the middle of serving, Noah could not chase after her, but he kept an eye on his CCTV screen.

The slippered escapee stopped in front of Harold's stand, but did not attempt to feed him. Eventually his dithering customer ordered a large bag of senior dog food and left; the transaction taking longer than normal, because both her glasses and her fingernails were more decorative than functional.

Noah added the dog food to his delivery list for Wednesday

and dashed into the street to see if the old lady's carer was nearby. The street was empty. He should have insisted on getting a contact number last time. When he got back into the shop, the woman was not bobbing around, as she had been before, but was standing quietly staring up at Harold. Even from the back she looked sad. Knowing how timid she was, Noah cleared his throat and called softly from archway, 'Excuse me.'

She ignored him. He sidled forwards and to the right to be within her eye-line and tried again, a little louder this time.

'Excuse me.'

She turned, taking a step backwards and pressing her hands to the scarf at her throat. A small nod indicated she had heard him.

Full of love and generosity of spirit, a legacy from his night with Aurora, Noah was overwhelmed with the need to cheer her up. She would have few pleasures in life. If being with his parrot was one of them, who was he to deny her? Dogs were used to enrich the lives of dementia sufferers; why not parrots too?

He took a piece of walnut out of his pocket and motioned giving it to Harold before holding it out to her.

'Would you like to give him a treat?'

Hesitating for only a moment she smiled, her whole face transforming like a flower opening in the spring. Taking the nut, she reached up to where Harold was sitting.

'Slowly,' said Noah, ready to leap forward if anything went wrong. Harold had only ever taken his treats gently, but any animal can be unpredictable.

Shuffling towards his benefactor, Harold leant down until he was almost hanging from the perch. Noah wondered how he managed not to fall when he did this. The bony hand remained steady despite the size of the beak approaching and didn't flinch when the walnut was gently removed. Harold righted himself, stepped back into the middle of the perch and took hold of the nut in his long-nailed claw.

'Thank you.' Nibbling off a piece, he gave a wiggle of pleasure; his first since he had spotted the parrot in the magazine.

The woman clapped her hands together silently and beamed.

A warm glow filled Noah. What a joy to give so much pleasure to this frail woman through such a small gesture. They watched together as Harold finished the morsel and climbed back down to the lowest rung, as if asking for more. Noah had never seen him on such a low perch when a stranger was in the shop. Maybe the woman's illness gave her a greater affinity with animals? A liver-spotted hand stretched out and gnarled fingers caressed Harold's neck. Parrot and woman closed their eyes, a sense of peace surrounding them. Appreciating the bliss of fingers buried deep in soft feathers, Noah almost closed his own eyes too.

The bell above the door tinkled breaking the mood and the woman's young carer bounded into the shop.

'There you are, Grace!' Noah recognised the dark plaits and open expression of the girl he had met three weeks ago.

'I'm so sorry,' she said. 'I turn my back for one second and she's absconded. Last time she was wandering around at the edge of the quay. What if she'd fallen in the water?' Her voice was high and breathy. Harold retreated to his highest perch.

'It's not a problem,' Noah soothed.

'It is a problem! I've been frantic.'

'I mean it's not a problem for me if she comes into the shop. I think she likes the parrot. You could bring her in now and again if you like. Maybe that would stop her making her own way here.'

'You wouldn't mind?' The young woman's voice had dropped about an octave and she stared at Noah, eyes round and wide.

'If you come when it's quiet, that would be fine.'

'That would be amazing,' her face shone with delight. 'I'd be happy to call ahead and make sure you're not too busy.'

'I've been wanting to get a contact number for someone who looks after her,' said Noah. 'This is the second time she's been in this week and I need to be able to let someone know if she's here on her own.'

'Oh God.' The carer covered her face with her hands. 'I'm so, so sorry.'

'If it brightens up her life to come here, I'm glad I can help.' Noah's chest swelled. It was so easy to bring happiness to others. He should do it more often.

'Did you say her name was Grace?' He pointed towards the old woman who was still watching Harold.

The young woman nodded, tears of gratitude in her eyes. 'Yes. My name's Tilly. I'm her niece. You're so kind.' She blew her nose. 'Life's difficult at the moment, what with her being so confused. And other stuff.' She paused and appeared to be gathering herself together. 'The only helper we had resigned yesterday, so it's back to me and Mum doing all the looking after.'

Noah guessed, the woman who had left was the one who had been so angry with Grace the previous day. He hoped the replacement, when they found one, would be more tolerant.

After they had exchanged phone numbers, Tilly left arm in arm with her aunt, promising to bring her back to see Harold soon.

Basking in the afterglow of doling out happiness, Noah decided he would do it more often, starting with Vera. She had been so kind and helpful to him. He would treat her to a coffee and a pastry from Brewberry tomorrow morning. She probably deserved flowers too, but coffee would be a start. Happiness glowed from his every pore. Was this why his uncle always seemed so cheerful? Maybe he spent a lot of time helping

151

others.

He was interrupted by the longed-for message arriving.

Come over at 6.30. Bring your toothbrush ;). No need for PJs xx

Noah read the message about eight times, did a little dance and then went to tell Harold.

'I'm sorry, but you're going to be on your own this evening. I have a special date.'

Harold waggled his head from side to side. 'Let's have dinner.'

'You can't come. It was a catastrophe last time. I can't risk that again. Not just yet anyway.'

'*Cat*-astrophe.' Harold gave a loud purr.

'You were the guilty one.' Noah admonished, offering Harold another piece of walnut. Refusing to take it, the parrot climbed to his highest perch and turned his back.

Dragging himself away from Aurora's the next morning, Noah longed to spend the whole day, or at least another hour there, but left early for The Ark. He needed to check on Harold, who had been alone since yesterday evening. Expecting him to be in a bad mood on account of being abandoned, Noah was pleased to come home to an excited bird running up and down his perch. Harold jumped straight out of the cage and onto Noah's shoulder the minute it was opened. In the aviary Noah worked on getting him to pick up brightly coloured plastic cups revealing the treats underneath – one of the enrichment activities suggested in *Parrots* magazine.

'You find this too easy, don't you?' he said.

'Easy, easy,' chanted Harold as Noah jumbled the cups in front of him. Leaping over to the one with a blueberry underneath, Harold threw it off the counter.

'Yum, yum.' The bird demolished his reward.

'That's it for the moment,' said Noah. 'I need to get a coffee for Vera before it's time to open.' Leaving Harold in the aviary, he strolled up to Brewberry.

Clutching a latte, a hot chocolate and two Danish pastries he knocked on the door of Vera's refill store.

'I've brought a little something say thank you for all your help and advice.'

Vera beamed. 'It's my pleasure. I'm lucky to have such a lovely neighbour.'

They sipped their drinks and chatted, Vera reminding him that the next business owners' meeting was the following day.

Out of the blue, she asked how it was going with Aurora. Noah blushed and mumbled, 'um, yes, really well,' while studying his hot chocolate.

Knowing when to move on, she said brightly, 'Could you do me a favour?'

'Sure.' Noah stood up, delighted at the change of subject.

'My picture of the glacier up there has got knocked askew. If I stand back and tell you when it's level, can you straighten it.'

Noah stepped behind the counter. On the wall above his head was a large canvas print of the Perito Moreno Glacier. It was one of many natural wonder prints around the shop. Their purpose was to remind Vera's customers why it's worth spending a little more on purchasing eco-friendly products.

Stretching up he could just reach the underside of the canvas with his fingertips. He gave one side of the canvas a prod. Vera called from the back of the shop.

'Right side down a bit. No the other side. Yes. Down a fraction on the left. Left. Oh, sorry, I mean the window side. Just another millimetre down on the window side. Perfect. Thank you.'

'You spotted I'm no good with left and right then.' Noah tried to look as though it didn't matter.

'My bad,' said Vera. 'Of course, left and right is difficult for you. Didn't I mention that one? It's common for people who have dyslexia to struggle differentiating right from left as well as following directions.'

Noah stared at her. 'You mentioned the directions thing, but not right and left. I just thought I was . . .' Noah shuffled his feet, '. . . stupid.'

Hand on hips and head tilted to one side, Vera sighed. 'You are an extremely intelligent young man. If there's anything you can't do, it's not because you're stupid. There'll be another explanation.'

There was a pause while Noah inspected his nails. Eventually he said, 'I guess it comes from school when people did think I was stupid. I've never got out of the mindset.' He looked up into Vera's kindly face. 'The whole right/left and directions thing causes me so many problems. When I'm doing deliveries, I always go wrong at some point. I've thought about giving up, but haven't because so many people depend on me delivering now.'

'How about feeling proud that you are prepared to do something that's tricky for you to make other people's lives easier?' said Vera.

'Um,' mumbled Noah.

She held his gaze, speaking calmly. 'It will take you longer than the average person to learn a route and you may struggle to correlate the map on your satnav with the roads in front of you. It's something you have to live with. But you haven't given up your deliveries because you are determined, caring, conscientious and capable and that's worth a lot. Never let anyone tell you otherwise.'

Noah's fists uncurled and he took a couple of deep breaths. Could it be that his difficulties made him a better person, rather than a worse one? 'Thank you. Talking to you always helps. I'm sure I'll find it easier to cope next time I go wrong. Which I will.' He gave a wry grin. 'I'll tell myself it's like reading, something I need to work harder at than everyone else in order

154

to get it right, but not insurmountable.'

'That's exactly it,' said Vera.

So many of the things he used to beat himself up about could be explained. His struggles were starting to make more sense.

Aurora was spending the weekend with her aunt in Cornwall, so Noah was grateful he had the business owners' meeting to occupy him that evening. It seemed unfair she had to go away just when their relationship was blossoming, but the trip had been arranged for some time.

He called, not sure if hearing her voice on the phone would make him feel better or worse.

'I'm missing you already,' she said, 'and I haven't even left yet. I'm still packing.'

'A weekend without you feels like a long time,' Noah agreed.

'Come over on Sunday, I'll be back early evening.'

'Are you sure, won't you be too tired?' Trying to sound solicitous, Noah hoped Aurora wouldn't make him wait an extra day.

She didn't disappoint. 'I've already told my aunt I need to get back before supper and it doesn't matter how tired I feel, I'll still want to see you.'

Her words sent a shiver down Noah's spine. 'I'll cook supper and bring it with me, then you won't have to worry about it'.

'You're my hero.' She blew kisses down the phone.

After the call, Noah leafed through his favourite cookbooks working out what to make on Sunday. By the time he needed to leave for the meeting a lengthy list of ingredients had been typed into his phone.

At the meeting there was a useful talk about the dos and don'ts of offsetting expenses against the business, followed by a lively question and answer session. Noah was shocked at some of the things people glibly put through their accounts. Later in the evening the subject of security came up again. Noah assured the group that since installing a new lock on the back door and CCTV he had experienced no further trouble with intruders. He also got the advice he needed on employing someone to help him over the summer.

He had just arrived home when his phone rang.

'Sorry it's so late, young lad, I meant to call you earlier,' boomed Uncle John's voice.

'No problem, I was up anyway.'

'Thanks, laddie. How's it going with the young lady then?' His uncle chuckled. 'Did the chocolates do the job?'

A stab of guilt hit Noah. He had completely forgotten to let his uncle know his relationship was back on track. 'Everything is great. She loved the chocolates, but in fact I didn't need them.' He told his uncle about Harold and the magazine article and Aurora helping him write to Doctor Little.

'What did I say? I knew you and that pretty girl would be alright,' said John, confident as ever that things would go well. 'I'm pleased you're getting rid of that parrot at last,' he continued. 'It's a bloody nuisance.'

Noah smiled to himself, remembering Harold mimicking John's 'bloody nuisance' phrase. He banished a pang of sadness at the thought Harold might not be his for much longer.

'I'm very fond of him,' he said, unable to explain what a massive understatement this was. 'And I don't know what's going to happen. I haven't heard back yet.'

'Anyway,' said John, 'the reason I'm calling is to see if you can give me a hand again on Sunday. I've got a few more things I need to move up to the barn and it'll be tricky to manage on my own. Back in my younger days it would have been alright, but I'm not the man I was.' It was the first time Noah had ever heard a downbeat tone in his uncle's voice.

'Of course I can help. What time shall I come over?'

'Does one o'clock suit you?'

'Sure.' If his uncle needed help, Noah wanted to be there.

Grace came in to see Harold again late on Saturday afternoon, this time accompanied by Tilly. Noah was relieved he didn't need to worry about searching for her carer. As it was a sunny morning, they went into the aviary, where Harold entertained them with his new trick of identifying which coloured pot contained a treat. Every time he got it right (which was every time), he shouted, 'easy, easy,' and hopped from foot to foot. Noah could hear laughter through the open window as he served his customers.

Mr Wainwright, flat cap resting on his bristling eyebrows, came in just as Tilly and Grace were leaving. He shook his head at their retreating backs before coming up to the counter and fixing Noah with a meaningful gaze.

'How can I help you, Mr Wainwright?' Noah put on his most business-like voice. Mr Wainwright's visits were always accompanied by long, rambling and often unintelligible tales about someone from the village. Noah had come to dread them. He wasn't interested in gossip, even when he did know who or what his customer was talking about.

'It's hard for 'er, you know.' Mr Wainwright shook his head.

'Oh dear,' said Noah. 'And how can I help you today?'

'Such a young 'un as well.'

Noah smiled politely.

'Lost her job, she did.' He took off his cap and turned it round in his hands, as if in respect for the dead.

'What a shame. Is it chicken feed you'd like?'

'Aye, when old Craddock's went out of business, she were left high and dry, along with the rest of 'em. No jobs for young people these days. She just looks after her crazy old aunt.'

Noah grimaced. It didn't seem appropriate to call someone with dementia a 'crazy old aunt'.

'Cheerful though,' continued Mr Wainwright, oblivious to Noah's discomfort.

Noah didn't know whether it was the girl or the old lady who was supposed to be cheerful. He looked past Mr Wainwright and nodded to the next customer. 'I'll be with you in a minute, sir.'

Mr Wainwright glared at the five people standing behind him in the queue, before buying chicken feed and leaving. Dealing with the queue as quickly as he could, Noah recognised many of the customers, even though he couldn't put a name to every face.

Just as he got down to the last person, a tall, dapper gentleman with thick round glasses, a check jacket and an old-fashioned leather briefcase came in. He didn't look like a typical customer. Nor did he act like one, pacing quickly up and down each aisle, before going into the back-room. Noah watched him on the CCTV. After a thorough inspection of Harold and his cage he peered into the aviary before striding back to the counter where the final customer was paying her bill.

A moment later, the shop was empty apart from Noah and the smartly dressed gentleman. The man stepped confidently up to the counter and held out his hand.

'Good afternoon, my name is Donovan Little.'

Noah gasped, belatedly clasping the proffered hand.

'That's amazing. I wasn't expecting you. I mean welcome. I . . . you . . . my letter . . .' This wasn't the impression he wanted to give the eminent parrot specialist. He cleared his throat and stood up straight.

'I'm Noah. Pleased to meet you. I'm honoured you've come to visit us. Are you here to see Harold?'

'It will be my pleasure to get to know both of you.' The man gave a formal bow. 'I was fascinated by your letter and happened to be at Exeter University this morning. I'm a regular speaker there and I made a spur of the moment detour to see you on the way back. I apologise for not giving prior warning.'

'I'm delighted you came.' Noah's heart pounded. Would this man want to take Harold away? Today? He couldn't cope with that. Trying to ignore his lurching stomach, Noah led the way to the back-room, where Harold was on his stand.

Noah offered his wrist and the parrot stepped onto it.

'What a fine specimen and in such magnificent condition. He's even more impressive than in his photographs. May I?' Doctor Little lifted his arm towards Harold, who stepped onto it without hesitation.

Anyone who thinks I'm a 'fine specimen' and 'magnificent' is a gentleman.

Harold behaved impeccably while the doctor inspected his eyes, beak, legs, wings and even bottom. Superlatives flowed like water from the doctor's lips. Placing Harold carefully back on his perch, he handed him a Brazil nut from his pocket.

Turning back to Noah he said, 'Tell me more about how you came to own such a glorious bird and your reasons for writing the letter.'

Harold fluffed his feathers noisily and stretched to his full height.

'Glorious bird.'

Doctor Little started. 'He talks?'

'Yes. He's got quite a large vocabulary.'

'That's unheard of in a kea.' The doctor looked at Harold with renewed admiration.

After detailing Harold's extensive vocabulary, Noah recounted the mystery around his acquisition of the bird and the relationship they had developed. He then described what had happened when Harold first saw Freya and his realisation that the parrot needed a mate. The doctor nodded his gaze alternating between Noah's glowing features and animated gestures and Harold's regal (possibly even magnificent) pose.

'And you're looking to rehome him?' he asked.

Noah rubbed his face in his hands. 'No . . . Well . . . it's difficult. I'll miss him terribly, but I want to do what's right for him. Kea aren't solitary birds and he's clearly shown he needs a mate. Much as I love him, if I felt someone could offer him a better home then I would have to let him go.'

'Indeed.' The parrot expert reached up to take Harold on his arm once more. He carefully stretched out one of Harold's glossy emerald wings, revealing the vibrant orange feathers underneath.

Noah couldn't believe Harold was letting the doctor do this. He was very particular about his wings, constantly preening them and flapping indignantly at any attempt to open them. The man's confidence and experience must shine through.

Doctor Little released the wing and produced a floret of broccoli from another pocket. Harold took it and flew up to his perch with an appreciative, 'Broccoli.'

'How much do you want for him?' asked the doctor, suddenly.

Noah stared. It hadn't crossed his mind to ask for money. 'Nothing,' he said. 'I just want to know he's going to a good home for the rest of his life.'

'You do understand he's a very valuable bird worth tens of thousands to an unscrupulous collector? His value is exceptionally high because he talks. Totally unheard of in a kea.'

'It's not about money,' said Noah. He swallowed. 'He's my friend.'

The doctor nodded and Noah felt he genuinely understood the breadth of feeling signified by '*he's my friend.*'

After a few more questions the doctor left, saying he couldn't promise anything, but would see what he could do about providing a suitable home for Harold.

Noah sunk on the stool behind his counter. He didn't know whether to be happy that Harold had the chance of a better life, or sad that he was going to lose him. He messaged Aurora, not

160

sure his voice was up to talking.

Taking Harold onto his knee, he re-watched the video of his parrot dancing on the picture of Freya and tried to be glad about Doctor Little's offer.

Noah dreamt about cages that night. Some empty, some containing only shadows and some containing dead animals which morphed into him being the one who was trapped. He woke more than once, unable to get the disturbing images out of his head.

On Sunday morning, at Harold's regular training session, he tried to get his bird to put the correct colour tiddlywinks into a bowl in return for a treat. Harold threw them on the floor and prodded Noah's pocket until he gave him the treat anyway. For some reason, he had an aversion to games with tiddlywinks. At midday Noah left for Abacus Antiques, glad he had a distraction to make the time pass until he saw Aurora that evening.

The anonymous country lane stretched ahead. Noah took a deep breath; his stomach was a balled fist. High Devon banks topped by hedges towered over him. Rolling fields stretched into the distance as far as the eye could see. He should be there by now. Listening to the radio rather than paying attention to the satnav, he must have missed a turn.

It's part of your condition. It will take you much longer than the average person to learn a route. You are determined, caring, conscientious and capable. Never let anyone tell you otherwise.' Repeating Vera's words like a mantra, his fingers loosened their hold on the steering wheel and his shoulders relaxed. Everyone had things they were good at and things they found more difficult. He was lucky he had a good brain for numbers and was fit and healthy. A few extra minutes driving through beautiful countryside was a small cross to bear.

Frustration subsiding, he drove back down the road, spotted a familiar landmark and arrived in Hatherleigh a few minutes later. Parking smoothly in a tight space directly opposite his uncle's shop, he reminded himself that parking was one of the things he was good at.

A large box van was positioned outside Abacus Antiques. John waved to Noah from the open back of the van.

'Hey there, lad, thanks for coming.' He stepped down, gripping the side of the van to aid his descent. Noah remembered his uncle's comment about not being as young as he was. He seemed to have aged by several years over the past few weeks.

'Let's jump to it,' said John. 'I need to get everything out of the shop and up to the barn today. There's not too much, so we'll only need a couple of trips.'

'Everything?' Noah looked around at the eclectic mix of treasures, scattered around the premises. 'You're not closing down, are you?'

'Nothing like that.' John clapped him on the back. 'That London dealer I was talking about, he wants the lot now. It's all a bargain to him, Devon prices you know. Spruced up and in some posh Knightsbridge store, he'll charge ten times what I'm selling it for. I need to have everything in one place for collection, so it's up to the barn with all of this. I've got a couple of house clearances and an auction coming up later this month. The shop will soon be busting at the seams again.'

'Okay. Let's get the big things in first,' said Noah. It seemed strange that a dealer would take absolutely everything, but John was a wily salesman. He must have negotiated a job lot.

It took all afternoon to move John's stock. Fragile items were wrapped in blankets or packing paper and everything had to be driven to the remote barn before being unloaded again. By the time they had finished, Noah was beginning to worry about getting back in time for supper at Aurora's.

'Well done, my boy. I couldn't have done all that without you.' John screwed up his face as he stretched. 'My back's not what it was, but nothing a pie and a pint won't cure. Let's get ourselves over to the pub.'

'I'm afraid I've got to get back,' said Noah. 'I'm seeing Aurora tonight.'

John guffawed. 'I'd forgotten, but I knew exactly what you were going to say the minute that starry-eyed look came over your face. Staying all night, are you?' John gave a wink and nudged Noah with his elbow.

'Um, yes.' Sometimes his uncle was a bit inappropriate.

'That parrot's not going to put a spanner in the works again is he?'

'I don't think I'll have him for much longer,' said Noah. 'The parrot expert I wrote to came to visit yesterday. He's going to see what he can do about finding a new home for Harold.'

'Excellent. Getting a good price for him are you?'

'Not really,' Noah couldn't meet his uncle's searching gaze.

'Come on, lad, where are your negotiating skills? Don't get ripped off. Experts are the worst for trying to beat you down.'

'I'll sort something out.' His uncle would never understand that he was giving Harold away for free. There was no point in trying to explain.

Having checked on Harold, Noah drove on to Aurora's, leaving the bird at the shop, where he couldn't cause another disaster. He was sure Aurora would understand why getting Harold the right home was so much more important than money, even if John didn't.

When he told her about the doctor's visit and his conversation with John, she insisted, 'You are totally right. Harold needs to go to Doctor Dolittle. I know you could never sell him.' Smiling and cupping his face in hers she said, 'knowing Harold is happy will give you all the riches you need.'

'Almost,' said Noah, bending to kiss her.

After supper they snuggled on the sofa, looking out over a

glorious melange of red, purple and gold, painting the sky. Noah kissed the top of Aurora's head, breathing in mango and coconut. He felt her curves mould themselves more closely into him. Life was perfect.

Trailing his fingers down her neck he felt rather than heard a murmur of pleasure. She turned her face towards him and their lips met; gently at first, then with more fervour. Small moans escaped from Aurora between kisses. Noah's breathing became heavy. He wanted to make love to her right there and then with a fierce urgency and at the same time he wanted to savour tender exploration forever. They had all night.

The following morning, standing on the pavement outside her flat, Aurora took Noah's face between her hands to give him a goodbye kiss. 'I need to get going. We've got a staff meeting before school this morning.'

Noah could still feel her touch on his face, although she had withdrawn her fingers. 'Okay, see you this evening. I'll cook something tasty for supper. Bring Buffy if you like. We'll see if she and Harold behave better at my place than they did at yours.' He grinned.

'I'll bring her if she's looking needy and leave her at home if she's asleep or out.' Aurora blew him a last kiss and set off down the street.

Noah knew something was wrong the moment he caught his first glimpse of Appledore. There were no mysterious signs, no palpable omens. He just knew. Belly taut and jaw clenched he ran from his car to the shop, telling himself he was being anxious for no reason. He had promised himself he would chase unnecessary worry out of his life. All his anxieties had proven groundless over the past few months.

He didn't slow down.

The sturdy frontage of Noah's Ark looked the same as always. The 17th century stone façade; the mullioned windows placidly reflecting the street; the solid front door. His hand trembled slowing down the process of fitting his heavy brass key into the lock. He ran through the shop leaving the key dangling. The door swung slowly on its hinge.

'Harold?'

Silence.

'Harold, where are you?' He was shouting now. The lump in his throat was unbearable.

Harold's stand had been knocked over. Shards of glass littered the floor showing where a panel in the back door had been smashed to gain entry. The cage door hung open. Food and water were scattered everywhere together with a few olive-coloured feathers. Noah picked up one of the feathers. He ran his fingers along the soft veins either side of the central shaft, oblivious to the tears running down his face. Harold was gone.

A big powerful bird, he must have fought and tried to escape his captors. That was why there was such a mess. Noah hoped his bird had crushed the fingers that tried to snatch him from his home. The vehemence with which he wished pain on the intruders made him catch his breath.

He searched the shop. Perhaps whoever it was had failed to capture him? Perhaps Harold was hiding waiting for Noah to find him. A flutter of hope kindled.

'Harold, it's me, Noah.' He tried to make his voice sound normal, but struggled to speak.

He would be up high. That was a bird's natural instinct. Noah turned on all the lights and paced the shop. Before long his neck ached from staring up into the corners. What if he were injured? He got on his hands and knees and crawled around peering under the shelves where his goods were displayed and calling Harold's name.

That was how Vera found him.

'Noah. What's wrong? I saw the door open and the key dangling, so I came in.'

He stood up, wiping the back of his hand across his face. 'It's Harold. He's gone. Stolen. There's been a break-in. I was checking in case he was still here and injured.'

Vera gasped. 'No. How awful. Did you hear anything?'

'I was at Aurora's last night.'

It was his fault. He had been out having a great time, leaving Harold unprotected. Now his beloved bird was gone.

'What about your flat? Has anything been stolen from there?'

'The flat?' He looked at her blankly.

'Has anything been stolen from there?' she repeated.

'I don't know. I haven't been upstairs.'

'Let's go together.' She took his arm.

The flat was untouched. Noah's laptop lay on the table where he had left it. Nothing was out of place.

'They only came for Harold,' he said.

'Perhaps the burglar alarm scared them off before they took anything else?'

'The CCTV,' said Noah, hope rising in his voice. 'Perhaps that will give us a clue.' He knew the theft had been all about Harold. His chest hurt. He wanted to call Aurora. He wanted to hear her telling him it would be okay. Feel her arms around him.

Vera put a 'closed due to family emergency' sign on the door, then put the same notice her own shop, while Noah checked his security system.

There it was. A hooded figure appeared from near the door and immediately stepped into a camera blind spot. A hand came up and placed a piece of sticky tape over the lens. It was still there when Noah went to look.

He inspected the yard. The back gate had been kicked open.

His call to Aurora went to voicemail. 'Hey, call me when you have a minute,' was all he said.

He called the police, who advised him they would send someone round as soon as an officer was available.

He called his mum, but her words gave no comfort. It was Aurora's voice he wanted to hear. He called James.

'No way! You loved that bird. The bastards. Is he worth a lot?'

'Yes,' said Noah miserably. 'He's an endangered species and it's illegal to trade them in the UK, so an unscrupulous collector would pay a lot. The fact that he talks and no other kea does makes him especially valuable.'

'At lot is how much?'

'I don't even know. Tens of thousands probably. I'm stupid, stupid, stupid. I had something wonderful and special and I just let a bunch of crooks walk in here and take him.'

'Hey. What's with the blaming yourself? I thought you'd stopped that? You've done everything you could. CCTV, burglar alarm, locked premises.'

'But I knew someone was interested in him. An intruder's been in a few times. They didn't take anything before, but they did hang around Harold's cage.'

'You did everything you could.' James's voice cracked with pain for his brother.

'I could have taken him with me to Aurora's, but no, I was too busy having a good time and thinking only of myself.' Noah put his head in his hands and dug his fingernails into his scalp. The pain wasn't enough to satisfy him. He needed to beat his head against the wall.

He called Javier, whose assurances that he would immediately get on to his extensive network of bird lovers gave some small comfort.

Slumped on his sofa and scrolling through photos and videos of Harold on his phone Noah smiled at the one of Harold leaping around next to the picture of Freya. A chilling thought came to him. Perhaps the article had been a scam to flush out other kea? Perhaps the revered Doctor Dolittle was a thief who traded in rare and valuable birds? Noah sunk his face into his hands. Had he been duped? The man had seemed genuine.

There was a knock at the door. Couldn't his customers read? He walked slowly down the stairs into the shop. Vera waving through the window. She had brought him coffee and a pastry.

'You have to eat. You're no good to Harold if you don't look after yourself.' She stayed until he had forced down both the coffee and the pastry.

Following a brief mid-morning conversation, Aurora appeared at lunchtime. 'I've only got a few minutes before I need to get back for my next class, but I wanted to come over.' They stood together, clutching hands, surveying the mess in the back-room of the shop.

'I'm leaving everything until the police have been,' said Noah.

'When's that?'

'I don't know. I guess people are more important than parrots, so I'm probably pretty far down the list.'

'Don't lose hope, Noah. You need hope to keep you going. I'll design some posters to put up around the area. Someone will spot him if he's nearby.'

'*If,*' thought Noah. Aurora's cheeks were wet with tears when she left to go back to school.

In the afternoon the police came to take a statement. They agreed with Noah that high value parrots are always at risk from theft and didn't seem hopeful he would ever see Harold again. Another shred of hope had been trampled on.

Seeing Aurora at lunchtime had made Noah realise that even her presence could not touch his misery. He asked her not to come over that evening, wanting to be alone with his wretchedness.

Hunched on the sofa, he now regretted choosing to be alone. Nothing distracted him. He couldn't watch TV, he certainly couldn't focus on reading, he didn't want to cook or eat. There was no-one he felt like calling. He went downstairs to search the shop again. Fruitless, he knew, but at least it was something to do. He was crawling round the storeroom when he heard his phone ringing from upstairs. A surge of hope went through him. Could it be good news?

Chapter 12

It was not good news.

Noah didn't know his uncle had listed him as next of kin on his medical records until the hospital called. John was in intensive care. He had suffered a heart attack.

Driving over straight away, Noah scoured every intersection for signs to Derriford Hospital, once he reached Plymouth. All he could think was, 'not my uncle as well as Harold'. He couldn't lose two loved ones in the same day. Why hadn't he spent more time with his uncle? Why didn't he didn't know about his heart issues?

The corridors were quiet when he arrived. Hushed footsteps, machines beeping and a sterile smell were his welcome. John was on a small ward of six people. He was connected to a drip with a machine monitoring his heartbeat. A tube, presumably providing oxygen had been inserted into his nose.

How could such a vibrant presence suddenly look so old and frail? Noah fought to steady his voice as he turned to the nurse.

'Will he be okay?'

'We're doing everything we can,' she replied. 'He's had a stent fitted and we're monitoring him very carefully.'

This hadn't really answered Noah's question. He tried again. 'I mean, is he likely to . . . will he . . .'

'He'll have quite a long recovery period and will have to look after his health, but his chances are good now that the surgery's been performed. The operation went as well as can be expected.' The nurse gave him a smile that was half kindly, half pitying.

Sitting on the edge of the bed, he took his uncle's hand.

What exactly did 'as well as can be expected' mean? Reconnecting with his uncle had been an unexpected bonus of moving to Devon. Was he to lose him now? Was he destined to lose everyone he loved one way or another?

He had called James and Aurora on the way to the hospital and messaged a brief update once he arrived. It felt inappropriate to make calls while patients were trying to sleep and he didn't want to leave his uncle's side. He let his mother's call go to voicemail. James must have spoken to her. Had her animosity towards John been quashed by his vulnerability, or was she was only calling to comfort Noah?

About four in the morning the same nurse who had answered his questions earlier suggested Noah leave and get some rest as John was stable. The drive back to Appledore was filled with the knowledge he was returning to an empty home. No parrot. No-one to comfort him. His brain tumbled with loss and longing. There was no room for any other thoughts. Dawn had already arrived before the oblivion of sleep overtook him.

He was still asleep when his doorbell rang the following morning. Eyes immediately wide, his first thought was that the sound might be Harold imitating the bell. Before the thought was fully formed, a vision of Harold's empty cage hit him with the force of a punchbag.

The doorbell rang again. Vera's 'closed due to family emergency' sign remained on the door, so he was not expecting to be disturbed. Stumbling down the stairs, he couldn't think who it might be.

He opened the door and his mum flung her arms around him.

'Noah, darling, we came to help.'

Radagast waved from over her shoulder. 'Hey dude.'

Noah blinked. His mother and Radagast? Was their visit because Harold was gone or because his uncle was in hospital?

171

Or neither. Closing the door behind them, Noah led the way upstairs. Once there, Shayleigh fished about in her handbag, 'Here we are, let's have some tea.' She brandished a bag of wilting nettles at Noah.

He needed caffeine.

'We planned to come and see you when we heard about Harold.' Shayleigh handed Noah a cup of something warm but insipid and continued, 'Then James phoned and told us about Uncle John's heart attack. You've got so much on your plate; we couldn't leave you to manage all on your own.'

'Thanks, Mum.' Noah made himself a coffee. He wasn't sure what help his mother and Radagast would be. No matter how well meaning, their idea of help could be somewhat random.

'We'll head off to see John after this cup of tea and you can open up the shop or rest, whatever suits you best.'

'Are you sure?' The last he knew, his mum still stiffened if John's name was even mentioned. Had she put all that behind her?

She must have seen the question in his face. 'Uncle John was good to us all when you and James were children and he's really helped you since you moved here. If he needs us, we should be there.' She crossed both hands over her breastbone taking a reverential pause. 'It's a long time now since . . . you know . . . everything.'

'Hatred is a burden. Love is power.' Radagast raised his hands in the air. 'Healing vibes have been sent to your uncle. They are working their magic right now.'

'What about Harold?' Noah couldn't help asking the question, although there was no way Radagast had any more idea than he did about the parrot's well-being.

'Harold is an old soul of great power and resource. His destiny is unchanged.' Radagast brought his hands into the prayer position and bowed his head.

Noah wished he hadn't asked.

Once his mum and Radagast had left for the hospital, Noah opened the shop. At least he would have something to do. Word had got around quickly about Harold and John and well-wishers arrived regularly. People Noah had never met expressed their sympathy and said they had been out looking for Harold or had shared Noah's posts on social media. Jemima brought him a hot chocolate mid-morning and a Moroccan tagine at lunchtime. Like Vera, she insisted Noah must eat to keep up his strength.

Aurora emailed Noah the poster she had designed. He printed it out and passed copies on to his customers so they could post them around the area. Despite having only lived there for a few months, he was touched by the amount of support. It did not bring Harold back or make John better, but knowing so many people cared tempered his grief.

Javier phoned to say that his contacts were on the lookout for a kea being offered for sale and he would let Noah know immediately if he heard anything. He also recommended putting Harold's small cage and favourite foods in the yard, as well as one of Noah's shirts. It would provide something for the parrot to recognise if he were on the loose and flew over. There was nothing more Noah could do, apart from look into the yard every few minutes. A pigeon flying past the window sent Noah leaping to his feet and flinging the door open, hope shining in his heart. The hope dropped like a stone into his belly at the sight of a still-empty yard.

The evening should have been happy with his mum, Radagast and Aurora all at the flat, but the mood was sombre. Noah couldn't decide whether having other people there helped or made him feel worse. It was such an effort to join in with the conversation.

Shayleigh and Radagast updated him on their hospital visit. John had been well enough to talk, although it required great effort and he became tired very quickly. He had told them that on the day before his heart attack, he had been evicted from his shop for non-payment of rent. Admitting his business had been failing for a couple of years, he said his financial affairs were in a mess, exacerbated by gambling in a misguided bid to resolve his difficulties. The only way to pay off the debts would be to sell his home. If he was lucky, he would have enough left over to buy a modest flat.

'He always seemed so cheerful and upbeat,' said Noah. 'I guess it was all a front and the alcohol was something that helped him cope.' How had he not seen through John's flamboyant insistence that everything was fine? He wondered if John's excessive drinking had been the cause or the result of his financial hardship? It was difficult enough for small businesses to make a profit, without their owners using alcohol to avoid tackling problems.

'He always had a cavalier attitude to life, but in the past luck seemed to smile on him and things worked out,' Shayleigh shook her head at John's misfortune.

'Perhaps I should have challenged him about his drinking,' mumbled Noah. Here was one more thing to beat himself up about.

'John's always done things his own way,' continued Shayleigh. 'He knew about his drink problem and his business issues. You can't take on the responsibilities of the world and anyway, it was probably too late by the time you got here.'

'He was so good to me. I should have done more.' Noah put his face in his hands.

'I don't think you could have done any more. You helped him moving stuff around whenever he asked,' said Aurora. 'I wonder if he was hiding it from the bailiffs or something like that. He'll need to come clean once he's out of hospital. We don't want him with criminal charges on top of everything else.'

With John's problems weighing him down on top of his

own, Noah couldn't summon the energy to make dinner. He could barely face doing anything.

Radagast offered to cook and made a surprisingly tasty lentil stew. It was the first practical thing Noah had ever seen him do. The only negative was that they didn't eat until late, because Radagast insisted on blessing The Ark before he started to cook. This involved going into every room, waving his arms and muttering unintelligible words.

'You're lucky to get such a boost for your business,' Shayleigh informed him.

Noah couldn't think of anything to say that wasn't rude and so said nothing.

Aurora threw him a sympathetic look and said, 'I'm sure Noah's very grateful.'

After supper Radagast's continuing cryptic remarks about Harold being 'in the hands of the universe' and 'imbued with unique powers' made Noah want to scream and throw something at him. He heaved a sigh of relief when conversation finally petered out and his mother and her partner left for their camper van.

Noah remained slumped on the sofa, not even noticing Aurora was clearing up.

'I told your mum to get Radagast to back off with the whole "Harold is magic" stuff' she said, 'I could see it was winding you up.'

'Thanks. I'm sure he means well, but it makes me feel worse, not better. I can't be done with all that mumbo jumbo; not when I'm feeling like this. It's useful he and mum are around to visit Uncle John though, because it means I can keep the shop open and be here if there's any news about Harold . . . or if he comes back.' His voice broke. The chances of Harold coming back were slim. Aurora put her arms around him and they sat in silence until it was time for bed.

By the next day, Noah and Harold had reached celebrity status in the town and a constant stream of people came in the shop, enquiring after the bird. Noah found the distraction of being busy helpful, but it was draining to keep repeating the same story over and over again. One minute he wanted everyone to leave him alone and the next he was grateful for their concern. Always there was a dull ache in his belly.

Tilly turned up at the end of the day, this time without Grace. She was so tearful Noah ended up comforting her. When five o'clock came around, he locked the door with a sigh of relief.

All Noah wanted to do was sit in solitude, but he hadn't seen John for a couple of days so, impelled by duty, he drove to the hospital.

'Hey lad, good to see you.' John's voice was feeble and croaky, his eyes sunken and dull, but he managed a faint smile.

Noah took his hand. 'I hear you're on the mend now.'

'In body, laddie, but I've made a bit of a mess of things. My life will take some putting back together.'

'You're a great person, I'm sure you can work it out. We'll help.'

'You're too kind, young Noah.' John's eyes filled with tears. 'I'm a stupid old man who doesn't deserve your help.'

'You're feeling down because of all this.' Noah waved his hand at the wires, tubes and machines. 'Once you're stronger you'll feel better.'

'What have I done?' John was openly crying now.

Noah, at a complete loss, patted his hand repeating, 'It'll be alright.' But he wasn't sure if he believed it. To see this strong and vibrant man so broken tore at his guts.

After a while John became still and calm. 'I need to sleep now, laddie. Go home and get some rest yourself.' John closed his eyes and turned his face to the wall and after a while Noah left.

The drive home was tormented by trying to think of ways he could help his uncle and at the same time fretting about raising the subject of the goods stored in the barn. Tired and stressed, he toyed with the idea of driving to Aurora's to feel the comfort of her arms around him, but went home instead – just in case Harold had found his way back to the yard and was waiting to be let in.

Walking from his car to the flat, Noah noticed a figure in a hoodie lurking near The Ark. His fists clenched. Was the thief returning to search his premises for other goods? Noah welcomed the idea of a confrontation. Something at which he could direct the pent-up emotion that was consuming him. He speeded up to get a better look at the man. Getting closer, Noah slowed down again. Even shrouded in a hoodie there was a familiarity about the person's shape and the way he moved . . . Alerted by Noah's footsteps the figure turned around.

'Bro! You're here.'

Noah's heart leapt. 'James!'

They hugged, Noah shaking his head in disbelief.

'How are you even in England?'

'It's the end of the season in Oz and there's a lot of shit going down here, so on the spur of the moment I came over. I'm here for a couple of weeks.'

'Did you arrive just now?'

'I was with Mum and Radagast in their van for a bit. I kept phoning but it went to voicemail, so came over in case you were in, but not answering.'

'I put my phone on silent in the hospital and haven't looked at it since.' Noah felt giddy. James was here. Everything would be alright now.

'I hope your spare room's free,' James tanned face broke into a grin. 'I don't fancy sleeping on the floor in the van.'

'Always.' Noah hugged his brother again.

Noah showed James round, while going over the break-in details and everything he had done to locate Harold. Even though James had no new ideas to offer, Noah felt more hopeful than at any time since the parrot's disappearance. If his brother could turn up unexpectedly, maybe Harold could too.

'How's Uncle John?' asked James. 'Mum said you saw him this evening.'

'He's very weak. Physically I think he's recovering, but mentally he's in a terrible state. It's hardly surprising having lost his business and likely to lose his home too. I never thought I'd see him cry.' A lump was burning in Noah's throat. 'He just sobbed and sobbed. I felt so helpless.'

'Poor chap. I can't imagine him being like that. I'll go and see him tomorrow,' said James. 'Maybe he'll feel better in the light of day.'

Noah shrugged. He didn't think so.

'Tell me about Aurora,' said James, trying to lighten the mood. 'Is it going well?'

A glimmer of light pierced the darkness in Noah's head. 'She's wonderful. I've never felt like this about anyone before. Ever. And she's been a rock since Harold disappeared.'

'Mum thinks she's your destiny,' James laughed. 'Whether you like it or not.'

Noah rolled his eyes. 'I'm amazed she hasn't been put off by Mum and Radagast's weirdo behaviour, but she gets on brilliantly with them. She really is special.' He gave his first genuine smile of the day.

'I'm happy for you, bro. We just need to find your parrot now.'

'Javier's my best bet for that. He's got so many contacts in the bird world.' A swathe of darkness settled over Noah once more. Even Javier had said the chances of seeing Harold again were slim.

The next morning, James helped Noah fit bars over the rear windows and put two sturdy bolts on the now repaired back gate. Shayleigh and Radagast looked after the shop. A carpenter was fitting a new solid back door later that afternoon. Noah could feel everyone thinking 'it's too late', but he needed to do it. Whether Harold came back or not, the shop had to be secure.

After lunch, James borrowed Noah's car to visit his uncle. Shayleigh and Radagast declared they would be most help by sending positive vibes to Harold and John, for which they needed peace and an open space.

'Whatever you like,' mumbled Noah. Why couldn't they do something useful like scouring the area with binoculars or putting up posters? Unsure if he was less tolerant than usual, or they were more irritating, he couldn't bring himself to thank them. On the plus side, he would be free from Radagast wittering on about Harold being looked after by mystic gods for a few hours. He gave a wry smile at finding something to be glad about.

Having explained for the hundredth time that morning that, no, the police had no new information about Harold, Noah was putting tins of cat food into Mrs Chalice's plaid trolley, when the door burst open and a breathless James charged into the shop.

'We've got to go. I know where he is.'

'What? Harold?'

'Yes. John stole him. Harold's at the barn where John stores his antiques. He says you know where it is.'

'What? John? Why would he steal him? I don't understand.'

'He needed the money. You'd told him you were getting rid of Harold anyway. That's how he'd justified it to himself. But he had no idea how attached you were to him.'

'Who stole him? What money?' Mrs Chalice was staring at them, eyes wide.

179

Noah was so focused on what James was saying, he had forgotten she was there.

'I was telling him how gutted you were at losing Harold,' continued James ignoring her, 'and all of a sudden, he grabbed my hand and confessed. He said he was so frantic about losing the business and his debts, he lost his mind. He's full of remorse.'

'No.' The room seemed to tilt. He felt sick. Remorse was no good. 'That was nearly four days ago. But . . . he . . . Parrots need . . .' He couldn't say it. Birds have an extremely fast metabolism and cannot last for long without food and water. Even if Harold had been left with fresh food and water, it was unlikely he could have survived four days.

'John was supposed to meet the purchaser at the barn on Monday, but then had the heart attack. Harold should still be in the barn.'

'Let's go,' said Noah.

'What's happening?' Mrs Chalice asked again. 'And I haven't paid you.' She started searching in her handbag for her purse.

'It doesn't matter.' Noah lifted her trolley onto the street and ushered her out of the shop. He locked the door and they ran to his car, leaving an open-mouthed Mrs Chalice with her questions unanswered.

In the car James filled his brother in on more details of their uncle's confession while Noah drove towards their destination.

'He cried. He said he had no idea you cared so much about Harold or he'd never have stolen him. He told me he took the spare key to the back door when he came in last week. Smashing the window was a ruse to make it look like a break-in.' James glanced at Noah's stricken face. 'He said he was desperate and the dealer was prepared to give him twenty grand. He thought it was his last chance to get back on an even keel.'

'Only until he'd squandered that money too,' said Noah bitterly. He gripped the steering wheel and concentrated on getting them to the barn.

James clutched the edges of his seat and closed his eyes. There was no point in asking Noah to slow down.

They had been on the road for an hour. Noah pulled over into a gateway and banged his head on the steering wheel. 'I'm so useless. Harold needs me and I can't remember where the bloody barn is. I've been there three times. It shouldn't be difficult.'

'It's not you. Everything looks the same around here, it's just hedges, trees and fields.'

'It is me. I'm hopeless.' Noah yelled, his hand trembling.

'We'll sort it. We could drive to the hospital and get directions from John,' suggested James. 'Then we'll be able to find it.'

'Every minute counts. It'll take ages to drive to Plymouth and back and even then, I probably won't be able to follow the directions. A couple of hours could make the difference between life and death for Harold.'

Somewhere in the blackness of his brain he heard a voice, *You are determined, caring, conscientious and capable. Never let anyone tell you otherwise.* He breathed deeply and pictured Vera. She was wearing her no-nonsense face. She believed in him.

'I can do this.' He turned around and drove back to a junction he recognised. It was left here and somewhere he had to turn right. Driving slowly, he intoned, 'I can do this.'

'I'm with you. I know you can.'

James believed in him too.

A jolt of recognition went through him. A wooden gate lying askew and a muddy track leading up to a barn on the brow of the hill. This was it. The corrugated roof flapped in the wind. A couple of the rusty side panels looked as if you could rip them off with your bare hands. He would do that, if necessary.

Noah jumped out, James following behind. The barn door swayed and creaked in the breeze. A broken padlock lay on the muddy ground. Reaching the door, he pushed it open; a strip of light fell across a mix of old dressers, cabinets, tables and antique farming equipment. The shelving where smaller items were stored remained in darkness. Rushing in, Noah strained his ears for any sound which might indicate his parrot was there.

'Harold. It's me.' He fumbled for the torch on his phone. James beat him to it and shone a thin beam of light around the space.

'There,' said Noah. In the shadows was a small parrot cage. There was no sound or sign of movement. Running over and fearing the worst, he pictured Harold's cold body lying on the bottom of the cage.

The door was open, its hinges askew. A number of small olive-green feathers together with several longer emerald flight feathers were scattered in and around the cage. The water and food bowls had been upended.

'Someone's tried to grab him from inside the cage. He wouldn't have liked that. You can see he put up a fight.' Noah's heart leapt with both hope and fear. 'The dealer who was buying him must have broken in when John didn't turn up.' Noah peered up at the rafters calling, 'Harold. Come on. I've got treats for you.'

'He might have escaped and flown away,' said James.

'He might be here.' Noah turned to James. 'There's a torch in the boot of the car. Go and fetch it.'

They had searched every bit of the barn. Noah had given up looking for a live bird and was crawling around looking under items of furniture for one which had crept away to die. Eventually, James pulled him upright.

'He's not here. We're wasting our time.'

Shoulders slumped; Noah shook his head from side to side. 'What if . . .'

'We should go. We can report to the police and Javier. The extra information might help them find him.'

'They won't find him now.' Noah clutched his brother's arm for support and peered once more around the barn. 'What will happen when the police see all this stuff? I'm sure John only put it here to hide it from the bailiffs. He'll get in trouble.'

James guided his brother to the car. 'The truth has got to come out, so the sooner the better.' He took the keys out of Noah's hand. 'I'll drive.'

The police took another statement and James sent them a pin with the location of the barn. They promised to take a look the following day, but as the barn had already been searched, they didn't expect to find any new evidence. The brothers made it clear they did not wish to press charges against their uncle.

Noah phoned Javier, who tried to comfort him by saying that if Harold had escaped, the cold wouldn't be a problem because kea are indigenous to a mountainous area. Noah wasn't in the mood to be consoled and for the rest of the day played out all the worst-case scenarios he could imagine, while muted conversation droned around him. Radagast seemed to be heeding Aurora's request and was no longer making unhelpful comments about Harold being in the lap of the gods.

Aurora, James, Shayleigh and Radagast ate take-away pizza. Noah picked at his toppings, while picturing Harold starving in a cold, dark barn, injured on a windswept hillside, cowering under a hedge and worse.

Chapter 13

It was Sunday and a week since Harold had been stolen. Noah was in the bedroom on the phone to Javier. Aurora and James were in the kitchen, clearing up after lunch.

'Just kicking around here is no fun,' said James.

'To be honest, not much is fun at the moment and it's worse for Noah.' Aurora glanced towards the bedroom.

'You're right. We've got to get him out of here. This waiting around is dragging us all down.'

Noah shuffled back into the room and slumped on the sofa.

'Any news from Javier?' asked Aurora.

He shook his head. 'Nothing.'

'Listen, bro,' James knelt in front of Noah. 'I know it's hard, but hanging around here is making it worse. We all need to get out.'

'But what if Harold comes back?'

'You can't stay here for ever waiting for "what if". You're more likely to have a new idea and you'll certainly feel better after going out. I'm taking you and Aurora down to the beach for some surfing. The fresh air and change of scene will do you good. Take your mind off your troubles.'

'I'll just feel guilty if I go out to enjoy myself,' muttered Noah.

Aurora sat down next to Noah and took his hand. 'James is right you know. We'll all feel better for getting out and it'll give us more energy to decide what to do next about Harold.'

Between James and Aurora they persuaded Noah to leave the flat. James drove them to the surf school (where he already seemed to know everyone) and organised wetsuits and boards.

Sitting in the beach café afterwards, Noah admitted, 'You

were right, I do feel better.' The dull ache in his belly had not gone, but his head felt less muzzy and he had more energy. He had eaten.

'I know it's hard, but you've got to start living life again. Feeling bad won't help Harold or change anything,' said James.

'It is early days. Cut Noah some slack,' said Aurora.

'He's right though,' Noah ran his fingers through his hair. 'I need to get on with life. I'll start by visiting Uncle John.'

His uncle had been asking to see him, wanting to apologise in person. It was a visit Noah had been putting off, but it had to be done. He declined James and Aurora's offer to come with him, thinking it would make the conversation less awkward and give him the freedom to leave in his own time.

John was out of intensive care and on a normal ward. Smells of disinfectant, despondency and poor coffee were overlaid with quiet chatter and the to and fro of nurses on duty. John was in the bed by the window. He looked frail, but some of the spark had come back into his voice.

Noah pulled the curtain part way across between him and the next bed to provide an illusion of privacy for their conversation.

'It's the biggest regret of my life,' John told him. 'I was out of my mind with the worry of losing the business and that made me do crazy things.'

Things? Had his uncle stolen from other people as well?

'What else did you do that was crazy?'

'So many things. I'm ashamed of the way I've behaved. I've done nothing but lie. Lied to the bank, to creditors, to customers. I've left other people in difficulties by not paying bills. I hid all that stuff in the barn. I don't even know what that was supposed to achieve.' He gave a hollow laugh. 'I was drinking to dull the anguish and gambling what little money I could get my hands on in the hope of a big win. Worst of all, I thought I could solve my problems by stealing from my nephew. My own flesh and blood.' John's face screwed up in pain.

Noah tried to say, 'it doesn't matter,' but the words wouldn't come out. He wanted to forgive his uncle but needed more time.

'You mean more to me than anyone, Noah. My brother's gone; my parents are gone. My wife left years ago. I've no kids.' The knuckles clutching the bedclothes were white. 'My happiest memories are times spent with you and James. I couldn't believe my luck when you said you were moving to the area. It gave me new hope.' He let go of the bedclothes and clasped Noah's long-fingered hands between his own meaty ones.

'I don't deserve you. I don't blame you if you never want to see me again.' Tears rolled down John's cheeks, no longer as grey and sunken as they had been a week ago, but his broken veins told the story of excessive drinking.

'I do want to keep seeing you.' Noah removed his hands and paced the room. 'Everything is so raw at the moment, but I'll help you get back on your feet if I can. We'll help each other.'

'You're too good, lad. Too good.'

What could he say in the face of such remorse? Noah's emotions swung between hating John for what he had done, pitying him for his circumstances and loving him for the childhood memories he had helped create. As soon as he could decently leave, Noah headed for the car park and the solitude of his car. Losing track of time, he wasn't sure how long he had been there staring blankly into nothing, when there was a tap on the window.

'Are you okay?' A kind-faced man peered through the glass.

'I'm fine,' mouthed Noah, giving the man a thumbs up.

He knocked again. 'Are you sure?'

Noah wound down the window. 'Thank you for asking. I'm feeling a bit emotional, that's all.'

'Drive safe and get yourself home,' said the man, patting Noah's arm. He waited for Noah's nod of agreement before walking off to his own car.

The kindness of strangers too much for him, Noah put his head on the steering wheel and let the tears flow.

Harold's cage was still on the table in the courtyard. Noah's shirt hung damply on the chair nearby. He put some fresh vegetables and nuts on the table and scanned the space for any sign of distinctive olive or emerald feathers. It was nearly two weeks since Harold had been stolen, but life moved relentlessly on. It felt weird to open the shop each day and make small talk with customers, when the heartache of losing Harold was still so intense, but what else could he do?

James only had a few more days in Devon and his mum and Radagast had left to run a 'Spirit of the Trees' retreat. Radagast had delivered a parting declaration about family joy being visible in the stars, Harold's spirit returning before the moon waned and the bird having many more lives to live.

Noah had closed his eyes and turned away. He didn't want many more lives for his parrot. He wanted this one. Aurora had said goodbye on his behalf.

Since James had moved in, Noah's flat was littered with used crockery, cutlery and clothing. The bathroom had developed a damp smell from the wetsuit that lived in there when James wasn't wearing it. Every surface was gritty with sand. Tidying up after his brother was a daily chore but Noah chose to do it without comment, rather than create bad feeling.

For the past week, James had been treating his time in the UK like a holiday, out surfing and socialising with new friends every day. Noah supposed this was fair enough, after all James had paid a lot for his flight, he was entitled to some fun. However, he couldn't suppress all his resentment at James spending so little time with him. His brother had flown to

England to be with him in his hour of need but seemed solely focused on having a good time.

Already in with most of the local surfers, James's social life was hectic. He regularly tried to persuade Noah to join him, insisting it would help the process of moving on. Noah would have preferred one on one time with his brother, but that option wasn't on offer.

On the plus side, the publicity around Harold had raised the profile of Noah's Ark and sales were booming. Serving customers helped him a little, because it gave Noah something to focus on, other than fretting about Harold. He forced himself to go through the motions of the day; opening the shop in the morning and closing it again at the end of the day.

Finally out of hospital, John was starting to organise his affairs. His house was going on the market and the items from the barn had been sent to a local auction house. Once his debts were paid off, he planned to buy a small flat. Somewhere other than Hatherleigh, where he felt he was too well-known. Meeting people every day who knew what a mess he had made of his life would be too much for him to bear. Despite pleas from Noah and James, he was back at the pub every evening.

'A man's got to have some pleasures in life,' was his refrain.

John's compromise was to promise he would never gamble again and that he would stay away from spirits. Keeping him on the straight and narrow was something for Noah and James to work on. At least they were pulling together.

The sun slipped behind the hill, the last of its rays sparkling and golden on the water. The sky was made up of layers of orange, indigo and grey. Hand in hand, Noah and Aurora strolled back to Noah's flat, having left James and his friends listening to a band at The Beaver. Noah's phone buzzed and he opened it to find a cryptic message from Javier.

Call me when you have a few minutes. I have some interesting news.

'I'll call as soon as we get home,' said Noah. 'The signal's rubbish in these narrow streets.' By the time they reached the flat his stomach was churning. The news must have something to do with Harold. Aurora was out of breath from trying to keep up as his stride became a jog.

There was no greeting, his first words were, 'What's the news?'

Javier picked up the note of hope in Noah's voice and started with, 'Harold's not been found, but I do have some news that might be relevant.'

Hope died. Noah stopped pacing and slumped onto the sofa. Aurora sat next to him.

'As you know,' said Javier, 'unregistered endangered birds can't be sold on the open market.'

'Yes.' Noah's heart thumped an irregular beat.

'One of my friends heard a rumour there was a kea for sale and managed to contact the dealer, posing as an interested buyer.' Javier paused. 'I'm telling you this because I think you need to know. It may be a pack of lies, or only some of it may be true. There's no way to tell.' His voice was flat.

'Spit it out,' said Noah. 'I can take it.' Aurora grasped his hand.

'As soon as my friend said he was after a kea, the seller went off on one. He said he would have had one, but the bird was rabid and had to be put down. He said he'd never come across a bird like it and as an "honest and upstanding dealer" (not), he wouldn't sell an animal unless it was suitable for private ownership.' Javier paused again.

'Go on.' Noah needed to know everything, even if the news was bad.

'He said the bird was, I quote, "a fucking savage". Apparently, the dealer ended up in A&E with two crushed fingers and severe gashes to his hands and face.'

'I hope he's scarred for life,' said Noah bitterly.

'To be honest, that doesn't sound like the Harold you've described to me, but I wanted you to know what I've heard. The dealer then went on to try and sell my friend a pair of hyacinth macaws. They had no paperwork.'

'He's obviously unscrupulous. I guess Harold could have been the kea he was talking about, although he's only ever been gentle with me.'

'Kea aren't known for aggressive behaviour, but Harold's a powerful bird, so it could have been him. I guess we'll never know.' Javier gave a sigh.

'Did your friend report the seller to the police? After all, he had illegal hyacinth macaws.'

'All my friend had was a mobile number. No address. These illicit dealers are careful. If anyone challenges him, he'll deny everything.'

'There must be something we can do?'

'I don't think so,' Javier's voice was soft and gentle.

'I guess you're right.' Noah felt bitter that there were to be no comebacks on someone who was trading endangered species. He ended the call, images of what might have happened to Harold going through his head. Every picture created new anguish.

They sat in silence for a while. Aurora picked up Buffy and settled the cat on her knee. She had got into the habit of bringing Buffy whenever she was staying over and the cat seemed happy with The Ark as her second home.

Eventually Aurora asked, 'Do you think the parrot Javier was talking about was Harold?'

Noah shook his head to clear the gruesome images circling there. 'It's hard to say. Harold's not aggressive, but there can't be many kea around and he would hate to be manhandled. Whether it was him or not, it sounds like I'll never see him again.' He stood up and paced the room again. Why had his uncle done this to him? He struggled to fight down his resentment. John was genuinely sorry and had been under a lot of stress when he took Harold. That didn't make things any better.

'I've got to accept he's gone now. If I can do that, it'll be easier to move on.'

'Take your time,' said Aurora. 'You can't hurry these things.'

The next morning Noah put Harold's cages and stands in the storeroom. Taking his first steps towards moving on made him feel worse rather than better. The back-room seemed strangely empty; the absence of Harold's paraphernalia accentuating his disappearance, rather than minimising it.

His phone beeped and he stared at the message. In the maelstrom of recent events Noah had completely forgotten about Doctor Little.

I would like to call in again tomorrow to further discuss arrangements for Harold. Would 6pm work for you? Donovan

Noah shuddered at the thought of explaining he no longer had the parrot. How careless he would look. What would the doctor think of him?

'What can I say?' he asked James.

James put down the bag containing his wetsuit and shrugged. 'You can't just send a message. The guy's gone to a lot of trouble to help you. You'll have to phone and explain everything in person.'

'Oh God.' Noah put his head in his hands. 'He'll think I'm some stupid, irresponsible owner who can't even keep his bird safe. He'll wish he'd taken Harold away with him when he was here. I wish he'd taken him away.'

'Stop beating yourself up,' said James. 'You owe the guy an explanation. He'll understand you've done everything you can. I know you'll handle it okay.'

191

He picked up his bag. 'I'm meeting someone at nine so I need to dash. I'm borrowing your car. I hope that's alright.' He waved Noah's car keys at him and disappeared out of the door.

Noah had expected more from his brother. He needed advice. He needed someone to talk things through with. How could he tell a world-renowned parrot specialist that his kea was gone? James had as good as said, 'it's your problem not mine' and disappeared. The surf would still be there in an hour's time. Was the world already fed up with him mourning Harold? It was only two weeks since he had disappeared. Surely James understood his pain.

By mid-morning Noah had summoned the courage to phone Doctor Little. Putting his 'Back in 5 minutes!' sign on his door, he locked it. There was no way he could deal with a customer half-way through the explanation.

The call went to voicemail and he left a message.

'It's Noah here about tomorrow. Would you call me back when you have a few minutes. Thank you.'

He tried calling twice more during the day but the call always went to voicemail. Mid-afternoon Noah decided to make one last attempt. If he still couldn't get through, he'd have to leave a message giving some sort of explanation and tell the man not to come. He locked the door and put up his sign again. Standing where Harold's cage used to be, he steeled himself for the conversation ahead.

There was a knock at the door.

'You'll have to wait,' he muttered to himself.

There was a second knock, more urgent this time.

Sticking his head around the archway, he could make out a pale face and long dark plaits peering through the window. Spotting him, Tilly waved furiously mouthing, 'open the door.'

He groaned and put his phone in his pocket. Closing his eyes, he took a deep breath before marching over and unlocking the door.

Tilly barged in followed by Mrs Chalice (without her plaid shopping trolley for a change). She was brandishing a cat carrier. Noah did not want a cat as a substitute for Harold. Buffy wouldn't be impressed either.

'He's here!' squealed Tilly, putting the cat carrier on the counter. There was a scuffling noise from the depths of the carrier. Heart hammering, Noah bent down and peered inside. He was having difficulty breathing.

There was his beloved bird. The anguish which had become part of his every day vanished. He knew but had to ask. 'Is that you, Harold?'

The bird eyed him, tipping its head slowly from side to side. Noah was becoming dizzy from lack of oxygen but couldn't work out what was causing the dizziness.

Eventually the bird spoke. 'Hello Noah.'

Noah gasped. His head cleared as oxygen flowed into his bloodstream. Hands trembling, he undid the door. Harold stepped onto his hand and climbed slowly up to his shoulder. Tilly clapped her hands in delight.

He knew immediately something was not right, his joy tempered by concern. One wing hung slightly lower than the other and Harold's gait was not as sprightly as usual. His feathers had lost their glossy shine. He would need to be checked by a vet. But his precious bird was back. That was the only thing that mattered. He reached up to dig his fingers into the soft feathers on Harold's neck and the bird bowed his head this way and that so the bits he most needed scratching could be reached.

Realising he had totally ignored Tilly and Mrs Chalice for the past few minutes, Noah turned to look at them. Two expectant faces were waiting for his reaction. His call to the vet would have to wait until they had told him the story of Harold's return.

'Thank you. Thank you so much. I can't believe he's back.

193

Where on earth did you find him?' He would have hugged them but didn't want to disturb Harold who was still on his shoulder. He needed physical contact with his bird to prove to himself that the parrot's return was real.

'He turned up on our kitchen windowsill,' said Tilly. 'Grace spotted him. We heard her shouting his name and when we opened the window he hopped inside. That was about twenty minutes ago.' She was blushing. Noah assumed it was excitement.

'Just turned up,' he repeated.

'It's not quite that simple,' interrupted Mrs Chalice. 'Tilly dear, why don't you lock the door and put up the closed sign. I think we've got some explaining to do and we can't be doing with interruptions.'

The whole story came out bit by bit. Harold had belonged to the previous owner of the pet shop, Mr Noah Gregory (hence the name of the shop), although he was known to everyone as Old Greg. He had been married to Mrs Chalice's sister, Grace, since they were in their twenties. Not long after Old Greg died, Grace's dementia became so pronounced that she could no longer live alone and Mrs Chalice and her daughter Tilly moved in to care for her.

They told Noah that Mr Gregory had acquired Harold as a young bird and kept him in an aviary at his home together with his African grey, Edith. He brought them both into the house in the evenings for company, in much the same way as Noah took Harold upstairs to his flat.

Old Greg had never revealed where Harold had come from. He had insisted on keeping the bird's existence secret from all but family and close friends for fear he would be confiscated because he was unregistered. When Old Greg became ill with cancer, they had rehomed Edith the elderly and docile African grey but had not known what to do with Harold.

Busy caring for Grace, Mrs Chalice and Tilly could not give Harold the attention he needed. Having lost his owner and his feathered companion, he became destructive and distressed. On more than one occasion he dismantled a section of the aviary and escaped, but always came back, tapping on the kitchen window asking to be let in. Mrs Chalice and Tilly were at a loss as to how to find him a good home – and then Noah arrived in town. Hearing that he was taking over the pet shop, they became convinced he would be the ideal new owner. Using the keypad on the back gate and Grace's spare set of keys, there was no problem sneaking Harold, his cage and his stands into the shop the night before Noah took ownership.

'So, you just dumped him in the shop for me to take care of?' Noah struggled to stop himself from yelling. 'You knew nothing about me.'

Although he was grateful to have his best friend back, Noah couldn't believe Mrs Chalice and Tilly had abandoned the parrot to the care of someone they had never met without even telling him.

'What was wrong with contacting a bird sanctuary?'

'We talked about that, but were afraid we'd get into trouble,' said Mrs Chalice.

'We were sure we'd found the perfect solution,' interrupted Tilly.

'I could have been anybody.'

'But we knew you weren't.' Tilly sounded triumphant. 'Aztec told us.'

'Aztec? The guy from the estate agents. How did he get involved? What does he know about parrots?'

Tilly blushed again. 'You told him how much you loved animals and about your work at the bird sanctuary and your friend Javier's parrots. It was meant to be.'

Surfer Dude. He had seemed so interested in Noah and his reasons for buying the pet shop. Fascinated to hear about

Noah's volunteering at the animal sanctuary and Javier's parrots. Now Noah knew why. 'But how did he know about Harold? I thought he was a secret.'

Tilly shuffled her feet. After a pause she admitted, 'Aztec's my boyfriend so he met Harold when he came to the house. They weren't on the best of terms. Harold demolished a few of his things including a wetsuit, a pair of trainers and a kayaking paddle. Aztec was furious. He was on a mission for you to be Harold's next owner and convinced us you were perfect.'

'That's outrageous,' snapped Noah.

'I'm sorry. I know we shouldn't have foisted Harold on you with no explanation, but we were desperate. Looking after Grace, working, sorting out a million things. It was too much. And Harold was distraught. He needed a better home.'

Noah stared at them, not knowing what to say.

'You're very fond of each other, aren't you?' Mrs Chalice looked pointedly at Noah's shoulder. Harold was nuzzled into his neck. Noah had his head on one side and was gently nuzzling him back. 'Aren't you glad we gave him to you?'

His anger subsided. They had done what they thought was right and Noah wouldn't have missed his few months with Harold at any price. 'I am glad,' he admitted, 'but he needs companionship of his own kind. I've been trying to find him a home where he'll have the company of other kea and be happy. I'd love to keep him, but like you I can't provide a suitable home.'

'But he's so content here,' gasped Tilly, 'I can tell.'

'He is content, but long-term that's not enough.' Noah explained about Freya and Doctor Little and that the doctor was calling in the next day to discuss Harold's future.

'That's so noble.' Mrs Chalice had tears in her eyes. 'Grace will be sad not to see him again – Harold was her link to her late husband. She was always calm and happy after she had visited. We won't be able to explain what's happened. She'd never understand.'

'I think it'll be a while before he goes,' said Noah. 'She can have a few more visits.'

Remembering the shadowy figure who had visited Harold in the night during the early days of his ownership, a thought struck him. 'Did Grace ever come here in the night to see Harold? You said she had keys. Could she have got in?'

Mrs Chalice swallowed nervously. 'I'm sorry. I didn't think you knew about that.'

'Not know,' Noah's temper rose again, 'I've got her on CCTV but had no idea who it was. I was worried sick.'

Unable to meet his eyes, she continued, 'Oh dear. She took the spare keys to your back door and sneaked out in the night a few times. As soon as we realised what she was doing we hid the keys and put an extra lock on our door so she couldn't get out unescorted. She might have dementia, but she's a determined lady. We've lost a couple of carers because she's so wilful.'

'The carers don't understand.' Tilly looked tearful. 'They get cross with her and cross with us, but she can't help it. She can't differentiate between right and wrong; she only knows what she wants to do.'

Noah sighed. They had a lot to cope with and despite everything, he was glad they had left Harold with him. In doing so, they gave him a friend. The stress caused by John stealing Harold wasn't their fault. How could he be angry with people who had only done their best to give the parrot a good home?

'I know everything you did was with the best intentions and I'm beyond grateful to have Harold back, so thank you. I'll keep you informed about Harold moving on, as soon as it's clear what's happening. Until then Grace is welcome anytime.'

Tilly picked up the cat carrier and Harold shot off to a high shelf at the back of the shop. He stumbled on landing reminding Noah about calling the vet.

Once Noah had the shop to himself, he tempted Harold down with some treats and sat quietly with his bird. It was only as the tension gradually left him that Noah recognised the extent of anxiety he had been carrying around for the past fortnight.

'I can't believe I've got you back. I've been so worried. I thought you were gone forever.'

Harold chewed on sunflower seeds, as if he had never been away. With the cage and stands retrieved from the storeroom, Noah's shop felt whole again. Relishing the comforting weight of Harold on his shoulder, he messaged Aurora, knowing she would call as soon as she was free. He then phoned Javier, filling him in on Harold's return and the subterfuge by which he had ended up with Noah in the first place.

To his relief, the vet agreed to see Harold that afternoon. She declared the wing sprained, rather than broken and reassured him it would recover over the next few weeks without further treatment.

That evening, everything felt so familiar and yet so strange after the stress of the past two weeks. How could he be preparing dinner with Harold watching his every move and Aurora feeding him way more treats than any bird needs, when only a few hours ago they feared the parrot was dead.

Harold was quieter than usual, but had flown over to Aurora saying, 'hello Sunshine,' as soon as she arrived. He landed with an ungainly thump, the injured wing hampering his normally perfect landings and nestled into her while she told him how much she had missed him. James was not yet back. Noah couldn't understand why he hadn't rushed back as soon as he found out Harold had returned. Surely James was as eager to meet Harold as Noah was to introduce them.

After dinner, Noah called his mum, but it was Radagast who answered the phone.

'The shaman has returned,' he announced, before Noah

could say anything.

'You mean Harold? How do you know?' Radagast couldn't know, but the question was out before Noah could stop himself.

'His long and arduous journey is over and the power of your love and the universe have guided him. A life-long relationship is cemented.'

Noah rolled his eyes at Aurora who was listening in. The guy came out with such gibberish.

'He is back and he's okay apart from a minor injury to his wing. Can I speak to Mum?'

'Your mother's meditating. She can't be disturbed.'

Noah refrained from slamming down the phone. 'She'll want to know about Harold.'

'I've already told her,' Radagast replied serenely.

'Fine.' This time Noah did slam down the phone.

'James probably texted them,' said Aurora.

'I guess so.'

A plate of supper for James was sitting on the side as he was still not back. Itching for his brother and Harold to meet each other, Noah couldn't understand the delay. Surely James knew how important Harold's return was? Reaching up to stroke the bird's beak Noah told himself he didn't care whether James was here or not.

'You were away such a long time,' he said to Harold. 'Did your injured wing make it difficult to fly or did you have trouble finding your way home?'

'Difficult,' said Harold.

'I wonder what happened?' Noah muttered, more to himself than Harold. 'Who hurt you?'

They sat in silence for a minute. Suddenly Harold raised himself to his full height and flapped his wings.

'Fucking savage! Fucking savage!' he shrieked.

Noah managed to get his hands around Harold's wings and

199

cradled him into his belly. 'It's alright. It's alright,' he soothed. Harold was trembling, his heart pounding against his ribcage. His eyes were wide and his powerful beak opened and closed, but no sound came out. It was several minutes before Noah felt the bird relax enough that he could release him. He could still feel tremors running through Harold's body where his feet rested on his arm. Whether it was fear or anger Noah didn't know.

'That was what Javier said the dealer called that kea wasn't it?' said Aurora.

'It was.' A muscle pulsed in Noah's taut jawline. 'Javier needs to know.'

'I'm sure you're right,' agreed Javier, 'but even if the guy can be tracked down, you'll never get a prosecution on the basis of a couple of words from a parrot.'

'It's proof though,' insisted Noah.

'Proof enough for me, but not proof enough for the law. Harold's back. You've got to let it go now.'

'It makes me so angry to know some crook got off scot-free. And he'll do it again with no regard for how endangered a species is, or how bereft the owner will be.'

'There's crooks in every walk of life,' said Javier philosophically. 'That reminds me, you'll need to upgrade your security. Harold's had a lot of publicity.'

'I've already done that,' said Noah. 'I thought I was shutting the door after the horse had bolted, but now I'm glad I got the window bars put on and a solid back door. There are bolts on the back gate too. The front of the property is secure enough and I'll make sure Harold's always with me at night. If I go anywhere, he's coming too.'

'That's the spirit,' said Javier. 'It's fantastic you've got him back. Not everyone's so lucky.'

It was ten o'clock before James strolled in saying he didn't need any food as he had already eaten. Noah tried to hide his irritation that James had not rushed back to meet Harold. After all, that was why he had come over in the first place.

As they had not met before, Noah got them to greet each other from a distance, assuming Harold would be particularly suspicious of strangers at the moment. It was clear he could inflict a lot of damage when alarmed. James gave him a respectful bow, which Harold returned, but he shied away when James reached out to touch him.

'We'll leave it there for today,' said Noah. 'He's pretty traumatised at the moment. I hope you two make friends before you leave though; it's not long now.'

'Only a couple of days,' said James. 'But I'll be back.' He grinned.

'Great.' Noah, tried to sound positive. It had been three years since James's last visit. How long would it be until the next one? Even though James had spent more time surfing and making new friends than he had spent with his brother, Noah was going to miss him. Just a few minutes of his brother's company lifted his spirits in a way no-one else did.

'I'll be back sooner than you think.' James looked almost gleeful.

'Great,' said Noah again. James was big on promises.

'Really. I know I've not spent enough time with you this week, but the reason I've been so busy is because I've been building contacts and checking out business opportunities. I'm selling my surf shop in Brisbane and moving to Devon.' James looked expectantly at Noah, who was staring at him, mouth open. Wide-eyed, Aurora glanced from one to the other.

'What? How?'

'I'm going into business with Aztec.'

'Aztec? You're going to be an estate agent?' Noah couldn't keep the incredulity out of his voice. He was delighted James wanted to move back to England, but as an estate agent? That would never work.

'Don't be ridiculous.' James's eyebrows shot up into his untidy fringe and a look of horror came over his face.

Noah relaxed a little.

'We've found premises in Westward Ho! and are setting up a surf shop together. It's low season for tourism in Australia, even though the waves are good' – a tiny flicker of regret passed over James's face – 'and it's coming into high season here. Now's a great time to make the move. And I'll be able to see my baby bro more often.' His look of delight returned.

'Are you sure?' It would be fantastic to have his brother nearby, but only if it was what James wanted for himself.

'I've been mulling over moving to the UK for some time now but didn't mention it before, because I didn't want to give you and Mum false hope. I know you'd both love me to move back. Chatting to you about Uncle John and the good times we had here as kids made me think more and more about moving. Hearing how much you loved it, I decided to bite the bullet and come back myself.'

'That's brilliant.' Aurora squeezed Noah's hand. He couldn't speak. His brother was moving to Devon. He felt as though his body were floating above the carpet.

'I put out feelers about selling the business in Brisbane before I left Australia and that's going ahead.' James was hopping from foot to foot in the same way Harold did when he was excited.

'What about your life out there? I thought it was perfect?'

'Life's never perfect,' laughed James. 'Being here the past couple of weeks has cemented my decision. I love it.'

Life's never perfect.

It was true. Noah had thought Uncle John's life was perfect but look at what had happened there. He had thought James's life was perfect and yet here he was, moving to the place Noah had chosen. Whatever happened in the future, he knew taking that leap of faith to change his life had been the right decision. Real life isn't perfect. It's a mixture of ups and downs and if you're lucky, you have family and friends to share those ups and downs.

James interrupted his thoughts. 'You're very pensive. I don't want to be big-headed, but I did expect you to be whooping and dancing round the room at my news. So much for that.' James pulled a rueful expression.

'It's amazing,' said Noah, his face lighting up. 'I can't think of anything better than you being nearby. I was just distracted mulling over what you said about life not being perfect. I wonder if I sometimes make things difficult for myself by striving for perfection.'

'That's you all over,' said James. 'I'm going to make it my mission to get you to lighten up.'

'I've been working on him.' Aurora gave a happy shrug.

'We'll be a team.' James put his arm around Aurora and they both hugged Noah.

'Didn't Radagast say something about your Devon family getting bigger?' said Aurora.

'Oh, he says all sorts of rubbish,' said Noah. He was still struggling to believe his brother's news. Was this really what James wanted? His chest felt tight.

'You really want to live here? You're not doing it for me are you?' He had to ask. He had to know. 'I'm fine with wherever you want to be.'

'Never fear,' James laughed. 'I love you, bro, but I do have a life and I know what I want. The surfing community around here is brilliant. I've made so many friends already and having Aztec as a business partner will be awesome. We've found a great location, right by the beach, I can't wait to show you.'

A serious look came over James's face. 'I'm sorry that getting everything sorted has meant I haven't been there for you as much as you deserved. I was desperate to get everything finalised before flying back and had so little time. I wanted to be sure it was going ahead before I left.'

How had he ever thought James didn't care? He hadn't been surfing and socialising, he had been setting up a whole new business, a whole new life, just a few miles down the road. James was looking at him expectantly and Noah suddenly realised what he was waiting for.

Whooping and dancing around the room he shouted, 'Welcome to Devon, big bro. You're the best!'

He grinned. 'Was that enthusiastic enough?'

Harold, having flown off to the curtain rail, certainly felt it was.

'So so,' said James. He then grabbed Aurora's hands and spun her around the room. 'You've got two of us to cope with now. How does that feel?'

'Twice the trouble and twice the joy,' she grinned.

'He's twice the trouble,' said Noah slapping James on the shoulder, 'and I'm twice the joy.' They collapsed on the sofa laughing.

Chapter 14

Well-wishers came in and out of the shop all of the next day. Vera brought round a hand-made 'welcome back Harold' card and Jemima and Alison delivered Noah's favourite hot chocolate with marshmallows and cream, a huge slice of chocolate cake and a nutty treat for Harold.

'If Harold likes it, we could start making luxury treats for parrots as well as dogs and cats,' said Alison. 'We could even put a picture of Harold on the front, now that he's a celebrity.'

'I'm not sure about that,' said Noah. 'I'm hoping he'll sink back into obscurity. The more people who know he's here, the more at risk he is.'

'They haven't caught the thieves then?' asked Jemima.

'That's not going to happen.' Just saying it made the anger flare in Noah's chest.

He and James had not told anyone about their uncle's culpability and everyone assumed Harold had been stolen by unknown burglars. It was only Mrs Chalice they had had to give some sort of explanation and she had agreed not to say anything. John would have enough difficulty getting his life back on track, without being branded a thief.

Early that evening, James was out with Aztec finalising plans for the surf shop and Aurora was at her flat. This suited Noah, because Doctor Little was arriving in a few minutes and he wanted to discuss Harold's future one to one. He had not yet told the doctor about the events of the past couple of weeks because he wanted to explain Harold's disappearance and return face to face.

Picking up the parrot, he kissed the top of his head.

'I'm going to miss you. Who will I talk to when you aren't around anymore? You're more special than I ever imagined. So much cleverer too.'

Harold fluffed his feathers and nodded.

'I know you understand me.' Noah held out his arm so he could look Harold directly in the eye. Harold looked back but said nothing. Feeling a lump forming in his throat, Noah put Harold on his stand. It wouldn't do to be tearful when the doctor arrived.

At that moment, there was a knock at the door. Noah's stomach churned. He could say he'd changed his mind. Mrs Chalice had given him a signed letter, confirming Harold had been gifted to him, so he was the parrot's legal owner. No-one could confiscate the bird unless Noah tried to sell him or breed from him.

Harold imitated the tinkling of the doorbell then flew out into the aviary. Noah watched him prancing in front of a large mirror – his substitute for another parrot. He could not offer Harold the life he deserved. He would have to let him move on. Straightening his shoulders he opened the front door.

Tall and dapper, Doctor Little stepped inside. Instead of his briefcase, he had a carrying cage in his hand. In the cage was a kea. Smaller and more fine-boned than Harold with a bright, enquiring eye, she sat quietly despite being in a strange environment.

'Good evening. This is Freya,' he announced, putting the cage on the counter. 'I thought it important to see if she and Harold get on before we make any decisions.'

'Of course,' said Noah, his heart hammering against his ribcage. 'I'll fetch him from the aviary.'

'Pop him straight in his cage,' advised the doctor. 'They'll need to get used to each other slowly and from a distance. It could take several days.'

Noah wanted to say that Harold had already made up his

mind about Freya, but thought this would sound presumptuous. He was not the expert.

Once Harold was locked in, Doctor Little brought Freya's carrying cage through from the counter and hung it from Harold's stand where they could see each other. Freya looked relaxed. Harold went rigid, then moved cautiously towards his new companion, tipping his head this way and that. Suddenly, he seemed to realise who it was and emitted a series of high-pitched warbling cries, a mew and a piercing 'keeaah'.

'Interesting,' said Doctor Little. 'These are typical kea cries. He's obviously excited to see another kea, but it's not wise to let them into the same space until they're completely familiar with each other.'

Harold leapt round his cage giving frequent warbling sounds interspersed with 'keeaahs'. He bobbed from foot to foot, ruffled his feathers and flapped his wings, displaying the vibrant under feathers. Freya fluffed herself up every now and again, giving a soft mew. Noah had never seen Harold so animated or vocal, even when presented with his favourite food or a new toy.

Walking up to Harold's cage the doctor peered into it. 'Is there something wrong with his wing?'

'He injured it recently,' said Noah. 'The vet says it's just a sprain and will get better on its own. It's a long story.'

'Perhaps you could tell me over a cup of tea?' The doctor raised his voice so it could be heard over the racket Harold was making. 'I think it's best to leave them alone to settle down.'

'Of course.' Noah had been so fascinated by Harold's reaction, he had forgotten about looking after his human guest. 'Come upstairs. The parrots can have some peace while we have our tea. I've got a lot to tell you.'

Over the next half hour, Noah told Donovan (he insisted Noah use his first name) about the break-in, Harold's return and everything in between.

The doctor listened intently while Noah told his story. A pained look came over his face when Noah described searching for Harold to no avail.

Once the story was at an end, Donovan filled Noah in on Freya's background. She had been in a consignment of illegally traded birds, which he had fostered until permanent homes were found. This had proved difficult with Freya because she was especially timid. She had not fared well when they introduced her to a circus of kea at a zoo.

'I've taken her back into my private collection,' said Donovan. 'I suspect she'll never thrive in a circus of kea but may be happy with a single companion.' He glanced at his watch. 'It's been quiet down there for a while. I think we should go and see how our birds are getting along.'

Noah jumped up. 'Are we going to try putting them together?'

'It's too soon. We'll need to leave them for a couple of days at least before they can be introduced at close quarters. I'm in the area all week, so I'll pop in again and help you with a controlled introduction.'

Needless to say, waiting wasn't Harold's thing. On this occasion, he had taken matters into his own claw (or beak). The door on his cage was open, as was the door to Freya's. Sitting together in her cage, they were taking it in turn to preen each other.

Noah glanced guiltily at the doctor. Would he be cross about Harold scuppering his careful planning? 'I don't know how he managed that. He's never unlocked his cage before.'

He reached into Freya's cage to collect Harold, but both birds shuffled away from him. The only way to remove Harold without a scene, was if he chose to step on to the offered hand. This was clearly not going to happen.

'So much for a controlled introduction,' laughed Donovan.

'That's quite a unique bird you've got there.'

'He's very special and exceptionally bright. He . . .' Noah couldn't speak. Doctor Little might want to take Harold away today, now they had established the two parrots were compatible. 'You don't want to take him now, do you?' He swallowed. 'I can't let him go straight away. I need time to say . . . to say goodbye.'

Harold seemed to sense Noah's distress and abandoned Freya to fly over and nuzzle his ear. Noah avoided Donovan's gaze by rubbing heads with Harold; he didn't want the raw emotion in his eyes on show.

'Will I be able to visit?' he asked in a muffled tone.

'Would you prefer to keep Harold?' asked Donovan.

'No.' The word came out as a croak. Noah tried again and spoke with more energy this time.

'No, I wouldn't. Harold needs a companion of his own species and I can't offer him that. I want what's best for him.'

'You are a thoughtful young man.' Donovan nodded approvingly. 'Harold has an excellent set up here with goings on for him to watch all day, access to an aviary and plenty of attention from you in the evenings. I'm very particular about the homes I deem appropriate for intelligent psittacine, but yours is one.'

'Thank you,' muttered Noah. All this made no difference, he had to let Harold go.

Donovan cleared his throat and caught Noah's eye. 'I'm prepared to gift you Freya as a companion for Harold, provided you promise never to sell either of them. Should you ever decide you can no longer keep them all I ask is that you to return them both to me. Would a solution like this be of interest?'

Noah gaped. Had he heard right? 'Gift me Freya? I can keep both of them?' The room seemed to get brighter, although the sun was low in the sky.

'That would be amazing. Beyond my wildest dreams. Are

you sure?' He needed to hear it again.

'I am sure.' Donovan was beaming. 'The bond you have with Harold is exceptional and Freya is not robust enough for a zoo environment. I think this is the perfect solution and I'm happy to leave her with you from today. I have more parrots than I can cope with at home.'

'That's wonderful.' Noah's hands shook as he clasped Doctor Little's. 'I can't thank you enough.'

Harold had flown back to Freya and was offering her a walnut.

'You're welcome to visit anytime you like,' gabbled Noah, remembering how desperate he had been to have visiting rights when he thought he was going to lose Harold.

'I've grown very fond of Freya, so I'd appreciate that,' said Donovan gravely.

Feeling an immense flow of warmth towards this serious and kindly man, Noah said, 'If there's anything I can do for you, please let me know. Would you at least stay for dinner? You could tell me more about Freya and meet my brother.'

'An excellent idea.' The doctor's eyes twinkled. 'I believe Harold helps you cook. I'd like to see that.'

Chapter 15

Noah had cleaned the flat and tagged a few of his brother's favourite recipes in his collection of cookbooks. In a few days' James was returning to England for good. Aurora agreed it made sense to plan ahead what he was going to cook, but said there was no point in cleaning or tidying before his brother arrived. Noah shrugged; he might as well start with a tidy home. James would only be with him for a few weeks. He was planning to share a place in Westward Ho! with Aztec as soon as they found somewhere suitable.

The sun was shining and Noah's business was booming. Holidaymakers strolled up and down Market Street looking for somewhere for breakfast or picking up essentials before they set off to the beach. The ones with dogs often called in at The Ark, tempted by the range of gifts and luxury items Noah had displayed in the window. The shop was so busy Noah couldn't put off recruiting an assistant any longer and had placed a colourful advert in the window. He didn't relish the thought of having someone he didn't know in his space all day, but could no longer manage on his own.

It was especially important to get the right person, because of the added complication of Harold and Freya. Freya took a long time to get used to new people. Some days she would not leave the cage unless Noah lifted her out and set her in the aviary or on the stand – something he only did when the shop was empty. She would not cope with the wrong person. Neither would Noah for that matter.

As for Harold, he was very particular about who he liked, but it would be difficult explaining to prospective applicants that they had to be vetted by a parrot. During the day, Harold shared his time between preening Freya in the cage, preening himself on his stand and imitating seagulls. He still sat on Noah's shoulder in the evenings while he cooked, occasionally taking a treat over to Freya who preferred to perch on the stand. If Aurora and Buffy were there, Harold would throw pieces of meat or fish to the cat. All attempts to prevent him from tossing treats to Buffy had failed.

'At least they get on well together,' Aurora had said.

'I am glad about that,' Noah replied, thinking how good he was getting at the 'glad game' and wondering if any other members of his book club were still following its principles.

He had missed the last book club meeting because he had to take James to the airport, but had made sure to listen to the book anyway. *The Midnight Library* was another novel that had given him food for thought. Just like Nora Seed, his life wasn't perfect, but it was the life he wanted and it was right for him. Vera had said she was sure the group would be happy to talk about it again next time, as it had generated an interesting discussion.

Today was particularly busy and by the time it got to mid-morning, Noah needed an energy boost. He messaged Jemima ordering a hot chocolate. Pre-ordered, he could pick up his drink and be back in the shop in less than a minute. Stepping outside on his way to collect it, he almost collided with Aztec, who was peering at the advertisement he had put in the window.

'That was close!' Aztec leant back, a drink in each hand. 'Your chocolate was ready when I called in at Brewberry, so I've brought it over.'

'Thanks. Come on in.' Noah took his drink and held the door open for Aztec. The smell of cocoa beans teased his nostrils. 'Have you finished at the estate agents yet?'

'Three days to go.' Aztec did a little jig. 'I finish the same day James gets back and a week later we open The Surf Shack.

Your brother's a dude. I can't wait to be out of that life-sucking office and selling surf-gear all day instead – when I'm not actually surfing, that is.' He grinned.

'I remember feeling like that when I realised I owned this pet shop and would never have to slave at a computer all day again,' said Noah. 'It was like a sunny morning bursting into my life.'

'I'm made up the shop's working out for you. I knew you'd smash it though.'

Noah laughed. 'You sound like my mum's boyfriend, Radagast. He's always mega positive.'

'The Radagast?' Aztec's eyes went round and his mouth fell open. 'The one on TikTok?'

'I'm not sure,' said Noah. 'He's some sort of guru. I don't really know what he does.'

Aztec whipped out his phone and pulled up a video. Sure enough, there was Radagast expounding on embracing the universe and achieving the ultimate in life.

'That's him,' said Noah.

'He's unbelievable.'

'He is,' replied Noah. Although he probably didn't mean it in quite the same way as Aztec.

Aztec goggled. 'Radagast,' he repeated, as if it were a holy word. 'He's got like twenty million followers. People's lives have been transformed by his teachings. He's the man.'

'Really?' James and his mum had both said something about Radagast being on TikTok, but Noah had not bothered to download the app. He'd normally had more than enough of Radagast by the time a face-to-face visit was over.

'I can't believe you've not seen his stuff.' A look of slavish admiration came over Aztec's face. 'If he's your mum's boyfriend, do you think I might get to meet him one day?'

Noah chuckled. He was about to make Aztec's day. 'Radagast and Mum will be here for The Surf Shack's opening day. Didn't James tell you?'

'He told me his mum was coming. But Radagast . . .' Aztec looked like he was going to pass out. 'Oh my God. I love you. Got to go. I need to tell people.' Aztec gave Noah a man hug and ran out of the shop leaving his untouched drink behind.

Downloading TikTok, Noah followed 'radagasttheguru'. The first message to pop up was 'Follow me for a life path that flows.'

Noah rolled his eyes, but noticed Aztec was right about his huge following. He scrolled through a number of videos. Surprisingly, some of the things Radagast said were almost sensible.

His scrolling was interrupted by Mr Wainwright.

'That there parrot's back then.' It was a statement, not a question.

'I'm very relieved,' said Noah. 'How can I help you?'

Mr Wainwright was not to be hurried. 'It were a right do, weren't it. I heard it were a local.'

'We've no idea,' said Noah quickly. His heart hammered. Had someone found out his uncle was involved?

'Who else would have known about that there bird?'

'Holidaymakers from all over the country are in here regularly,' Noah pointed out.

'Ah . . .' Mr Wainwright pondered for a moment. 'But that bird must 'ave been hidden round 'ere or 'ee wouldn't have found his way back. 'Ee's not a homing pigeon, is 'ee?' He guffawed at his own joke.

Perhaps everything Mr Wainwright said was guesswork. Noah stood tall and spoke with confidence. 'Harold is exceptionally intelligent. He could have found his way back from anywhere.'

'Exceptionally, eh?'

'Absolutely,' confirmed Noah.

''Ee can't help with yer spelling though, can 'ee?'

214

'Well, no. Parrots can't spell.'

'Nor their owners,' Mr Wainwright roared with laughter. 'Get your favORite dog treats here.' He quoted from Noah's A-board. 'FavOURite. There's a 'U' int' middle. Didn't yer go to school?'

Vera's conviction rang in Noah's head: '. . . *intelligent . . . capable . . . don't underestimate yourself.*' He breathed slowly in and out before replying.

'I did well at school despite having dyslexia. I'm proud of what I've achieved and don't think it matters if I spell something wrong now and again.'

'Oh.' Mr Wainwright took a step backwards and looked sheepish. 'Very good.'

Noah's confidence had obviously wrong-footed him.

'That'll just be my normal bag of chicken feed then young man.' Mr Wainwright didn't say another thing until he had hefted the chicken feed onto his shoulder.

'You're doing a good job here. You're an asset to the town. Keep it up.'

'Thank you.' Noah resisted punching the air with his fist. He had conquered his demons and impressed this cantankerous man. Not bad for a morning's work. He took a well-deserved sip of hot chocolate.

Tilly and Grace were due to call in at the end of the day. Noah smiled to himself at the thought of their faces when he showed them his latest acquisition. It was a comfortable and brightly coloured tub chair he had found on eBay. Grace would now be able to sit down and relax while she enjoyed Harold and Freya's company. Although watching them made her laugh and clap her hands, she was too frail to stand for long. Noah had even bought a small side table to go with the chair. He had put the latest *Parrots* magazine out on the table yesterday. Inexplicably Harold had demolished it. Noah had been planning to read the article advertised on the front cover: 'African greys – the world's most intelligent parrot.' Sometimes he just didn't understand what got into Harold's head.

Tilly and Grace arrived at five o'clock bringing a handful of mangetout. Noah led them through to the back of the shop, where the new chair faced the cage that Harold and Freya now shared.

'This chair is for you, Grace,' he said. 'Or any other customer who needs a rest,' he added.

After looking at Tilly, who nodded furiously, Grace sat down.

'You're so thoughtful.' Tilly had tears in her eyes.

Blushing, Noah placed Harold's small stand next to the chair so Grace could feed him without getting up. Freya remained in the cage but accepted a mangetout from Noah. He left his visitors and went back to finish the daily admin. After a few minutes Tilly appeared at the counter.

'Are you busy? Can I talk to you?'

Noah closed his laptop. 'Of course. What is it?'

'I know we didn't get off on the best start, what with foisting Harold on you and everything, but I'm hoping that's all in the past now.' She shuffled from foot to foot making her pigtails dance.

'Absolutely. I love Harold and it's even better now I've got Freya as well. Things have worked out perfectly.'

'I'm so glad.' Tilly produced an envelope from her pocket. 'Aztec told me about the job you're advertising in the window and I'd like to apply. I've brought a copy of my CV.' She put the envelope on the counter and pushed it towards him. 'I've not worked in a shop before, but I'm sure I could learn.' Her voice was breathy and anxious and she was talking at top speed. There was no opportunity for Noah to butt in.

'I worked as a receptionist at Craddock's until last month, but it's closed down and I've been made redundant. It would be fantastic to work here with you and it's so close to home. I don't want you to feel obliged or anything. I'll totally understand if you find someone more suitable.' She stopped gabbling and chewed her lip.

'That would be perfect.' A weight lifted off Noah's shoulders. Here was someone he would be happy to work with. She was friendly, polite and got on well with Harold and Freya. From observing the way she looked after Grace, he knew she'd be good with customers. He remembered Mr Wainwright saying something about Tilly losing her job, but it hadn't occurred to him she might want to work in The Ark. He didn't need to look at her CV.

They chatted about duties, working hours and pay and it was soon agreed that Tilly would start in a couple of days' time. Part of the deal was that she would go home for lunch, so her mum could have a break from looking after Grace in the middle of the day. Another solution had just slotted into place.

Radagast's words popped into his mind: 'Follow me for a life path that flows.' Noah shook his head. He was becoming quite fanciful.

Finally, it was the grand opening day of The Surf Shack in Westward Ho! Noah could hardly believe his brother was back after all these years. Not only back in England but his new business would be a few miles down the road. James's friends from the local surf school were coming along to help celebrate the opening and they were expecting the local newspaper and possibly even Radio Devon to be there too.

It was a sunny Saturday morning and parking spaces were almost non-existent. Noah and Aurora had been driving around for several minutes before Noah spotted a space.

'That was lucky. They're opening in twenty minutes,' said Aurora. 'I wonder what's going on. The schools haven't even broken up and the town's gridlocked.'

Noah shrugged. 'Perhaps there's a pop-up market or something.'

Aurora fished in her bag for sunglasses. 'It's a shame Tilly can't be here as well.'

'I hope she's alright,' Noah glanced at his phone, checking for messages. 'It's the first time she's been on her own at The Ark.'

'You're not fretting, are you?' Aurora raised an eyebrow at him.

'Only a little bit,' Noah grinned. 'It's great I can be here for James though and I'm glad you're here to share the moment too.' He put an arm around her waist, and she leant into him.

'My life is complete,' he said, kissing the top of her head.

'Mine too,' she said.

Approaching The Surf Shack, it became clear to Noah and Aurora that something huge was going on. No-one could get in or out of the small car park opposite the new shop because of the throng outside. Cars lined the approach road, despite double yellow lines. Camera crews were everywhere and large fluffy microphones on long booms reached over the crowd. Reporters sporting logos from national newspapers hovered at the car park entrance and people of all ages were craning their necks; children sitting on the shoulders of their parents. A contingent of druids waited patiently near the sea wall.

'What is happening?' Shorter than Noah, Aurora jumped up and down trying to see over the heads of the crowds. Even Noah couldn't see much apart from the banner over James and Aztec's shop, which announced: *The Surf Shack – opening 10am today*.

The door opened and a hush fell over the crowd. A tall figure wearing a purple robe stepped outside. His dreadlocks with their multi-coloured beads, swung from side to side as he searched the crowd. Spotting Noah and Aurora, Radagast stretched his hands towards them.

'Patience begets spirituality, my friends,' he announced to the crowd. 'We will be with you at the allotted hour.' The last few low voices fell silent.

Radagast paused for dramatic effect, surveying the onlookers. Beckoning Noah and Aurora he declared, 'Make way. My kin need free passage.'

People in the vicinity turned to look where he was pointing.

'I think that means us,' said Noah, pushing Aurora forward. The crowd parted creating a path to Radagast and The Surf Shack.

'Namaste, my children.' Radagast gave a bow.

Noah and Aurora scuttled inside.

James was punching the air. 'Have you seen all those people? This is the launch of the century.'

Uncle John, who had come along to support the opening, slapped him on the back. 'You've smashed it, young James.'

Shayleigh gave a serene smile. 'It's lovely all these people have turned up.'

Aztec was staring at Radagast, his mouth agape. Noah half expected him to kneel and kiss the hem of Radagast's robe.

A few minutes later Radagast, James and Aztec went outside to announce the shop was now open. James and Aztec returned to the shop so they could welcome their first customers. Radagast wandered into the crowd, speaking to his devotees, signing autographs, posing for selfies and touching the occasional person on the forehead or bowing to them, his hands in the prayer position.

James and Aztec found they had to answer more questions about their relationship with Radagast than they did about surfing gear, but despite this sold almost as much on their first day as they had expected to sell in the first month.

'I hope you're getting photos of this for your social media pages,' Aztec said to Noah. 'Tag it with @radagasttheguru and you'll get loads of new customers next week.'

Noah looked doubtful. 'Do you think so? Would any of these people even want anything from a pet shop?'

'Look at all these guys,' Aztec hissed waving his hand at the queue. 'People are going mental because of our Radagast connection.'

'I suppose.' Noah wasn't sure the extra customers were worth the inconvenience of celebrity by proxy. He preferred a quiet life. Anyway, business was more than good enough for him. He had a flashback to Radagast blessing The Ark. If anything he told himself, it was Harold that had brought in extra business.

That evening they all returned to Noah's flat for supper, except Uncle John who had gone home early as he still tired easily. Tilly joined them and it was a squeeze fitting everyone in. Noah had been cooking all week in preparation (much to Harold and Buffy's delight) and after warming up a few things in the oven, the spread was ready. Freya remained downstairs; the flat being too crowded for her to cope with.

There had been a minor fracas when Aztec walked in. Harold had risen up, flapping his wings and shrieking, 'You're dead meat.'

'Oh dear.' Aztec looked sheepish. 'I'm afraid I lost the plot with him when he trashed my wetsuit.'

'He trashes wetsuits?' Looking horrified, James grabbed his bag from the corner of the lounge and threw it in his bedroom.

Noah wondered if the threat of precious surf gear being destroyed would encourage his brother to be tidier around the flat.

Aztec expounded on Harold's destructive tendencies. '. . . And a load of other things too. I don't think there's anything that bird couldn't destroy if he put his mind to it.'

James eyed Harold warily.

'As soon as we find somewhere to live in Westward Ho! your stuff'll be safe,' Aztec consoled him.

'I think I'll leave my gear in the shop storeroom until then,' said James. 'Just in case.'

'Hurrah,' thought Noah.

Aurora gave him a surreptitious thumbs up.

Supper was over and they were reminiscing on the success of the day, when Noah's phone rang. He was about to let it go to voicemail when he saw Javier's name and snatched it up.

Without preamble Javier announced, 'I've got news for you.'

Noah's hand tightened on his phone. Harold was safely back. What news could Javier have?

'Justice has been done my friend,' announced Radagast holding out an arm. Harold swept over and landed on it.

Noah scowled. Couldn't Radagast leave it out for just one evening?

'It's Javier. I'll take this in my room,' he said.

It was some time before he returned.

'What did he say,' asked Aurora and the room went quiet.

'They've caught the dealer who tried to take Harold from the barn,' he announced.

Aurora clapped her hands in excitement. 'That's fantastic. I thought Javier said the police wouldn't be able to do anything, because there was no proof he tried to take Harold.'

'That's right, but Javier's contact managed to discover the crooked dealer's address and tipped off the RSPCA and the police. They raided the premises and found a whole raft of endangered birds, none of which he had licences for. The RSPCA are in the process of rehoming them.'

'What's going to happen to the dealer?' asked Tilly.

'He's on bail, but a prison sentence is likely because it's not the first time he's been caught with unlicensed birds. There's not enough evidence to press charges concerning Harold's abduction, but it was the scars on his face and hands that helped Javier's network identify the guilty party.'

'Hurrah for Harold.' James raised his glass and they all followed suit.

'Do you hear that, Harold,' said Noah. 'You helped catch your attacker.'

'Fucking savage,' squawked Harold.

'Language!' said Noah. Everyone else laughed.

Radagast made a mystic sign above Harold's head.

Later that evening, when Aurora and Noah were alone, she mused, 'Do you think Radagast can really predict things?'

'Nah,' said Noah. 'He's a nice guy, loads of charisma, but a complete charlatan.'

'I'm not so sure,' she said. 'He seems to have an uncanny knack of getting things right.'

She had a point, but Noah wasn't going to admit it.

'Tasmai śrī-gurave namah,' said Harold.

To that glorious Guru, my salutations.

Dear Reader

I loved writing this book and drawing on my own experience of keeping parrots to bring Harold's personality to life. The book is based in Devon, where I am lucky enough to live and I hope my deep affection for this beautiful part of the world shines through.

As an indie author, it would mean a lot to me if you would help others to enjoy this book by leaving a review.

If you want to know more about me and my forthcoming books, or sign-up for special offers and freebies, check out my website.

www.ebberleyfinch.com

Acknowledgements

Heartfelt thanks to everyone who has helped in the creation of this book. Without your support, encouragement and feedback my journey would have been lonely and hard.

There are too many people to mention them all, but special thanks go to my Devon Novelists group, Angie Chadwick, Jonathan Posner and Jane Rayner. Their eagle-eyed critique and invaluable advice were the perfect guide as I took my first steps into the world of publishing. Thank you also to Jenny Kane from Imagine Creative Writing for imparting her knowledge and experience so freely and to my editor, Cassandra Rigg, for understanding my characters and helping make this book the best it could possibly be.

Finally, I would like to thank my partner, Kevin, who has given me the time, space and IT support ☺ that has allowed me to pursue my dream.

Made in the USA
Coppell, TX
13 December 2024

42426683R00128